Clash

Clash

The First Novel in the Two Worlds Trilogy

Tara Orfani

CLASH
THE FIRST NOVEL IN THE TWO WORLDS TRILOGY

iUniverse books may be ordered through booksellers or by contacting:

iUniverse
1663 Liberty Drive
Bloomington, IN 47403
www.iuniverse.com
1-800-Authors (1-800-288-4677)

ISBN: 978-1-5320-2800-7 (sc)
ISBN: 978-1-5320-2801-4 (e)

Library of Congress Control Number: 2017910974

Print information available on the last page.

iUniverse rev. date: 07/15/2017

PROLOGUE

Imagine the worst horror you can possibly think of-then multiply it by about a thousand. It still won't even come close to what I have been forced to live through.

There is something to be said for losing everyone you ever cared about and being betrayed by everyone you'd ever trusted. When I was young and naive, I never would have thought that such things could ever happen to someone like me.

I was horribly, hilariously wrong.

I was forced to kill everyone I ever loved, betrayed by people who were meant to be my friends and discouraged from caring for anyone ever again. Moreover, I had been killed by three men who I had truly thought I could trust. And that wasn't even the worst part.

If you're looking for a story with a happy ending, then I'm afraid you've come to the wrong place. Happiness said goodbye to me the moment my parents were killed when I was only seven; so, if that's what you're looking for, then I suggest you put this book down right now.

On the other hand, if you wanted a story about redemption, death, betrayal, destruction, and doomed love, then read on. This is my story and I can say, with absolute authority, that there is a lot of all of that.

But enough of my rambling, You wanted to hear about my life? Well, here it is, in all its tragic, heart-wrenching and bloody glory.

CHAPTER 1

To Be a Murderer

The rain beat down a tattoo on the grimy window as the steady pouring reflected in the soulless eyes staring out at it.

Those eyes were redder than blood and betrayed so little emotion, they could have belonged to a machine.

A prolonged sigh left a patch of fog on the grey-tinged window as he finally tore his eyes away from it.

Brushing back a lock of slate hair, he let a second, slightly shorter sigh escape his bloodless lips and focused his gaze on the room he was in.

It wasn't a terribly large room, but it was large enough to still look spacious even with all of the things he had piled up on the floor and against the walls.

Books and scrolls in various languages littered the grey stone floor, all stacked and tossed haphazardly across it.

A bare, colourless cot was pushed carelessly up against the far wall, beside the window he had been staring out of, serving as his bed, though the fact that it was bare was a testimony of how little he slept.

The thing referred to as the window was actually just a clumsy rectangle cut into the peeling wall, filled with cracked, grimy glass and usually covered with a translucent grey cloth.

It had been ages since he'd actually left the building except for the occasional venture down to the water for a cigarette.

It wasn't that he didn't want to leave; it was just that there was never a reason for him to leave the *room*, much less the building.

Staring out of the window or at the mirror in the adjoining bathroom were his main sources of consuming time when he wasn't poring over the books and scrolls covering the floor.

The disadvantage of being a wanted criminal; the only one, actually.

To take a step on that stone floor would be the sound equivalent of banging a metal cymbal, but for him, it was as soundless as if he hadn't moved at all.

Years of practice and discipline had trained him to move quickly and silently, faster than the eye could track. It was almost inhuman, how fast and silent they were forced to become. But to become otherwise in this world was to have a death wish.

He let out a breath of cold, humourless laughter as his mind turned to his training days. A death wish was the one thing he didn't have.

As he turned from the hole in the wall, aka window, his pale hand swept the grey material back over it, effectively eliciting the last remnants of light from the room and causing his crimson eyes to practically glow in the dark as the result of his night vision abilities; another residual effect of his training.

What was he trained as, you ask?

Well, what his title throughout Vanadis so obviously suggested:

Varros Hawk, legendary assassin.

CHAPTER 2

The Gate of Souls

At the precipice of the two worlds, there is a gate.

It is fashioned out of a supernatural iron and interwoven with the sins of man and other beings to keep out the untainted.

This gate is called the Gate of Souls. It protects the innocent from what lurks within.

A figure cloaked in black, with their face covered by dark rimless glasses and the hood attached to the cloak, skulks outside the gate.

No skin is visible of this figure's person, except for a vague patch beneath the glasses; that patch is the colour of bronze and the figure that it belongs to watches as the gate gleams eerily in the moonlight, invisible to all but those who have been on the other side.

"*Have you located the Gate*?" a male voice asks from the com in the figure's ear.

The figure places a gloved finger to the ear piece and replies, "Yes, my lord,"

The voice on the other end chuckles without humour.

"Any activity? And remember, Therrian, I want to know if there's even a rat loitering by the latch."

"No activity. The air is as still and silent as the grave," Therrian answers calmly, barely moving his lips as his eyes behind the black lenses of his glasses stay trained on the seemingly harmless gate in front of him.

"Remember, the Gate of Souls is imperative to our plans. Make sure you remain in position because even the most insignificant thing going on at any given time could be vital to know for our success."

The speaker paused.

"And try to get one of our operatives on Hawk. I think it's time we got him out of hiding."

Rain streamed down from the tumultuous black sky, pelting her like liquid golf balls. She wanted so badly to stop and catch her breath, but she couldn't-not when the Devil himself was on her heels.

Putting on an extra burst of speed, she tore off into the abandoned alley, chest heaving with the effort of retaining her equilibrium. Her clothes clung wetly to her body and she was having to fight just to stay conscious.

The storm raged on overhead, claps of thunder reverberating in her ears and illuminating the dark streets in brief, violent flashes of white light. Her eyelids were heavy; her arms and legs ached and she was about a second away from passing out due to exhaustion; but still, she continued to run.

A gunshot shattered a metal trashcan in her path and she screamed when the loud clanging punctuated the cacophony of sounds filling the air. She urged herself faster, praying that she would make it out of this alive.

Please, please let me live through this. Let me live to see another day. *She pleaded silently to any higher power that might be listening, fighting back another scream as a second bullet glanced off the brick wall two feet to her left.*

She felt tears springing to her eyes as her thighs began to burn and her arms began to weaken. The world blurred around her and she gritted her teeth, praying harder, practically begging for some divine intervention.

Her prayer went unanswered.

He materialized suddenly, cutting her off and causing her to stumble and skid on the damp ground. A hood covered the top half of his face so that all she could see of her assassin was his sculpted brownish chin and the chapped, wide-set mouth. She frowned; those features seemed extremely familiar for some reason.

"Jarl?"she called out uneasily, hardly daring to believe her eyes and dreading that her impression was correct.

The cracked, dark lips curled into a slow smile as the assassin removed his dark hood and drew his silver revolver.

"Hello, little sister."

"No," she whispered in horror, shaking her head fiercely, refusing to accept what her eyes were seeing, "Why? Why are you here?" "I would think it's obvious," He cocked the silver gun. "I have orders-and I intend to follow them."

She shook her head a second time, moisture trailing involuntarily down her cheeks. "Jarl, please," she begged desperately, anguish and betrayal evident in her voice.

The tall black boy grinned savagely at her misery, raising the revolver until the barrel was aimed directly at her chest.

"Say hi to our parents for me, sis," Jarl said mockingly an instant before he pulled the trigger.

The last thing Nyle saw before she died was her brother's twisted, smirking face and the muzzle of his revolver as he shot her, point-blank, in the heart.

I touch the cigarette to my parted lips and blow out a perfect smoke ring, which condenses in the damp night air and I watch the smoke through the clear rain; I know there are probably goosebumps rising on the back of my neck from the cold, yet I feel nothing: not the rain nor the cold it results in.

There's something to be said for being a heavy smoker living in a house near the water.

I should probably introduce myself, shouldn't I?

My name is Varros Hawk.

I am just over 18 years old with slate-coloured hair, naturally crimson eyes, and skin pale as the moon and... that's pretty much all you need to know about me.

Oh, except that I'm a-former-legendary assassin.

It was hardly my choice to enter the assassin's guild at the age of, yes, only seven, but that was just it; I didn't have a choice. I was marked with the assassin's blood infusion from the second I was conceived. Killing is in my blood.

Of course, that's not to say I wasn't good at assassinations. The case was quite the contrary: I didn't become a legend for nothing. I excelled at every field the guild trained us in and slew more victims before I hit my teens than any other assassin had in their entire life.

But despite being the top member, the assassin's guild still had one very fatal flaw: its leader.

When his true reason for forming the guild came to light, I wanted no part of it anymore and quit, forcing me to have to go into hiding from doing so.

So now I'm a wanted criminal, selectively immortal at 18 and above all, the heaviest drinker and smoker you will ever meet, except for maybe my old friend Candor, who went the whole hog and did things like cocaine and marijuana as well as smoked and drank like he was sponsored by vodka and cigarette companies.

Sadly, I haven't seen Candor since I left the guild and he's probably in a lot better shape than I am-which is a sad commentary in and of itself.

The rain drenches my paper-thin black trenchcoat and seeps through to the dark muscle top underneath, but I don't even twitch. I am loath to let myself be shaken by a sensation as trivial as the cold, much less trifles such as emotions.

The way the guild was taught, emotions were burdens that you dealt with by keeping them locked up. If even a smile or flinch snuck through, you were beaten within an inch of your life.

That is why I still don't allow myself to feel. Never did, not even when I had only just been born. My face had always remained a bloodless, empty mask; no emotion, no expression.

Because if you look like you feel nothing, you don't feel anything; you don't care and that is the code I've lived by for the last seven years.

Because if you didn't care, it didn't hurt when you lost.

And I, I lost everything the second my soul was promised to the assassin's guild.

I was thrown to the ground next to a boy with dark blue, almost black hair and olive eyes that were, oddly enough, alight with excitement, matching the grin he wore over his folded, dark-skinned arms.

There was no smile on my lips and absolutely nothing on my face. Figuratively speaking, of course.

"So, this is the new crop, hmm?" a silky, hissing voice came out of the blackness, followed almost immediately by practically soundless footsteps.

The speaker was the epitome of a snake in human flesh. Olive-coloured, almost reptilian, skin covered the rearing, slim-necked and emerald-ebony haired head above a dark, obviously high quality, green suit, matched with emerald leather boots.

He gave all us cowering, grinning and some simply staring children an oily smile. Well, it was oily in my opinion, anyways.

"I don't think I've ever seen so many children in one place before," he commented silkily. "But that is a good thing. It means we have seen much more potential-and it's only your potential that has brought you here."

His smile grew.

"My name is Lord Niral-my last name is of no consequence. Yours, however, will be your title. Mine from the likes of you shall be Lord Niral or my lord while you are here. I assume you all know why you're here?"

"Yes, Lord Niral," everyone droned back at him without conviction.

Everyone except me, that is.

I didn't speak at all, keeping my pale lips stubbornly compressed while my crimson eyes coolly surveyed "Lord Niral" with careful scrutiny. I could see his hooded, torpid eyes glaring at me and had to resist a smirk. He was obviously the type of man who was used to getting what he wanted-and what he wanted was obviously complete obedience.

He had obviously noticed my lack of submission when he asked to be called "Lord". Good. *I had thought. Niral had needed to recognize that I was not one to grant status to anyone unless they earned it first-even if I was only seven and he looked closer to forty-five, nearly four decades my senior.*

While the other children had fallen silent, Niral headed directly for me and I straightened my back to look him in the eyes. Those eyes were merciless as they bore down on me, plainly conveying that he didn't think I was worthy to shine his boots, let alone ignore his commands.

*"**You,**" he said, switching languages to Vandais, "**What is your name?**" "**Hawk,**" I replied in the same language, tone completely metronomic, my accent flawless.*

I watched tranquilly as one of his eyebrows cranked up a fraction; clearly, this was the biggest display of emotion he was capable of.

*"**You are one of the birth-marked, aren't you?**" Niral questioned coldly.*

I tilted my head slightly downward in an affirmative, still expressionless.

*"**So you will swear loyalty now.**"*

It wasn't a question, but I tilted my head a second time all the same. He nodded, apparently satisfied.

*"**Good. Your soul belongs to the guild now.**"*

And with that, he left.

I feel a slight twitching at the corners of my mouth at the memory, but resist the urge to smile.

Niral Lione.

The Devil in human form; the bane of my existence and a more despicable man, if you can even call him that, I have never met.

It was his plan that forced me to give up on my only calling in life and his reputation that keeps me from regaining any semblance of a normal life now.

I toss my still-burning cigarette to the ground and turn away from the rolling water.

For too long, the majority of my life has been spent either standing here or drinking until a normal person would pass out.

One day, I will break out of this cycle.

The worlds can count on that.

CHAPTER 3

Dark Angel

There are many reasons why one might choose to adorn oneself with the garment known as the cloak.

It could be a mundane reason, such as protecting yourself from the cold, but in such a case, one would eventually remove it at other times, rather than just when sleeping.

It could be a more gruesome reason, such as hiding an unsightly injury or scar on one's body, but even in that case, one would eventually remove it; either to treat the injury or simply to make sure it hadn't gotten any worse.

The final reason is one you can be sure no one has ever thought of before: to conceal one's identity as a dark angel.

And this is precisely the reason why Therrian Shalis is never seen during waking hours without his dark cloak: he hides his wings, except during rare moments when he needs utilize his "special" talents.

The cloak falls to the damp ground along with his dark glasses and onyx wings splay out, covered with similarly-coloured thorns and soft, shadowy feathers. And the eyes a sharp contrast: electric-white and utterly devoid of pupils and emotion. Thorns identical to the ones on his wings jut out of his bare coffee-coloured chest and his victim gasps with fear.

"W-what are you?" he stutters shakily, raising a hand in a vain attempt to defend himself.

Black-tinged lips curl in a sneer.

"Your worst nightmare," he declares in a satisfied hiss before launching.

The bloodcurdling scream of the man beneath him rings out through the silence of the night.

Screaming.

Tearing.

Blood.

Skin.

And then...blackness.

Therrian turns away from the mangled body now lying prone across the ground and once again dons his cloak and glasses, cleaning the blood and skin from his pointed canines. His wings fold back into the cloak and the glowing light from his eyes fades as he replaces his dark glasses and hood over them, leaving the deserted terrain in its previous darkness.

A slight smile tugs at the corners of his inked lips.

It had been quite a long while since the last time he had fed on a live one since Lord Niral had been keeping him in check with a supply of dead bodies; leftover corpses from the guild's victims.

The metallic tang of his victim's blood lingers on his tongue and Therrian grimaces.

As soon as his watch duty is over, he resolves to wash out his mouth. Blood was not a taste he was fond of.

"What...was that, Therrian?" Niral's obviously irate hiss erupts in his ear as his com crackles to life.

Therrian sighs and simply deigns not answer at that moment as there are still faint traces of blood remaining on his teeth and having the viscous red liquid in his mouth tended to make him slur his words, even if there were only just a few small traces.

He runs the tip of his tongue over the bottoms of his front teeth, removing all remnants of the man's blood, before replying. "There was an intrusion and I took care of it," he says quietly, voice empty of emotion.

He hears Niral struggles to restrain himself from yelling, "And I commend you for that, but must you so openly display your inhumanity to every intrusion that comes along?"

Therrian can't help smirking.

"One might think you didn't want to advertise the fact that you have a dark angel as your weapon, the way you keep me under wraps, my lord," he comments in a low voice, as he returns to his watching position behind a tree near the Gate.

Niral's exaggerated sigh was emphasized static through Therrian's earpiece; "You are a *secret* weapon, Therrian, to only be revealed at the opportune moment. And getting rid of minor annoyances is most definitely *not* the opportune moment,"

The dark angel rolls his eyes and cuts off the connection by way of a response.

She wakes up on the other side of the gate of Souls, clothed only in shadows and standing before a row of four aged immortals, two male and two female, seated at a long, cylindrical glass table, all surveying her impassively.

"Nyle Candor," the man at the head of the table announces coolly, steepling his translucent fingers together and resting his chin on top of them.

The three others make similar motions and before long, Nyle is beginning to feel rather uncomfortable. She shifts nervously, unsure if she should broach a reply or not.

Luckily, the man who had just spoken takes the decision out of her hands, so to speak.

"You have been brought before the underworld council for a single reason. Do you know what that reason is?" he asks her shortly.

Nyle shakes her black head, though her brain is telling her to do exactly the opposite.

The man sighs and inhales deeply, clearly annoyed by her answer.

"You are here because your life and death were different: you lived relatively unsullied and innocent, but your untimely death has the taint of the assassin's guild on it. Which brings up the question of the underworld you belong on," he declares neutrally, as if it doesn't matter to him one way or the other.

Again, Nyle shuffles uncomfortably under his piercing gaze "I was killed by my elder brother; he shot me," she pipes up tentatively, not sure if this information will make a difference or not.

A barely visible eyebrow arches in what can only be described as ill-concealed surprise.

"And what do you think you did to him that permitted such an act?" the man wonders politely, but escaping her notice are his eyes burning with malice and anticipation.

She shrugs, clueless, biting her bottom lip in obvious distress.

The immortal strains to hide the smile steadily building on his pale lips.

"Then, there is but one course of action, should you choose to take it: you shall become an assailant of the underworld in order to keep yourself from the fate that will befall your victims, and your brother," He turns to face her fully. "Do you accept?"

Nyle raises her head, olive eyes blazing with the fires of the gruesome and macabre.

"I accept,"

CHAPTER 4

Puppet

"There is no safe haven left for you, dear Hawk, for many are after you," Niral crooned to himself as he shut off the connection with Therrian, an almost lustful gleam in his scaly, insipid eyes.

He turned away from the aerial and activated his earpiece. "Candor, I want a word with you," he said, enunciating his words carefully, lest he be misheard.

In an instant, said dark-skinned youth was in his doorway, clad in the customary black leather pants and jacket over bared chest of male members of the guild.

The guild's leader had to restrain himself from growling in arousal at the sight of that dark-skinned, muscular chest and forced himself to adopt a professional expression, instead.

Candor sank onto one knee, head tilted in a low bow that only enticed Niral further.

"You summoned me, my lord?" he questioned, arching a blue-ebony eyebrow in silent query at his master.

Niral's expression turned into an almost feral grin.

"Yes, Candor," he said, brow low and voice husky, "I find myself in need of satisfaction and you were, of course, the first person I thought of. So, if you wouldn't mind,"

Candor grinned, "As you wish, my lord," and he obediently stripped of his jacket and pants, leaving him standing in the middle of the room, clad in only a pair of black briefs.

Niral's eyes roved hungrily over the man's sculpted body; the toned chest, the defined stomach, the muscular arms and powerfully built legs, all a rich dark brown colour. But what always caught Niral's eye the most was the almost inhuman bulge at the front of his briefs.

He advanced towards the half-naked man, fingers hooking in the waist of his own dark green pants. When he had closed the distance between him and Candor, he pushed his pants off his hips and they fell to the floor with a soft thump. Candor's olive eyes watched the snake pull his shirt over his head and toss it carelessly onto the floor next to his pants.

With a casual flick of Niral's head, Candor dropped to his knees, positioning his legs so they were slightly apart. Niral sidled up in front of him and removed his boxers, leaving the assumption hanging out in an air of perverse thoughts and forbidden thrills. "Suck," he said simply and Candor obeyed, pulling the taller man's throbbing erection into his mouth, sucking hard.

Niral bucked his hips and thrusted vigorously into the younger's mouth while Candor's tongue ran over the bottom of his shaft slowly. Before he was brought to his release, though, Candor backed off and gave him a pointed look, signalling Niral to press him into the cold floor, one hand pinning his wrists above his head and the other slipping his boxers off so Niral could enter him fully.

Without warning, Niral pushed himself deeper, thrusting and grinding his hips into the younger man's roughly, causing him to cry out-whether in pleasure or pain, it was unclear; most likely a little bit of both.

The snake's cruel chuckle hissed into Candor's ear as Niral's teeth sank into the lobe, scissoring through the flesh and before long, Candor felt something warm trickling down the side of his face. Niral chuckled again and let his tongue flick out to catch the blood as it fell, leaving a thin trail of saliva in its wake. When the blood was gone, though, the snakelike tongue didn't stop its descent and continued over the length of Candor's neck, stopping at the nape, where he bit down on the skin, just barely leaving it intact.

He slammed into Candor's exposed opening, eliciting a sharp, ragged scream from the dark-skinned male's mouth. He continued to ram into Candor brutally, each thrust punctuated by a loud, almost agonized yell.

Finally, he reached his climax and bit into a dark shoulder in the heat of the moment, feeling himself release deep within Candor's ass. When he had ridden out every last drop, he slid out easily, but remained pinning Candor to the floor.

"Damn," Candor muttered before saying in a more normal voice, "So was I really the only fuck available?"

Niral laughed without humour and looked at the naked man beneath him seriously. "Well, Therrian's still on watch duty, so, yes."

With a harsh sneer, he released Candor's wrists and got to his feet, beginning to pull his clothes back on. Candor redressed quickly and left the room without another word.

As I was making my way back to my hideout, I felt the sudden, familiar press of cold metal against the back of my neck.

"Oh, shit," I swore under my breath before my would-be killer spoke.

"Hawk," a female voice that I, unfortunately, recognized, greeted me sneeringly.

I whipped around, instantly knocking the gun pressed to my skin out of its wielders hand with a swift spinning kick. I caught the gun and had it pointed at the assailant before they had a chance to recover.

They raised their arms in mock surrender and lifted their ebony head to the light.

My shock didn't show on my face, but I had to force myself not to drop the gun in astonishment: I knew this dark-skinned profile all too well.

Candor's little sister grinned at me, her olive eyes gleaming with malevolence.

"Hello, ***sandres***," she said, spitting out the Vandais word for "brother" with a fierce snarl, causing me to actually take a step back from her seething form.

"Nyle," I uttered mechanically, my stunned disbelief effectively preventing me from saying anything more.

"Wondering why I'm here, are you?" she curled her lips coldly, glaring at me.

I deigned not to answer, fearing my voice would crack from the severe stupefaction I was currently experiencing.

Nyle laughed, a rough, throaty cackle that was completely opposite from the laugh I remembered her having and advanced toward me menacingly as she drew a second gun from her belt.

She directed the barrel of the pistol between my eyes before speaking again, "My brother shot me and forced me to be brought before the underworld council. And now their power has given me a second life so he can pay for what he did to me and the guild can pay for what they did to him. And, of course, you were at the top of my list as a victim; after all, it was your influence that drove Jarl into becoming the monster he is today."

I folded my arms across my chest; now that just wasn't true.

"I'm flattered you thought I had so much influence on your brother," I commented dryly, "But Candor was a monster long before he ever met me. When the guild took him, he went willingly because he *wanted* to be an assassin."

"You're lying!" Nyle spat lividly, "He was captured just like all the others and then he became who he is today to impress you because you were the guild's best!"

I stared coolly back at her and uttered two words; "Bull. Shit."

She roared almost inhumanly and disappeared with a blast like a cannon, leaving behind a suspicious scent in her previous spot.

My crimson eyes narrowed at her vacated position. I unfolded my arms and knelt down next to it for closer examination.

A strangely familiar aroma lingered in the air around it and I thought carefully for a moment, attempting to place it.

"Oh, *crap,*" I muttered mutinously when I finally remembered where I recognized the unseemly smell of fire and rotting flesh from.

Nyle had become one of the dreaded underworld assailants so she could get revenge on Candor for killing her.

I got back on my feet, lost in thought.

Had Candor really become so hard-hearted since I left the guild? Because, the last time I had seen him, he absolutely coveted his younger sister and wouldn't have ever even thought about killing her, even if he was ordered to.

Something really wasn't right about this.

I mentally groaned.

I had been looking forward to one day of staying outside without having my life threatened, but no, instead, it was back into the old hideout to try and find out what could have happened to Candor to make him ruthless enough to kill the last surviving member of his family.

It looked like I'd finally found a use for that laptop he "bought" for me all those years ago.

CHAPTER 5

The Other Side

The underworld council had been in existence for hundreds of years, but it hadn't always guarded the Gate of Souls.

It was developed when the original assassin's guild was formed and there was a true need for judgement, because before then, the hosts of the Gate were convinced that everyone who died deserved to die in purgatory.

But that changed.

The council started out unbiased and with good intentions, wanting only to serve justice and righteousness.

But now, they serve their own ends by creating the underworld assailants: revenge-driven lost souls, consumed by insatiable lust with extraordinary demonic powers.

And to have the powers of a demon from the underworld was to become virtually indestructible.

The man turned from the table, rising from his seat, a malevolent smile playing uncharacteristically onto his translucent grey lips.

"That is another assailant we have produced from our dear friend, Candor," he declared, sounding almost gleeful. The others, not so much.

"And how does that help us with the judging of the departed?" the youngest woman questioned, artfully raising an invisible eyebrow at him, causing his smile to expand.

"We are no longer simply the judges, Maiaa; we can influence things now, and the guild has made enemies of us," he chided mockingly. "Lione's plane to unleash his power on the underworld with that foolish dark angel at the helm will fail,"

Maiaa shook her great white head. "Though it is our place to protect the world from minions like that, it is not our place to be creating the assailants and in turn, create even more victims. You know this, Caius."

Caius turned around to face her, his clear eyes glowing eerily, "We do not create victims, we take care of them. The assailants are our form of a second chance for people who have been unjustly murdered by one of the guild."

"Your opinion of a second chance is transforming innocent people into monsters with a lust for flesh, physically and otherwise, so that you can have an army to destroy the guild with," Maiaa argued valiantly, but anyone could see she just wasn't going to get through to him. He was done listening.

He turned away from her and declared in a soft, sibilant voice, "The guild is an embarrassment and it needs to be eliminated."

Nyle landed outside of the bowels of the flames that served as her chambers in the underworld after leaving Varros behind.

Her meal was waiting; she could smell the live specimen inside her room, healthy and terrified.

A cruel smile crossed her lips; that was exactly how she liked them.

She entered her bedchamber, eagerly searching the room for her victim.

She found him sitting in the corner, arms and legs crossed, eyes closed and blonde head bowed low.

~A blonde.~*Nyle observed with a satisfied growl, rubbing her hands together in anticipation.*

"So why has the underworld council condemned you to being my meal for tonight?" she asked him coldly, feeling herself beginning to transform.

The man lifted his eyelids and head just in time to see her transition from a normal teenage girl into underworld assailant.

Long and spiked black leather wings sprung from her back, ripping slits in the back of her shirt; a sharp contrast to her now blood-coloured eyes. The whites and pupils of her eyes retreated into the pools of red and left them filling her entire eye socket.

Her nails turned jet black and grew to the size of long daggers; her front teeth lengthened considerably into sharp fangs.

The man raised a light eyebrow in incredulity, hardly believing what he had just seen. "What are you?" he questioned in a strangely calm tone, folding his arms tighter across his chest.

Nyle laughed icily, sharpening her claws against her knife with a sharp, grinding sound.

"You'd think most people would know an underworld assailant when they see one,"Nyle commented, faking hurt as she advanced toward her prey threateningly.

He watched her slightly horned tongue glide sinuously over her lips with bile rising at the back of his throat at the sight.

"And how am I your meal again?" he quipped disgustedly, his second eyebrow rising to join the first.

"Don't you know your history?" Nyle pretended to chastise him, "Underworld assailants "service" most of their victims before flaying the flesh from their bodies and devouring it. And the council has provided you as my victim for tonight, which essentially makes you my meal. Now, if you'd be so kind," She gestured to his arms, "I do prefer victims who fight back, but I'm already exhausted and don't have the energy to subdue you, so..."

The man lowered his eyebrows and surrendered, getting to his feet before raising his arms above his head and pressing them against the wall.

Quick as a flash, Nyle was directly in front of him and she held his arms above his head with one hand, while the other reached for his belt buckle.

When I got back to my hideout, I sat down on my bed, placing the laptop in front of me before opening it and switching it on to Candor's creation: the guild website.

It was meant as a joke, but he had taken it seriously and used it as his own personal outlet for all the things that went on in the guild that Niral didn't want the members to know.

Hopefully, now it would tell me why Candor had just suddenly up and scrapped the only personal value that he had had left.

The layout of the website was pretty basic, but I do recall Candor setting up all sorts of precautions so that he and I were the only ones who could access it; him to update it, me because he knew I needed a good laugh every once in a while, even it was just a sardonic snort.

It was a miracle that I still remembered my password after four years without needing it; I entered it and found the page completely different from what I had known it to be.

It was no longer solely dedicated to mock-bashing the guild; it was now totally for it, posting the names of recent victims and such.

I let my eyes wander over that because something else caught my attention: a small, flashing headline in the corner that read "personal attachments", and against my better judgement, I clicked on it.

What came up on the screen then burned itself permanently into my brain; of this, I kid you not.

Filling the screen were all sorts of images that I swear made me want to throw up.

Because they were all of Niral and his ungodly reptilian-like looks.

Worse, they were poor shots of him and Candor doing-I didn't even want to know what.

At seeing all of these pictures, it hit me all at once what had forced the last of my old friend's humanity to go down the drain-even after witnessing firsthand the damage it had done to me, he had become Niral's puppet.

No, even worse than that, he had become Niral's *sex toy.*

~*Ugh.*~I groaned in my head, slightly wanting to retch as memories of what that had been like for me began to cloud my mind.

I inwardly shuddered, not wanting to recall what it had felt like to be used like that. I bet I knew why the snake had chosen Candor, too; because Candor and I had been friends and Niral wanted to suck out everything good about my life.

Now I knew my composure was going to go out the window at this prospect, so I didn't try to delay the inevitable and groaned aloud.

Very unbecoming of me, I knew, but it was bound to happen sooner or later, so I decided I might as well get it out now.

So, Candor belonged to Niral now and he was no longer even the slightest bit human anymore.

The question was, what was I intending to do about it with me in hiding and him still a very prime part of the dreaded guild?

The Gate of Souls was almost always still, but now that events were being set in motion to bypass it, that was all about to change.

A loud clang rang off its iron rungs as an unearthly blast of wind violently slammed it open.

Therrian's fingers twitched, but he restrained himself with a massive effort.

Now was when the "watching" part of his watch duty came into play.

Black forms appeared, seemingly out of thin air, heading for the Gate. Leathery wings sprouted out of their back and spheres of red glowed menacingly where their eyes should have been.

Underworld assailants. Therrian concluded with a slight smile.

The assailants entered the open gateway, smoothly and silently, each of them dragging a long, pointed stick behind them. *Now there's something new.* Therrian observed, arching an immaculate steel-white eyebrow behind his dark glasses as he watched the scene unfolding before him.

Every one of the assailants stood firmly in the gateway, holding their left-hand claws in a forked position by their heads, the "sticks", for lack of a better word, scraped the ground and hung motionless.

And then it began.

A hoarse, bone-rattling cry rose from the assailants' mouths, causing Therrian's other eyebrow to join the first in disbelief.

A tall assailant, this one evidently a female, appeared at the Gate and Therrian once again had to restrain himself from activating his earpiece and contacting Niral. Quiet and inconspicuous as he was, his voice could still attract unwanted attention from the assailants and he couldn't risk giving away his position. At least, not yet.

"Our masters are waiting," the female assailant in the front, presumably their leader, announced, her voice a grating hiss through the hoarse cry the others were continuing to emit. And all the others bowed their heads and followed her through the gateway and the Gate slammed shut behind them, leaving a sharp, billowing silence in place of the assailants' cry.

Therrian's eyebrows dropped down as he recomposed himself to contact Niral.

He pressed a gloved finger to the com and flicked it on. "Lord Niral, I think there's some feed you might want to have a look at," he declared, softly and offhandedly."

"*Time frame*?"

"The last fifteen minutes," Therrian said in a bored voice.

He heard Niral swear.

"That's not a time frame, you overdeveloped, single-cell Cro-Magnon," Therrian rolled his eyes at the insult. "I mean, from when to when."

"O:15 to 0:30," Therrian amended his statement, hiding a smirk and switching the earpiece off.

CHAPTER 6

Action on All Fronts

Later that night, Niral lay out the guild's entire arsenal of weapons before the members and turned impassively to face them, drawing his own revolver from its holster and raising it in front of his face.

He spoke then, carefully measuring every one of his words. "You have all heard my plan to unleash the full might of the guild on the underworld council," he began calmly, his olive-coloured face expressionless. "The council has now decided to strike back with their newly developed weapons: the underworld assailants. I trust you are all aware of the creatures of which I speak?"

"Yes, Lord Niral," the members of the guild responded immediately. Niral grinned, "I hoped you would be, Candor in particular,"

Candor's blue-ebony head swivelled around rapidly to face the sneering snake.

"Oh yes, Candor-I think you'd like to hear this, actually," Niral mused, drab eyes flashing with what could only be described as amusement, "Your younger sister–Nyle, I believe her name is–the one you were previously assigned to kill, is now one of the prime assailants of the underworld."

The male assassin folded his arms across his bare chest and turned away. "Just get on with it, Niral."

Niral resisted a smirk. "Well, now that the underworld council is planning to strike back, we have no choice but to put our plan into action," he said, "Gather every working weapon from the armoury. We move now."

I knew they were still after me; why else would Niral have chosen Candor as his "puppet"? Hiding is no longer an option, though. So, what was there left for me to do?

I'd been sitting on my bed, staring blankly at the laptop screen, still and silent as I contemplated my next move for the last few hours. Candor obviously wasn't going to respond to ordinary means of confrontation, so I think it's time to think outside the box.

I slammed the laptop screen shut and stood, reaching over my bedpost for my black cloak.

I threw the cloak back on and opened the drawer under my "bed", withdrawing my two guild-issued guns and a knife. The guns I deposited into the empty holsters attached to my belt and the knife I tucked into my left boot.

The final thing was to stuff the laptop down the front of my cloak and dispose of all evidence of my presence in this building. With a quick flick of my fingers, the books and scrolls previously scattered across the floor were swept into an untidy pile in the centre of the room; I flicked my fingers a second time, and they disappeared entirely.

Throwing my hood up over my slate hair, I placed on my black gloves and transported myself out of the building.

Watch out, Niral, because, not only was I not in hiding anymore, but you're going to pay for corrupting my only real friend.

Through the mazes of the underworld, Nyle lead the newly arrived army of underworld assailants to where the council was waiting for them. Her mind was empty, except for a single thought: the massacre they were about to unleash on the world of the living was going to be nothing compared to what she had in store for her notoriously bloodthirsty brother.

She wasn't going to feed on him; oh, no, he deserved so much worse than that. He was far too despicable for her taste, but her plan would make him wish she'd chosen him for her meal. He was going to pay dearly for killing her.

The double doors swung inward of their own accord, admitting the army without question.

"All assailants gather in the entrance hall," Caius' easily recognizable voice rang out, seeming to emit from the stone walls themselves.

Nyle bypassed the marble staircase and entered the scarcely lit corridor with her other brethren following close behind her. "Raise your pikes, my friends, because now the underworld fights back," she announced with passion, "And the heads of those who dare to proclaim themselves our masters will be erected on these pikes for eternity!"

An almost ungodly cheer filled that corridor, reverberating off of the walls and surrounding them with an inescapable rush of noise.

Down the corridor, they travelled, still cheering and now jabbing their pikes repeatedly into the air in time with their cheers. The call echoed throughout the hallway, but came to an abrupt halt when they reached the council hall, where Caius and Maiaa and the rest of the council stood, waiting with varied expressions; Caius, a fiercely triumphant one; Maiaa, one of ill-concealed distaste; Livden, one of cool indifference and Yyx, one of obvious anger.

Nyle brought the group to a stop in front of Caius and knelt at his feet.

"Master," she greeted him and the other assailants mimicked her actions. Caius waved the formalities away and gestured for them to stand up.

"You were all turned into these weapons of mass destruction because you wanted vengeance on those who dared to steal from you the gift that was your life. But now you have a greater calling," Caius cleared his throat before elaborating, "The hated assassin's guild is planning to use their power to gain dominion over the underworld. Once upon a time, the council would've just sat back and let them do so because we were contrite, and if they were meant to have the underworld, we could not change that. But now we have the power to influence events and the underworld will not fall into those blasphemers' clutches- which is why I created you, my friends. The underworld assailants shall become the instrument of demise for the world of the living."

Again, the cheer rose up explosively, the assailants punching the air and Caius smirking right up to his clear, achromatic eyes. "Yes, my friends, revel in the dawning of a new age," His smile dissipated. "But not yet. First, we must rid the world of these tiresome assassins and the terror their existence has caused."

The cheer grew, while Nyle stood in the front, keeping silent but smirking with anticipation.

"Therrian, it's time," Niral's oily voice crackled through the earpiece an hour after the events at the Gate, tense with excitement.

Black-tinged lips creased in a sly smile. "So, the underworld council has opted for war over peaceful surrender?" Therrian commented, playing with the clasp of his cloak.

Niral chuckled without humour.

"Indeed, they have," he confirmed smoothly, "So we begin now. Your watch duty is over,"

Thank God. Therrian thought with relief.

The connection was suddenly cut off then, though, before Niral could relay any further instructions on what Therrian was to do now, and the dark angel frowned.

Then, static sounded over the com and an unfamiliar voice rang out in Therrian's ear.

"This channel now belongs to me, dark angel," The voice was male and a harsher voice Therrian had never heard before in his entire existence.

"And how, exactly, is that?" Therrian questioned fluidly out of the corner of his mouth, his gloved fingers twitching toward the revolver holstered beneath his cloak.

The voice laughed mirthlessly. "Simple. When you communicate on a private channel, there's no one to prevent it from being infiltrated."

"And who are you, the master hacker?" Therrian retaliated dryly, moving for his dagger instead of his gun.

"You could say that," the voice said evasively.

Therrian had had enough. He withdrew the dagger from his belt and plunged the tip into the centre of the earpiece, effectively cutting the power completely.

He tossed the now inactive earpiece onto the ground before stowing his dagger back in his belt and pulling out an older com-link to contact Niral.

The com link flashed to life and Niral's irate voice came through, "What happened, Therrian?" "The channel was hacked. I had to deactivate the ear-piece's power and revert to the older com-link," Therrian explained truthfully.

"And who, pray tell, hacked the communication channel?" Niral asked. "That, I don't know; but if I had to guess, I would say probably someone who's very good with a computer," the dark angel replied calmly.

"Whatever. Get back to base, Therrian, so we can start this damn operation already," Niral ordered with a rather unnerving return to his usual emotionless tone, and he terminated the conversation.

Therrian dropped the com link back into his pocket and disappeared with a whirl of his cloak.

Hacking Niral and the dark angel's communication channel had been almost too easy. Turned out that that laptop had more than one convenient use.

I scrolled down through the lines and found the video feed. *This might be interesting.* I decided, clicking on it without hesitation.

The screen now showed the Gate of Souls, eerily immobile as ever. Then, an unearthly scream of wind violently blasted it open with a loud clang. Black forms materialized out of the dense air, carrying with them sinister-looking pikes and with pupiless pools of blood filling their eye sockets.

One of the black forms moved to the head of the group and spoke.

"Our masters are waiting."

It was a female whose voice I, unfortunately, recognized. *Nyle.* I mentally cursed, swearing under my breath. The feed ended there.

I steeled myself to loosen my grip on the edge of the laptop and let my fingers glide over the keys in a swift sequence that allowed me to connect to Niral's end of the channel. I chuckled smoothly through the link.

"If you were wondering who hacked your communication link with the dark angel, you can stop wondering, Niral," I taunted, completely taking control of the connection so Niral wouldn't be able to deactivate the earpiece like Therrian had.

"***Hello, Hawk,***" Niral's nauseating voice greeted me slyly in the language he knew I despised him using, "***Glad to hear you're out of hiding. Up to your old computer tricks, are you***?"

I allowed a faint smirk to briefly cross my lips before responding, "I wouldn't call them *old,* exactly. I just thought I'd let you know that there was someone else out there who could hack a communication channel, besides your latest puppet." "***Oh, so you do know your old friend has taken the honour that you effectively lost when you decided to quit the guild!***" Niral exclaimed with what sounded sickeningly like glee.

I had to force myself not to gag. "I'm watching you, Niral, and when we meet again, you're going to pay for corrupting Candor," I vowed and with that, I terminated the connection.

This was the problem; Niral always knew exactly which buttons to push because of all the years I had spent in the same position that Candor was in now. He knew me too well. But I was going to change that.

I was no longer the obedient little assassin he had trained me to be; I knew why I was doing things, and my trust lay with no one but myself.

But Candor was a friend. He had helped me while I was in the guild, and kept me from completely losing my humanity. And now he was losing his. Niral had corrupted him so much that he'd killed the last living member of his family, the only person that had stopped him from becoming a complete monster.

I needed to stop him before Nyle, in her underworld assailant form, destroyed what was left of him.

CHAPTER 7

The Serpent and the Hawk

I could feel my laptop sagging down in my cloak, but attempted to ignore it. After all, there wasn't much I could do about it while transporting. The trees and other such things passed by me in a whirlwind of disoriented images.

When I landed, for the first time in I don't know how long, I actually had to take a minute to recompose myself afterwards.

I guessed it was probably a residual effect of not having gone anywhere that couldn't be reached by simply walking in the longest time; my two destinations had mainly consisted of my hideout and the "beach" in front of it for the last four years.

But I was going to have to get used to this mode of transportation again since I wouldn't be going back into hiding again.

Not while Niral was still at large.

Once I'd finally managed to regain some semblance of dignity and had straightened myself out, I pulled my laptop out of the front of my cloak and switched it on again to the hacked channel that Niral and Therrian had been using to communicate.

Through some very elaborate hacking manoeuvres that are far too complex to explain, I was able to turn the earpiece that Niral possessed that was connected to this channel into a tracking device, because, where Niral was, most likely that was where Candor would be as well.

My crimson pools quickly scanned the readings pasted across the screen, and from them I was able to discern Niral's current location-about a day's walk from the Gate of Souls.

Now what could Niral be doing there? I thought caustically, rolling my eyes as I snapped the thin screen shut and stowed the laptop back where it was before, heading in the direction of where it had said Niral was.

I wasn't usually one to go looking for trouble, but someone had to stop Niral from putting his plan to overthrow the underworld council into action.

And that someone was going to be me-one way or another.

The journey to the Gate of Souls continued. And hanging in the air was an impending sense of foreboding that had everyone, even Niral, on edge. Wind tore through the trees, emitting a restless rustling.

"Your operation ends here, Lione."

Niral halted in his tracks at the familiar voice, drawing every member of the guild's attention to the front of the queue.

Out of the corner of his eye, Niral saw Candor fight to suppress what was evidently a gasp.

Because blocking their path, dark cloak rippling in the building wind, was Varros Hawk, the guild's estranged legend.

"So, you really are out of hiding," Niral observed softly, his hooded eyes flickering maliciously.

"Hawk, what are you doing here?" Candor demanded in a bark, his facial muscles working furiously to conceal his shock.

Varros pushed back his black hood and turned the piercing crimson pools underneath on his former friend impassively.

"I think the real question here, Candor, is what are *you* doing?" he retorted smoothly, sounding as though he didn't actually care about the answer.

The question threw Candor completely off-guard- and this time, everyone could see him struggling not to show it.

"What do you care? You're no longer a member of the guild and I don't owe you a damn thing. So, get the hell out of my life and stay out," he snarled coldly, olive eyes dark with hatred.

But Varros saw something else, too-he just couldn't identify it. Could Candor really be hurt that he had quit the guild?

Niral interrupted his musings with a click of his tongue.

"Hardly a friendly reunion," he commented, shaking his head with mock disapproval, "Clearly, the two of you are missing something."

"Shut up, asshole. This whole thing is your fault, anyways, so butt the fuck out," Varros snapped acidly, before turning back to the dark-skinned male in front of him, who had folded his arms across his bared chest. "And as for you, do you want to know *why* I quit this goddamned guild? Because of what you're about to do this very moment!"

"You can't stop us, Hawk," Niral cut him off calmly, staring him down. "And Candor here belongs to me now, so your coming here was a colossal waste of time, except to allow me to capture you again-but if you stand down, I might reconsider, so step aside,"

Varros looked disgusted.

"Candor doesn't belong to you, you sicko, and you're wrong; I *can* stop you," he drew out both of the guns from his belt and pointed them forward. "Take one more step towards the Gate and I'll blow every last one of your damned heads off."

CHAPTER 8

Time For Armageddon

"Take one more step towards the Gate and I'll blow every last one of your damned heads off," I growled threateningly, daring any of them to move even an inch.

I wasn't bluffing, either-I'd had it up to here with Niral and his drones, and I would have gladly shot every one of these dumbasses.

But I never got the chance to carry out my threat, because at that exact moment, a gun was jabbed painfully into the side of my head and a familiar voice hissed into my ear, "Drop the guns, Hawk."

I couldn't resist a smirk. "Or what?"

Nyle chuckled throatily. "Or you'll get to experience firsthand the savagery of an underworld assailant."

"Why, do you *want* them to overthrow your masters?" I retorted, stubbornly refusing to let go of my guns.

"Quite the contrary, actually. The second they enter Master Caius' domain, they will be getting a very nasty surprise. Now kindly drop the guns because I would prefer not to kill you now," Nyle said with false sweetness.

I finally surrendered and allowed the iron grip I had on my guns to go completely slack, causing them to fall to the ground. "Now kindly remove the gun from my head because I would prefer not to get shot," I ordered smoothly, mocking her previous statement.

The female underworld assailant snorted, but complied. The second her gun was no longer in contact with my head, I transported and grabbed Candor-as well as my guns off of the ground-before transporting us both to somewhere Niral would hold no sway over what my old friend said and couldn't make any more interruptions.

"All right, Jarl, no more screwing around. What the hell's going on with you?"

Candor had the nerve to pretend to look confused. "Why, Varros, whatever do you mean by that?" he questioned innocently, faking hurt.

"Don't mess with me, Jarl, you and I both know what I'm talking about," I said, my voice dangerously low. "I know you're Lione's puppet now and that you shot your sister. So, what gives?"

"You quit, so how could you possibly know either one of those things?" Candor all but growled, raising a dark blue eyebrow.

"Three words: your guild website," I stated simply, rolling my eyes in exasperation.

Candor swore. "I knew I should've gone with my gut and deleted that shit, rather than changing it to support the guild."

It was my turn to raise an eyebrow.

"So why didn't you? Who convinced you to do otherwise?" I wondered, though I was pretty sure I already knew what Candor's answer was going to be.

And I was right. "Niral," Candor admitted quietly, confirming my suspicions that he was indeed said vile assassin guild leader's "puppet" through and through.

There was still something bothering me about that, however. Why would Niral persuade Candor to change the website instead of deleting it completely? Wouldn't he want it gone? Unless he knew I'd have it to see it at some point and it was all some sick ploy to coax me out of hiding.

But Niral couldn't have known that I was the only other person who had access to it. Could he?

"Did you tell Niral that I was the only other who could get on to that website?" I asked him sharply, my voice now frigidly calm-the only alternative I had to keep my anger in check.

My eyes closed then, because I didn't want to see my old friend's face when he responded, no matter what he said.

Then, he uttered the single word I was so utterly dreading; "Yes."

I inhaled deeply though my nose and didn't even bother to open my eyes before speaking. "You fucking *moron*."

In my mind's eye, I could almost see Candor wincing at the emphasis I put on "moron" and had to refrain from allowing a sneer to cross my bloodless lips, "Do you even know what 's going to happen now?" My eyelids practically flew open now to reveal my crimson eyes burning with ferocity.

"The guild isn't even going to have a *chance* against the council. They have an army of underworld assailants and the only way to stop one is by removing the spell with Eidolon powers. And, in case you hadn't noticed, the Eidolon guild isn't exactly a public group, so it's not like they're freely available to be at your disposal. So how exactly do you suppose the assassin's guild is going to overthrow the underworld council?" I folded my arms across my chest.

Candor, to his credit, managed to keep the astonishment I thought he was feeling off of his face. But it was in his eyes. He knew that the guild had set itself up for what could only be complete and utter Armageddon.

Niral raised his own revolver at Nyle, hardly even noticing that neither Varros nor Candor was no longer in the vicinity. "Why did you stop Hawk from carrying out his threat, assailant?" he questioned coldly

She laughed without humour, "So Master Caius can have the pleasure of eliminating you himself, Niral Lione."

The leader of the assassin's guild visibly tensed, raising an eyebrow at the familiarity with which the underworld assailant spoke his name.

"I'm sorry, have we met?" he asked fluidly, masking his shock well.

Nyle let out a second mirthless chuckle and stared him hard in the eyes. "And here I thought you prided yourself on knowing and remembering every victim of your precious guild," she commented, voice thick with disdain.

"Well, if I could do that, I'd have to have some sort of super memory, wouldn't I?" Niral shot back, not missing a beat.

The female assailant rolled her eyes, those twin spheres of blood now positively glowing with scorn.

"Take a good look, Niral, at Nyle Candor, leader of the underworld assailants and whose brother was forced to shoot her by *you*," Nyle declared, viciously extending her claws, "And you're lucky that the council wants to take you out themselves, or I'd have let Hawk carry out his threat and blow all of your heads off right here. Sadly, that won't be the case, so." She turned around, "Continue to the Gate of souls and," she snickered, "Your doom."

And she was gone.

Shaking the remaining shock out of his system, Niral stowed his revolver back in his belt.

"My lord?" the tentative voice of one of the other members of the guild piped up from behind him, sounding slightly shaken.

"Yes, Mihd, what is it?" Niral replied nonchalantly, not really caring what the younger man had to say.

"We are continuing, aren't we?" Mihd questioned, sounding vaguely apprehensive.

"Don't ask stupid questions," Niral bit back irritably, "Of course we're continuing. Did you really think that I'd let a minor threat by Hawk and the pitiful underworld assailants deter my operation from being put into action?"

Mihd didn't answer and the leader of the guild let out a derisive snort before he began heading toward the Gate once again.

Silence reigned until one of the female assassins deigned to voice another concern. "My lord."

Niral stopped in his tracks a second time and actually bothered to turn around this time. "What is it now, Ilyx?" he quite literally spat through his now forcibly clenched teeth, forcing himself not to yell.

Ilyx, to her credit, didn't waver in the slightest when she spoke the words, "Candor's gone."

"So, when did you happen to find out the only way to take the underworld assailant out of someone was with the powers of a member of the Eidolon guild?" Candor asked, attempting civil conversation. Man, was he ever dense. Anyone with even an ounce of sense could tell that I wasn't in the mood at this point.

My eyes were closed, my arms folded over my chest, my back leaning against the wall and my legs crossed casually at the ankles; my classic anti-social pose. I reserved it specially for situations like this.

So, I deigned not to answer, but instead unfolded my arm and pulled out a cigarette. Normally, I would've had a drink instead, but I had left my flask behind, so I would just to have to make due with a smoke. I raised the thin white stick to my lips as I pulled my lighter out and lit the tip before letting out a puff of smoke.

That was when I sensed Candor coming towards me, clearly looking for his answer. His arms extended forward, but without even opening my eyes and before he had a chance to retract his arm, I grabbed the outstretched limb and had him in a wrist lock that drove him to his knees.

"You can't force an answer out of me, Jarl. Or did you think that just because I've been in hiding for the past four years that I'd forgotten my assassin's training?" I asked him coolly, lifting my eyelids again to the man in front of me. And I say "man" for lack of a more derogatory term.

"No," Candor just barely managed to choke out, face contorted in suppressed pain, "But I wanted an answer,"

"I wasn't the guild's best for nothing, so I'll answer when I'm good and ready."

I released my death grip on Candor's wrist and refolded my arms while he rubbed his wrist in an attempt to get the circulation back.

Once he'd done that, he worked himself into a sitting position and repeated his previous question. "So, really, when did you find out?"

I sighed, but decided that if Candor was going to try to be at least civil, then I should at least give him a straight answer. But it did strike me as slightly odd that he didn't know this, even though he had been there when I'd found it out.

"Are you telling me you don't remember, Jarl, or did Niral really take away, not only your humanity but your memories, too?" I replied, arching a slate eyebrow fractionally.

Candor looked taken aback. "I knew about this, too?" he quipped incredulously, sounding as if he couldn't believe his ears.

I gave a non-committal shrug.

"I don't know if you actually knew specifically about how to take the underworld assailant out of someone, but you were there when I found out. It was right after I was attacked by an assailant for the first time and you let me study them on your laptop, remember?"

There was absolutely no sign of recognition on Candor's dark-skinned face and I started to get slightly frightened. How could he forget something that important when it hadn't even happened all that long ago?

A grim thought filled my head.

It looked as though Niral's corruption of Candor's mind, body and soul had gone further than even I could ever have imagined.

I unfolded my arms and went to kneel in front of my former friend, deciding in that moment that it was time to get to the bottom of this situation.

But when I faced him fully, I discovered something I definitely didn't expect to see in those familiar olive eyes: traces of painful recognition, affirming that he did, in fact, remember.

"I blocked all of my good memories of you, Varros, so that it wouldn't hurt so much that you left," he confessed shamefacedly, answering my unspoken question. He'd been faking from the beginning.

I should have been angry, but all I felt was one of the emotions I just could never stand: confusion. Because I'd had no idea that my quitting the guild would have caused anyone pain.

"Is that why you became Niral's puppet, too? To forget about me?" I asked quietly, fighting to keep my voice under control. Candor turned away from me, obviously unable to bring himself to answer-which I took as a "yes".

"Candor, look at me," I commanded softly, reverting back to using his surname for the time being.

When he didn't move, I jammed my gloved hand underneath his chin and then forcefully turned his head around so he was facing me. I saw clearly the hurt burning in his eyes, but didn't acknowledge it.

"The guild is wrong to try to overthrow the underworld council, Candor," I started plaintively. "By doing so, they're disrupting the natural balance of our two worlds. And with the assailants on the council's side, they don't stand a chance. Once they are defeated, the gate of Souls will be destroyed and the border between the land of the living and the land of the dead will be as well,"

I knew my words had shaken him, but they had needed to be said, so he could understand the reasons why I had quit the guild.

I could see him thinking out of the corner of my eyes; then, after a long silence, he spoke.

"So that's really why you quit?" he said at last, looking disbelieving.

I nodded truthfully, "Yes, it is."

Candor raised his chin slightly. "Then we can't let what you said happen. So, I'm quitting the guild, too. And you and I, we're going to do something to stop it,"

"What are you proposing we do?" I asked him carefully, though I was pretty sure I already knew.

Candor grinned. "We find a way to contact the Eidolon guild."

CHAPTER 9

The Eidolon Guild

Even after so many years apart, I still had yet to forget how good Candor was in these types of situations; he'd taken my laptop out of my cloak, hacked one of the Eidolon communication channels, contacted them via earpiece and set up a meeting at a nearby bar. Not your typical place to meet a vampire, but Candor and I both needed a drink, so the Eidolon guild members would just have to deal.

"So here's how things are going to go down," Candor started to explain, adopting what he must have thought was a professional tone, but really just made him sound extremely pompous. "The Eidolon guild is going to have a representative waiting for us at the bar's corner. We're going to march over there, subtle as we are, and present him with our guild-issued guns so they know who we are and then hopefully we can get down to business." He met my eyes. "What do you think?"

I gave him a slight nod by way of a response. "That'll work. So, now, then?"

"Well, no. I mean, we could go now, but they said their representative wouldn't be able to get there before midnight and it's only about eleven now," Candor reasoned with a shrug.

I crossed my arms. "Are you planning to wait and then transport, then?" I quipped dully and nonchalantly, staring Candor down.

He shifted slightly under my razor-sharp gaze, like I was making him uncomfortable. "That was my plan, yeah,"

I stared at him hard for a few more minutes, then gave a non-committal jerk of my head. "Whatever."

I withdrew from my chest pocket my second cigarette in the last, I think half hour. I could see Candor's heavily lidded olive eyes following every motion of my figure as I lit the cigarette between my bloodless lips and lifted it with my two gloved fingers to blow out a smoke ring, but pretended not to notice. After all, it was out of my hands what effect this was having on my former friend.

But after a couple of minutes, I did get rather tired of feeling his eyes on me and swivelled my head around to face him.

"Something wrong, Candor?" I asked him coolly, my eyes glittering with vague amusement.

Candor hastily averted his gaze and moved it onto the floor. "No," he mumbled defensively.

I hid a slight laugh. "Maybe we ought to go now so you can find someone as interesting as me to stare at,"

I took his silence after my suggestion as an agreement and transported to the aforementioned bar.

It wasn't a very large, or indeed conspicuous building and could easily be mistaken for a tacky house or shop that served beer. I wondered if the owner was aware that we lived on Vanadis, not Earth, where the general consensus for alcoholic drinks was Inarian volic.

Maybe that was why I'd never come here before.

I think it was safe to say Candor had, though, because when he arrived, he strode right in, looking all sorts of comfortable. Unfortunately, I had no choice but to follow him.

I knew from the first second I walked through those wooden doors that any hopes of being inconspicuous were all but completely void.

Every head whirled instantly in my direction and every face was immediately contorted into expressions of intense dislike. There were only two exceptions: Candor, up at the bar's counter, swilling some clear liquid straight from the bottle, and a muscled, hooded figure sitting at a table in the far corner.

The figure sat with one leg crossed over the other, arms folded, head tilted downward and not even touching the drink on the table next to them-coolly.

That must be the Eidolon guild representative. I concluded to myself, heading for the counter with my gaze focused straight ahead, deliberately avoiding anyone else's eyes.

When I arrived at the counter, Candor spoke up. "Hey bartender, get my friend here a drink. I think he needs it after that entrance,"

I kept my head down and muttered a "thank you" when the bartender plonked down a clear bottle full of equally clear liquid in front of me and then disappeared into the back of the bar.

I raised the bottle to eye-level, scrutinizing the liquid inside critically. Candor noticed this and snorted.

"Don't worry, Hawk, it's not poison; it's vodka and it'll take the edge off. Go on and take a drink," he reassured me, downing the remainder of his own bottle all in one gulp. I shrugged and uncorked the bottle.

Candor was wrong about one thing because the contents of the bottle sure as hell smelled like poison-but since I didn't really have the patience to be picky, I raised the bottle to my lips and took a sip.

One thing I could say about vodka, it was definitely a lot stronger than Inarian volic and believe me, that was saying something-although my assassin's training still prevented me from getting drunk, so I could drink as much as I liked.

Once I had roughly around half the bottle in me, Candor spoke again. "I take it you noticed the only other person who didn't dislike you from the second you walked in here?" he questioned me in an undertone after making sure the bartender was still out of earshot.

I nodded and Candor gave me a crooked smile. "Good. Now the bartender's still in the back, so we're going to go over there with our drinks and do what I said before, got it?" he instructed, keeping one eye behind the counter while he talked.

I nodded a second time and used my unoccupied hand to pull myself to my feet.

"We're going to walk side-by-side so people think we're all friends, yeah?" Candor said, picking up the empty bottle in front of him. I couldn't resist making a snide comment; "Oh, yeah, because the three of us make such a compatible group; me being pretty much the bane of everyone's existence, you in your assassin's garb, and him or her in the corner over there with the lone wolf position,"

Candor snorted a second time, and just started walking so I had to keep pace with him in order to abide by his plan.

The figure didn't even look up once we reached their table-if anything, they lowered their head even more; at least, until we drew our guild-issue guns and set them down next to their drink-all five of them.

I was wondering at that moment of why Candor carried three guns instead of the standard two, but I didn't have long to contemplate before the hooded figure spoke.

"Assassins who have left the guild are still in possession of their guild-issued guns?"

It was a man and his voice was deep, fluid and completely devoid of emotion-he spoke in a cold, nonchalant drawl that just barely rivalled my own guarded tone.

"Some of us still require them," I retorted evenly with a sideways glance in Candor's direction.

The man let out a singularly humourless laugh, "I expected no less an answer from you," he inclined his hooded head in my direction. "Hawk."

I arched a slate eyebrow at the familiar way the Eidolon said my name. "Have we met before?"

"You wouldn't remember even if we had," the man said smoothly. "But that is neither here nor there. So, how about you and your friend take a seat and we can get down to business?"

I didn't see what else there was to do, so I complied and nudged out a chair with my booted foot, setting my vodka bottle down on the table as I did so. Candor, being the ever-graceful person he was, dropped himself unceremoniously into a chair between the man and myself and slouched down the back, stretching his legs out under the table and crossing them at the ankles.

"Okay, it's clear that you already know our names, so how about you give us yours so that we can be on level terms here?" Candor suggested without preamble, facing the man fully.

For the second time, the man inclined his concealed head.

"A fair question. I am known as Uronis and I am a part of the drakkhons," he introduced himself placidly, finally looking up, but still not at us. "You, Jarl Candor, issued my summons here. What is it you want from the Eidolons?"

Candor struggled to sit up straight before answering. "I quit the assassin's guild because of their plan to overthrow the underworld council. The council is using underworld assailants as ammunition against the guild and the only way to defeat them is by using Eidolon powers to extract the assailant spell out of people."

"So you want the Eidolon guild to aid you in saving the assassin's guild?" Uronis surmised coldly, turning the back of his head on me to look at Candor.

"It's not the guild I'm worried about," Candor said quietly and matter-of-factly. "They mean nothing to me."

I could see the narrowing of his eyes at that second comment and knew that it wasn't entirely true. And with building fury, I realized I also knew exactly who the exception was.

"Your friend there doesn't believe you," Uronis pointed out as if reading my mind and I reeled inwardly. How had he known what I was thinking?

"Drakkhons have more abilities than you can even begin to fathom, Hawk," he supplied dully, again answering my unspoken question.

I frowned with confusion-something I didn't do very often-and shook my head, deciding to pursue this matter at a later time.

"Alright, maybe I'm not being totally honest," Candor confessed shamefacedly. "There is one person in the guild I do actually care somewhat about."

"And this person would be Niral Lione, am I not correct?" Uronis finished without emotion.

Candor hung his head under my livid glare. "Yes,"

Uronis nodded as if satisfied. "Well then, if saving the guild isn't why you want the Eidolons' help with destroying the underworld assailants, what is your reason?"

Now I was curious. I mean, I knew why I wanted to stop the assailants-because I didn't want the dead to walk among the living-but Candor, well, it just seemed like he wanted the same thing, but with him, there was always an underlying reason for everything.

My dark-skinned former friend swallowed hard. "The land of the dead and the land of the living are meant to remain separate," he mumbled without any real conviction. I could tell he was lying, though. I knew that wasn't the real reason for his sudden defection.

Something wasn't right here. Candor was lying, and to someone who could read his mind, too. But if Uronis knew Candor wasn't telling the truth, he didn't show it. He simply nodded again and said, "I'll convince the other members of my guild to aid you. But in return, you won't begrudge us preying on members of the assassin's guild."

I shrugged my shoulders and Candor mumbled. "Whatever."

The three of us transported back to our previous location from the bar and I dumped my cloak on the floor in front of one of the doors.

"We might as well stay here for a while," I decided. "We're not going to get around to anything else tonight. And even if Niral does manage to reach the Gate before morning, it won't be open and it'll take him at least an hour or two to open it, so that gives us some time to rest." *And check up on him while we're at it.* I added silently to myself, heading for the room in front of which I had put my cloak.

Candor cleared his throat awkwardly and I realized he hadn't even moved once since we had returned here. "There's something I should tell you, Hawk," he began quietly, burying his hands in his jacket pockets and looking at the floor.

"Yeah, what?" I asked, feigning a calm I definitely didn't feel.

Candor shifted his feet. "Back there, when the drakkhon asked what my reason for wanting to destroy the assailants was, I lied," he admitted, "I mean, don't get me wrong, I don't want the land of the dead and the living to merge, but that's not the main reason. I also, umm, want to save Nyle. I think I owe it to her for being the one who turned her into an assailant in the first place,"

You couldn't even imagine how badly I wanted to yell at him that he shouldn't have shot her at all; but I knew that wouldn't achieve anything. So I just shrugged and entered the other room without a backward glance.

I shut the door behind me and opened my laptop, switching it onto Niral's hacked channel, aka my new tracking device.

I scanned it and found that Niral was getting dangerously close to the Gate of Souls. But even from where he was now, he couldn't reach it before morning, which was a good thing.

I was about to check something else when the screen suddenly went haywire and Niral's rough, grating laughter crackled through the speakers.

"Didn't Candor ever teach you, Hawk, that where there's a way out, there's a way back in as well?" The screen was then dominated by Niral's snake-skinned visage, wearing the smuggest smile I had ever seen in my life. "So how is dear Candor, you know, since you kidnapped him?" he asked conversationally as if he were merely asking how a sick cousin was feeling or something.

I snorted.

"You're one to talk, Lione," I spat in disgust, "Assassin recruitment sweep, anyone? You've kidnapped more people than I've met."

Niral chuckled coldly. "Yes, but this isn't about me-it's about you." His smile grew wider, exposing his incisors. "In fact, it's always been about you-right from the beginning."

"What are you talking about?" I said as if it were a throwaway question of no real importance, but my hands had gone numb beyond reason.

Another cold emitted from the snake's scaly lips. "Really, Hawk, I thought you were smarter than that," he chided. "Did you really think that the fact that all of the things happening have a lot to do with you was just a coincidence?"

"What are you talking about, Niral?" I repeated lividly, clenching my gloved fists over the handles of my guns.

"Just look at the facts, Hawk: you and Candor were taken at the same time and the two of you became friends; you killed a man called Caius Halcott, who is now the one who creates the underworld assailants; my covert operation came to light while you were in the guild; I chose Candor as my puppet after you went into hiding and made him shoot his sister, thus, causing her to become an underworld assailant and she came after you first," Niral listed calmly. "Everything has been about getting to you from the start,"

I gritted my teeth. "And why, pray tell, have you been so eager to get to me?"

"Isn't it obvious?" The snake smirked. "You possess powers like no other-powers of destruction. Think what someone like me could achieve with powers like that. Everyone has just been an instrument in my game of harnessing your power."

I snapped the laptop screen shut, cutting Niral off, and turned on my heel to leave.

And found Candor behind me, looking completely dumbstruck.

"Candor," I said dumbly, my heart pounding in my ears. Then I shook my head helplessly and left the room, blowing past him without another word.

CHAPTER 10

Different

The steam from the shower followed me out of the glass cubicle and clung to the air as I stepped out and wrapped a towel around my waist. I pulled a second towel from the rack, moved to stand in front of the sink and began to towel my damp slate locks dry.

My pale eyelids fell shut, trying in vain to rid myself of the memories that were currently plaguing my mind.

What Niral had said, that everything had been all about getting to me from the beginning was still haunting me. Because why? Why would anyone be so anxious to get to me at all? I mean, I realized I was not a regular person, but I was still nothing but a lowly assassin. So how could I possibly possess power "like no other"?

It didn't really matter, though; whether I did or not, it still all came back down to the fact that everything was my fault. I condemned Candor to becoming Niral's puppet and Nyle to becoming an underworld assailant.

My train of thought was then interrupted by the sound of the bathroom door thudding open, causing my eyelids to snap upward.

Candor stood there in the doorway, olive eyes subconsciously roving over my dripping, half-naked body.

Fighting down a blush, I cleared my throat pointedly. "Can I help you with something?"

Candor jolted, shaking himself and I could see him struggling to tear his gaze away from my pale, glistening, bare chest. "Sorry," he apologized quietly, "I thought you were asleep and I suddenly felt the need to wash my hands."

I stepped smoothly away from the sink and said, "Go right ahead. Don't let my being here stop you."

Candor took my vacated spot and I turned in the opposite direction as he switched the faucet on.

I felt his eyes on me the entire time and when I heard the sink shut off, he tentatively placed his hand on my naked shoulder. "Is something wrong, Hawk?" he questioned me softly, sounding genuinely concerned.

Now, usually I had a very tight hold on my emotions, but all of tonight's events seemed to have finally caught up with me and broken that hold, because everything came pouring out.

"I'm losing it, Candor," I declared miserably. "Everything up to this point has been my fault. Your sorry predicament in being Niral's puppet, Nyle becoming one of those abominations, the underworld assailants, and this entire plot to overthrow the underworld council, it's always just been about Niral getting to me. I don't even know how you can stand to look at me, knowing that it's my fault your little sister became an undead monster."

I threw his hand off of my shoulder and slumped, dejected, against the tiled wall.

Candor knelt down in front of me, pulling a black metal hip-flask from the inside pocket of his jacket and handing it to me. "I think you might need that more than I do," he chuckled slightly. When I looked sceptical, he added, "It's much stronger vodka than the stuff you had at the bar, so our assassin's training will pretty much go out the window."

I rolled my eyes doubtfully at that, but took a long draught out of the black flask, anyways.

Candor turned out to be right; my assassin's training went pretty much out the window after downing about three-quarters of that flask.

My vision started severely fuzzing and my senses began to dull. Ah, sweet numbness. Now Candor wasn't the only one who was drunk. "Thanks, Jarl," I said gratefully, somehow managing not to slur my words.

Candor shook his head, "You know, no one's ever really called me that, except, well... you know." He looked down guiltily.

I watched his face fall and without thinking, I uttered the words, "We can save her,", trying to reassure him and causing him to meet my eyes.

I watched his eyes flicker back and forth over my face a couple of times and then he did something I definitely wasn't expecting: he leaned forward and pressed his lips to mine.

Maybe it was just the influence of the alcohol, but when he made to pull away, I clamped my free hand to the back of his head and didn't let him, kissing back almost urgently.

The metal flask dropped out of my other hand and that hand moved to push Candor's leather jacket off of his shoulders, exposing his dark-skinned, muscled arms. His tongue ran slowly over my bottom lip as he guided my free hand to his belt buckle, clearly enjoying it travelling south of his pants line.

I unbuckled his belt, pulling it out of his belt loops and heard it hit the floor with a slight clang.

When we broke apart for lack of air, I couldn't take my eyes off of his hands as they pushed his black leather pants off, leaving him clad in his black boxers and nothing else-which suddenly made me all too aware of the fact that I happened to be clad in nothing but a loosely tied towel.

Apparently, this occurred to Candor as well because he reached for said towel, untied it from around my waist and let it fall off, completely broadcasting my entire body to him.

"Damn. If I'd know all these years that you looked this good under those clothes, I would've tried this sooner," he commented huskily, looking me over with a vaguely lascivious grin.

I had to smirk. "Now it's your turn. Show me what you've got, Candor,"

His grin widened. "As you wish, Hawk." He stripped off his boxers, chuckling when my eyes almost popped out of their sockets.

"Like what you see, then?" he questioned slyly, placing his hands on the wall on either side of my head, trapping me between his body and the wall.

I gave him a cocky smile and waggled my eyebrows. "Maybe."

My cockiness vanished, however, when Candor pressed closer, angling his head, and trailing his lips slowly down my neck, causing me to positively arch with pleasure.

This was most definitely a far cry from what I was used to when it came to sex. I could feel Candor's cock pushing suggestively at my entrance and I completely surrendered myself, allowing him to enter me fully.

I was absolutely gone with that first thrust and cried out his name repeatedly to punctuate each and every thrust. Candor clearly wasn't satisfied that he had pleasured me enough, though, because his lips moved down my bare torso, capturing one of my erect nipples between his teeth and causing it to harden even further.

He pushed my body further up the wall, making my knees meet his hips and I wrapped them around his waist as he continued to thrust into me with steadily increasing speed.

Then, before I could blink, my arms were pinned above my head and Candor began to slam into me in large, claiming thrusts that made my head spin.

"Candor, God, Candor, "I groaned passionately, unable to hold it back.

It was Candor's turn to smirk. "And the difference is?"

I couldn't hold back at that and came, shutting my eyes. I felt Candor's hot breath on my skin as he joined me in orgasm and moaned when I felt his teeth break the skin of my left shoulder.

When Candor finally pulled out, I could barely stand and my knees gave way, causing me to fall onto the cold floor, panting and trying desperately to get my breath back.

Candor pulled his clothes back on in front of me and when he was once again fully dressed, he turned.

"Though I don't mind the sight of your naked body, you might want to put some clothes on," he pointed out with a wry smile, arms folded across his bare chest.

I picked my towel up off of the floor, stood, tied it back around my waist, retrieved my clothes from behind the door and left the room without another word. There was no way I was getting to sleep now.

"I take it the guild accepted our little challenge," Caius observed calmly as Nyle re-entered the council hall, looking vaguely satisfied.

She nodded. "I had to make a few threats, but I think it's safe to say they'll be getting their war and we'll be getting our massacre."

Caius couldn't resist a smirk. "Excellent."

"No, Caius, it is most certainly not *excellent.* As a matter of fact, it is about as far from *excellent* as is possible," Maiaa cut in sharply, her transparent features completely livid.

"And why, pray tell, is that, Maiaa?" the male immortal shot at her coldly, raising his silvery eyebrows.

"Because we are meant to remain neutral in wars, not start them!" she burst out furiously, clenching her fists. "This massacre of yours is going to disrupt the very balance between Vanadis, Earth and the underworld-"

"Exactly my point," Caius interrupted swiftly. "That balance has given us nothing and therefore, it means nothing. The world would be no worse off under our rule than it is now under the rule of the guild. And we've sat idly by, letting them systematically take over, for far too long. Now it's finally our turn and you expect me to pass up that chance?"

Maiaa shook her head at him almost pityingly. "I know that's not really why you're doing this. This isn't even about the entire assassin's guild; it's all about getting to the one who killed us, isn't it?"

Caius turned away, averting his eyes from her. He didn't want to reveal the truth-because the truth was, he was still angry about being killed by Hawk and volunteered for the underworld council just over ten years ago. And after everything he'd done for that ungrateful brat, too.

"This has nothing to do with that" he growled in a low voice; but that was a lie.

It had everything to do with getting to Varros Hawk.

Everything.

And Maiaa apparently picked up on that because she said, "I don't believe that for a second,"

Caius faced her again, folding his arms defiantly across his chest. "I don't particularly give a damn *what* you believe, Maiaa, because I happen to be the leader of this council and if you refuse to participate in this, I will be forced to view it as insubordination."

The female immortal stepped back as if she had been slapped and Caius smirked, knowing his words had struck a very vulnerable chord. "So you can continue to argue with me and risk exile-or you can keep your mouth shut and remain where you now stand. Which is it going to be?"

He took a menacing step forward and his hand shot out, closing around her throat and holding her against the stone wall, "Because I promise you, if you choose the former, you won't be around for very much longer,"

Maiaa closed her eyes in acquiescence and Caius released her, leaving her clutching at her throat in an attempt to get her breath back.

Uronis ran a hand through his teal hair as he pushed his dark hood back.

His scaled amber orbs glowed in the dimly lit room, putting its features into sharp focus. The chamber was empty, save for a bare bookshelf and sparse bed both pushed carelessly up against the white wall.

Hardly complimentary accommodations. he commented to himself, letting a slight smirk briefly touch his pale lips.

The door behind him opened at that moment, but he didn't have to turn around to know who it was. Even so, he didn't acknowledge the intrusion and waited for them to speak.

"Why are you helping us, drakkhon?" Candor's deep voice asked quietly, sounding legitimately confused.

Uronis turned his head, meeting Candor's olive eyes with a piercing stare. "You want to save your sister,"

It was not a question, but a statement and Candor looked guiltily at the floor.

He'd known the drakkhon would've seen through his lie at the bar, "She became an underworld assailant because I killed her and I want to make up for my mistake,"

Since his back was turned, he didn't see the lean, hooded figure disappearing down the hallway after he said those words.

I think this was the first time in my entire life that I could honestly say that I was wrong about something. And believe me, that was saying something.

I re-entered my room and leaned against the back of the door as it clicked shut behind me.

I'd thought Candor had lost his humanity when I had found out that he'd shot his sister. I'd assumed he didn't regret it-but, since we'd been reunited, I'd not only discovered that he *did* regret it, but also that he wanted to fix it.

Could it be that his shooting her was yet another attempt at forgetting me after I left the guild?

I winced inwardly at how sickeningly possible that looked from where I was currently standing.

The impact of what I'd just heard him tell Uronis was so incredible that it caused me to slump down to the floor. Hearing that made me see that I had to face the truth: this had all been about me from the start. All of it. From Candor being taken by the guild and the plan to overthrow the underworld council to Candor becoming Niral's puppet and shooting Nyle in the first place; it had all been in order to get to me.

And all because I had some power that I didn't even know about that Niral wanted to get his filthy hands on. Well, he wasn't going to. Get his hands on it, that is. Since this "power" resided within me, I would be the one to decide what it was going to be used for; even though Niral insisted that they were powers of destruction. My powers to my purposes; not his, whether he liked it-or not.

It was times like these that I really wished I wasn't drunk. I still managed to be an excellent eavesdropper under such circumstances, but it did play hell with my ability to think clearly and hold back my emotions the way I'd been trained to.

I think that was pretty clear from the fact that I had just let my former friend screw me earlier.

No, actually, it was worse than that; I had reciprocated his actions willingly-and now I was blaming it on the alcohol, which had definitely played a part, but wasn't entirely at fault.

I sighed, because I knew the lion's share of the blame fell on me. I had been in the middle of an extreme emotional upheaval and had been too vulnerable to combat the alcohol's demand for physical contact-so when Candor had kissed me, I had let things go a lot further than they ever should have with him.

Now I didn't know what was going to happen between us and I didn't particularly relish finding out. But I would have to face it when it came, no matter what-and that single prospect terrified me more than an entire legion of rival assassins did right then.

I pulled myself to my feet and leaned heavily back against the door, plunging my gloved hands deep into the pockets of my cloak and letting my pale eyelids fall shut over my garnet orbs.

My breath caught slightly as my mind once again replayed what had happened in the bathroom, confirming what I had already known: I hadn't even tried to stop Candor or myself and had surrendered completely. There was no escaping that.

Candor hadn't forced himself on me. He'd given me the chance to stop him after he'd kissed me; he'd made to pull away, but I hadn't let him-and I'd kissed him back.

Both actions on my part had been totally unexpected, especially when you considered that only a couple of hours ago I was thinking Candor wasn't even human anymore.

This was seeing years and years of rigorous training go out the window for one night of misguided vulnerability-and it had been quite the night, too.

If I was honest with myself, no matter how wrong I knew having sex with Candor was, I had enjoyed it in the moment. After being Niral's plaything for nearly half my life, what I'd experienced with Candor was about as far from what I was used to as was possible. I couldn't resist letting out a faint breath of laughter escape from my bloodless lips; that was an understatement.

I had had a chance to back out with Candor; with Niral, if I had tried to stop him, he would've killed me-or worse.

But this was even more complicated because, although I had had the chance to back out, I hadn't taken it.

It was then that I realized why: I'd wanted Candor, just as much as he, apparently, had wanted me.

With that thought ringing in my head, I drifted into a fitful sleep.

CHAPTER 11

Attempting to Balance the Scales

"Sleep" was not a word with much meaning to members of the assassin's guild-even former ones.

As such, even after quitting, Candor still remained awake, watching the oncoming storm through his rain-drenched window, his olive eyes hooded and darker than ever.

He was really beginning to regret having given Hawk the rest of the contents of his flask as well as leaving the aforementioned flask in the bathroom.

Candor cursed under his breath.

No matter how hard he tried not to think about what happened in that bathroom, his mind kept returning to it.

What in the worlds had he been thinking in that moment, making a move on his best friend?

He hadn't been thinking-that was just it. He hadn't *let* himself think about what he was doing and that was the problem.

Something had just pushed him into kissing Varros when he'd said that there was a way to save Nyle. Just like

Varros had wanted to know he didn't hate him, Candor had wanted to grasp onto the hope of saving his younger sister from the plague of being an underworld assailant-the plague he'd condemned her to.

It was his fault she'd become one in the first place-he had been the one who killed her and forced her to be brought before the council.

But that was no excuse for what he and Varros had done; things shouldn't have gone that far. He should've stopped himself after they'd kissed, but in the heat of the moment, he hadn't thought about how wrong it was.

They were both at fault.

His thoughts were cut short then by a soft knock at his door.

Bewildered, and slightly apprehensive, Candor rose to his feet and walked over to the door.

When it opened, Varros was standing there, hands deep in his pockets and expression more uncomfortable than Candor had ever seen it look before in his life.

Varros looked at the floor and said quietly, "Can we talk?"

Candor stepped aside wordlessly to let Varros in and closed the door behind him once he'd entered.

The younger man sat down in the chair next to his bed and put his hands on his thighs. And wildly, all Candor could think about as he sat down across from Varros on his bed was how good it had felt to be between those thighs barely five hours ago.

He lifted one of his legs over the other, mentally shaking himself. "So what's up?" he asked in as composed a tone as he could muster.

When Varros answered, his voice was low and uncharacteristically tentative, "I think we need to talk about what happened in the bathroom earlier."

Candor couldn't pretend he was surprised and he nodded in agreement. "Yeah, I think we do, too. And let's stop calling it "what happened in the bathroom": We slept together," Candor stated bluntly. "There. It's out there. Because that's the truth, that is "what happened": we had sex,"

"Yes, I'm aware of that fact, Candor," Varros cut him off sharply. Then, his voice dropped again, "And I'm also aware of the fact that we both enjoyed it."

This time, Candor didn't have to pretend that he was shocked.

When those words came out of his friend's mouth, his own fell open while his brain went into overdrive.

Hawk had enjoyed it as much as he had?

He'd thought that had just been a show, but it had been genuine passion; genuine enjoyment coming from his stone-cold friend.

He forced himself to get a grip and snapped his jaw shut abruptly, taking a deep breath.

Once he finally managed to get back in control, he spoke, struggling to keep calm, "So what exactly does that mean?"

"It could mean a lot of things," Varros replied slowly. "But the one thing that seems the most likely is that you and I might actually have feelings for each other that go beyond friendship; and if that's true, then we need to figure out what to do about it."

"And how are we going to find out if that's true?" Candor quipped with a salacious smirk playing onto his dark lips.

Varros stood up, bent down, grabbed the collar of Candor's leather jacket and pulled him forward so that their lips met in what had obviously been his plan from the start: a kiss.

As soon as their mouths touched, Candor knew where he stood; he definitely felt for Varros in a way that went far beyond friendship. He kissed back fiercely, pulling Varros closer by hooking a finger through one of his belt loops.

Even so, it was a complete surprise when Varros' tongue pressed against his lips, asking permission.

That action in and of itself was more of a demonstration of how he felt than anything.

Candor parted his lips, allowing Varros' tongue to roam his mouth while his free hand closed over the front of Varros' cloak, allowing him a second degree of control.

They broke apart then, but Candor's hands kept Varros where he was and Varros didn't appear to mind.

"So," Candor whispered, leaning his forehead against Varros'. "You have feelings for me,"

The former assassin smiled with silent laughter. "Yeah, I guess I do," he admitted, the hand holding Candor's collar sliding down to his leg.

Candor completely released him then, but placed his hand on top of Varros', intertwining their fingers before staring hard into the garnet orbs in front of him.

In those crimson depths, he saw something he had never seen there before: fear. Varros was scared.

As if he knew what Candor was seeing, Varros answered his unspoken question, "I'm not a real person, Jarl. I was created to be an assassin, created to have no emotions whatsoever. And the only reason that that fell through was because of the people who raised me. They were human and I loved them-then I was forced to kill them. Now that I've admitted I love you, too, I'm afraid the same thing's going to happen again."

Candor measured his words carefully before responding, "You may have been created as an assassin, Varros, but you aren't one anymore. And no one can make you do anything you don't want to do."

To emphasize this, Candor curled his fingers through Varros' and gave his hand a reassuring squeeze.

Varros shook his slate head, his smile returning, "Now I know why I feel the way I do about you; you always know what to say to show me that I'm being an idiot,"

"That's my job, isn't it?" Candor grinned before capturing Varros' lips with his own again as he fell back onto the bed and tangled one of his hands in Varros' slate locks.

Now it's time to add yet another character to our ensemble cast and his name is Iove-with no last name because his last name is unimportant as of yet.

From an early age, Iove was instructed in the many-layered art of prophecy-keeping. He had seen through each and every prophecy written in the Destiny Tower, but only a single one remained that still had yet to come to pass: the prophecy of the Guardians-possibly the only prophecy that involved both Earth and Vanadis in its contents.

It foretold of three men who had extraordinary powers and embodied the elements of blood, darkness and ice-the elements needed to permanently seal the border between the two worlds and stop them from colliding.

Our subject had spent multiple years of his life attempting to discover the identities of these three men, and he had discovered all but one: the guardian of ice was still unknown.

All Iove had managed to discover was that he resided on Earth, and was the head of some mundane company, completely unaware of the fact that he was one of three keys needed for saving the worlds from catastrophe.

"Have you made any progress with finding the third Guardian at all, Iove?" the master asked sternly.

Iove shook his head. "Not since I learned of his location on Earth."

The master sighed. "You know we need that information," he reprimanded. "Without it, we're sunk and won't be able to gather all three Guardians before it's too late,"

"I know, master. I'm working as hard as I can, but it seems that this man prefers total anonymity to what the others have going for them," Iove commented, allowing his evident frustration to surface.

"Well, work harder," the master commanded bluntly before he disappeared into the rain.

CHAPTER 12

Operation Underworld Takeover Begins

The entire legion of the assassin's guild stood directly in front of the gate of Souls, awaiting their leader, Niral's orders.

Of course, the gate was only visible to Therrian and only he had the power to open it.

Niral turned on his heel, beckoning the dark angel to his side. "This is the moment where all of my most momentous plans will come to a final head," he said in a soft, but carrying voice.

Therrian stared at him from behind his dark hood and glasses, clearly waiting for him to continue.

Niral's voice increased in volume and he announced, "Operation Underworld Takeover begins now!" He faced Therrian, his colourless eyes dead focused. "Therrian, open the gate."

Therrian bowed his head and marched forward until he was positioned directly in front of the iron gate.

He curled his gloved fingers over the front of his glasses and lowered them to reveal his glowing, electric-white orbs, flashing with energy and power.

From within them, an almost transparent beam of light escaped, heading for the gate of Souls. It collided with the gate, dead center, creating a sort of chip in the iron rungs.

Its whitish glow spread across the gate steadily, illuminating it so that it was visible to the others as well. "Holy shit," Therrian distinctly heard one of the members of the guild breathe in obvious awe.

But what Niral's eyes were drawn to was the fact that the illumination also seemed to be gaining substance; when it reached the gate's latch, the latch appeared to disintegrate away from the iron.

In minutes, the latch had completely disappeared and the gate of Souls loomed before the guild, finally ajar.

"And now it's time the underworld council finally learn exactly who they're messing with," Niral muttered confidently to himself, striding over the threshold of the gate as his silenced pistol effectively cleared its holster.

The rest of the guild followed suit, but the dark angel hung back, pushing his dark glasses back up his nose and over his eyes. Niral noticed this and cut through the members of the guild until they were standing face-to-face.

"Is there a problem, Therrian?" the guild leader asked mildly, looking vaguely abashed for the first time in his life.

Therrian wasn't immediately forthcoming with a response, but when he replied, he met Niral's emotionless voids coldly. "Only that I've decided that this is no longer the way I wish to settle my score with the underworld council-which means I have no remaining allegiances to you and you'll have to continue this operation without me."

Niral blinked at this announcement, clearly thinking he'd misheard.

"Did you just say what I think you just said?" he quipped, his abashment steadily growing.

"Yes, Niral. I quit being your servant," Therrian confirmed in a deliberately patronizing tone, surveying the guild leader coolly, waiting for his reaction.

And he got the very reaction he was expecting: anger.

"You treacherous son of a bitch," he hissed, undoing the safety catch of his silencer and directing the barrel at Therrian's forehead. "I'm the only reason you are even able to exist in this world and now you're reneging on our agreement? I reincarnated you to do my bidding, not to settle your bullshit score with underworld council,"

"And that, Lione, is exactly the problem," the dark angel pointed out calmly, apparently unperturbed by the fact that there was a gun to his head.

Niral was apoplectic now and he blew a gasket. "I'll shoot you right back to the underworld, you idiot freak, I swear I will!"

Therrian merely shook his head as if dealing with an annoying child-instead of a homicidal maniac on the verge of having an aneurysm.

"Now you don't want to add me to the council's arsenal of underworld assailants, do you?" he commented slyly, and when Niral didn't reply, he chuckled, "I didn't think so. So, this is the end, Lione. I'm no longer your servant; it's over."

I was vaguely aware of someone coming to the door before it opened silently to reveal Uronis standing on the threshold, his tanned visage utterly devoid of emotion.

"What?" I asked without preamble, slipping out of Candor's leather-clad arms and sitting up on the bed the two of us were currently occupying.

The drakkhon didn't even comment on Candor and I sharing a bed and instead simply stated, "I thought you might like to know that the assassin's guild has breached the gate of Souls and is heading for the underworld."

"Oh, son of a bitch!" I cursed mutinously, getting to my feet abruptly, all thoughts of actually getting a good night's sleep for once evaporating immediately.

My raised voice roused Candor and his dark eyelids blinked blearily. "What's up, Hawk?" he questioned as he gradually sat up and rubbed the sleep from his olive eyes.

I had difficulty not rolling my own eyes and responded tensely, "The guild's gone through the gate."

Candor shot up as if he'd been electrocuted. "*What?!*" he exclaimed in obvious horror.

"Apparently, we overestimated the time it would take them to get there and open the gate," I surmised dispassionately, making for the door.

Uronis' gloved hand closed over my arm lightning fast before I could reach it, though, and my head swivelled around to face him.

He spoke before I had a chance to. "What, exactly, do you plan on doing, Hawk?"

His amber slits bored into my eyes as he said this, clearly seeking to make sure I told him the truth.

I wrenched my arm out of his grip-or rather, I attempted to, but he was just too strong, so I abandoned that and shrugged. "I don't know, something to stop the guild before this gets any more out of hand."

"So you don't have a plan," Uronis concluded, the dull tone not quite reaching his flashing eyes.

"Well, no, not really," I admitted, inwardly wincing; the drakkhon's grip on my arm was beginning to get just a tad bit painful.

"If we're going to stop them, we're going to need a plan, Hawk, and a good one at that," Uronis said seriously, his eyes now virtually glowing beneath his dark hood.

I stared back at him coldly. "I am aware of that, Eidolon, but no plan will be thought of if you do not release me," I declared with as much dignity as I could muster in spite of the fact that my arm had gone numb where Uronis' gloved hand was gripping it.

Uronis' dark lips curled in what could only be described as a sneer and he bowed his hooded head mockingly, finally releasing my arm in a single fluid motion, amber slits blazing with danger.

I resisted the urge to rub my prostrate limb in order to get the circulation back, instead clenching my fist in the pocket of my cloak and turning to face Candor. "What do you think we should do, Jarl?" I asked.

Candor hesitated for about a fraction of a second before answering, "I wasn't expecting this, but I did have a contingency plan just in case the guild bypassed the gate earlier than expected."

His olive eyes flicked toward the motionless drakkhon, whose tanned face was once again devoid of expression. "Are you wearing an earpiece?" he questioned authoritatively, pushing himself off of the bed we'd been sharing.

Uronis' response was utterly monosyllabic; "Yes,"

"Is it activated?" Candor wondered, prodding me into wondering where he was going with this.

"Not at the moment," the Eidolon's face was completely deadpan now-or it would've been if not for his burning amber orbs, now virtually spitting sparks from their sockets.

Candor cinched his weapons belt back around his waist and drew a bronze stiletto blade from it, tossing it in the air, then catching it and pointing the tip of the blade at Uronis. "Then activate it. We're in need of some Eidolon reinforcements; the strongest members from each type."

Uronis nodded his understanding and left the room in order to do as Candor said.

"What are you planning, Jarl?" I questioned my lover, arching a slate eyebrow in his direction.

He wagged a reproving finger at me, grinning slightly. "Come on, Varros, that would be telling. Now where has your laptop gotten to?"

"It's in one of the other rooms, but what do you need it for?" I prodded curiously, my second eyebrow rising to join the first in confusion.

What a landmark day this was becoming for my life, being utterly puzzled for a whole day and letting a total stranger get the better of me at the same time.

I mentally shook my head and waited. "Just be good and get it for me, yeah? Then maybe I'll tell you what I've got planned," Candor had barely finished his sentence before I was out of the room, heading for one on the opposite side of the, well, I won't call it a house; "hideout" would be a more appropriate term.

My laptop was sitting exactly where I had left it: on the wooden table, where Niral's face had filled the screen and, in essence, basically told me that I'd been born a condemned man.

I shook off the unpleasant memory, and closed the laptop's lid before picking it up and exiting the room, kicking the door shut behind me.

Candor was waiting in the center room, leaning almost casually up against the wall, but his expression was dead serious; clearly, any remaining aftereffects of drinking so much had evaporated and Candor was, for once, completely sober.

When he caught sight of me, he held out his hand for the laptop wordlessly and I handed it to him in equal silence, still curious as to exactly what he was intending to do with it.

He opened the screen and switched it back on, but that was all I could tell since the screen's back was to me.

"Okay, Hawk, we have our reinforcements from the Eidolon guild," Candor announced in a low voice, his eyes riveted on the laptop screen, the light emitting from it throwing his dark features into sharp focus, so I had no trouble looking him in the face when he spoke again.

"The three of them, plus Uronis, and us are going to breach the gate of Souls ourselves and see if we can't stop that war," he summarized swiftly, looking up from my laptop to gauge my reaction.

I shrugged my shoulders, unsure of what he wanted me to say about this plan.

It definitely had its merits, but with the aid of only four Eidolons, including the drakkhon, I didn't see how we could take on an entire army of underworld assailants *and,* to all intents and purposes, the entire assassin's guild, including Niral himself, the snake I had never been able to fight.

"If you don't think it's going to work, now's the time to tell me, Hawk," Candor told me seriously, surveying me over the laptop screen.

I shrugged a second time, still thinking of how I could tactfully put the doubt I was feeling into words.

But unfortunately, my brain came up short, so I settled for stating bluntly, "That plan has little to no chance of succeeding, you do know that, Candor?"

Candor rolled his eyes expressively. "Trust you to be so rude," he chided. "Here I am, trying to save all our skins and all you can manage to do is criticize me. I'm hurt, Hawk, I really am."

I had difficulty not rolling my eyes when Candor finished his little speech and put a hand over his chest, pretending to be wounded. "Spare me the theatrics, Candor," I said, throwing him a withering glance. "You *know* your plan won't work,"

Candor cocked his head to the side like a curious child. "And why ever not?"

I stared at him incredulously. "Are you serious? Two renegade assassins and four Eidolons with questionable loyalties against the underworld council, their army of underworld assailants and, more likely than not, Niral and the entire assassin's guild? Suicide would be less life-threatening than this," I exclaimed, running a hand through my slate bangs.

Candor's response to my utter rejection of his plan was totally not what I was expecting. "That's not all," he stated enigmatically.

"What do you mean?" I asked suspiciously.

Candor grinned. "We have Niral's dark angel servant on our side."

Wind tore ruthlessly through the back of Therrian's black cloak, causing it to billow out behind him in a similar fashion to his wings.

"So it's true," a vaguely familiar male voice commented, "Niral's dark angel servant has deserted him."

Therrian fluidly turned his head in the direction of the voice and found himself facing three men, only one which looked even remotely familiar. "Candor," he drawled tonelessly. "I see you got my message."

"Oh, so you do speak," the dark-skinned youth quipped sardonically, cocking a blue-black eyebrow.

"Obviously," Therrian stated in an ironic tone, surveying Candor dispassionately over his folded arms.

So that's Therrian Shalis, then. Varros mentally observed, scrutinizing the dark angel carefully.

"To answer your question, yes, I did get your message," Candor confirmed. "And I must admit, my friends and I were rather shocked, to put it mildly."

Varros shook his head as Uronis corrected, "*They* were shocked. Such emotions do not become me."

"Well, I've decided that Niral's plans are no longer relevant to my reason for a second life, so I quit being his servant and decided to shift my allegiances to destroy some underworld assailants," Therrian explained smoothly.

Both of Candor's eyebrows shot up beyond his hairline once Candor finished his sentence. "Hang on, I though the only way to take down an underworld assailant was with Eidolon powers?" he said, confused, turning his head accusingly in Varros' direction.

"That would most probably be the only way whoever told you that knows of," Therrian contradicted him coolly, sliding his dark glasses down his nose to provide Candor with a clear view with his ocular enigmas of eyes.

The renegade's own eyes widened considerably. "Damn," Varros exclaimed simply, no doubt voicing exactly what his lover was thinking.

Therrian chuckled without humour before pushing his dark glasses back in place. "Dark angels are creatures of which barely anything definite is known. From being one, I know a lot more than most and one of the powers we possess is the ability to draw things out of people; creatures, diseases...and the underworld assailant curse."

Varros shrugged. "Well, that would explain why that web-page never mentioned this since so little is known about dark angels," he observed, jamming his gloved hands in his pockets before turning to look directly at Therrian.

"So does that mean you've decided to side with us then, even though to all intents and purposes, we will be fighting Niral as well as the underworld assailants and council?"

Therrian tilted his head forward in an affirmative. "It matters not who *else* we are fighting, just as long as my score with the council will finally be settled," he declared in a voice that was almost eerily calm.

There was almost no question as to what would happen now that the mismatched band of somewhat do-gooders had gained another weapon against the underworld assailants.

Candor shot a quick glance at Uronis. "When are your friends arriving?" "

"Friends" is a rather loose term. But the three other representatives from the Eidolon guild will be here once they sense that the gate has been revealed once again," Uronis replied dully without meeting anyone's eyes.

"And that signal falls to our new member here. If you wouldn't mind, dark angel?" Candor faced Therrian expectantly.

Therrian bowed his head in acquiescence before turning on his heel to once again face the gate.

For the third time that night, he lowered his glasses, directing his powers at the gate. In a matter of minutes, it was, once again, completely visible-and with its visibility came the immediate appearance of three more cloaked and hooded figures.

CHAPTER 13

"War" Takes On a Whole New Meaning

Losing the most important person in your life is like watching a sinking stone, completely powerless to halt its descent through the water below.

Down...

Down...

Down it goes as the final breaths of the person's life are taken, slowly and laboriously. And then comes the final plummet: the person's heart will stop just as the stone hits the bottom of the water and just like that, it's over.

The seven of us walked through the iron gate unhindered; but there was something nagging at the back of my mind as we crossed the threshold between the land of the living and the land of the dead. Somehow, this was all just too easy.

And in my experience, when things were this easy, it usually meant something bad was about to happen.

Candor, the one who'd known me the longest out of all the members of our motley group, obviously picked up on my negative thoughts because he sidled up beside me at that moment, looking concerned. "Something's up with you," he said, facing me seriously.

When I didn't supply an immediate response, instead running an uncomfortable hand through my slate locks, Candor nudged me in the ribs.

"Come on, Hawk, I can't convince you you're being an idiot if I don't know what idiotic things you're currently thinking," he cajoled, attempting a grin.

I sighed grudgingly and told him what was on my mind, "Am I the only one who thinks that this has been just a little too easy? I mean, we've assembled quite the formidable little group here without very much trouble and, if there's anything I've learned from being a part of the guild, it's that nothing is ever easy unless there's something you don't know."

I could see Candor processing this carefully, his questioning look morphing into one of intense concentration as he lapsed into silence.

He halted in his tracks to do this, and out of the corner of my eye, I saw our five companions raising their eyebrows in his direction, obviously wondering what the hell Candor was doing.

But whatever they were thinking wasn't important to me because I wanted to know if my theory had any validation at all.

Finally, after what felt like the longest minutes of my life, Candor spoke. "I think, at this point, we all definitely need to be on our guard," he concluded firmly. "Especially if your theory proves valid."

With those words, he turned and began to walk forward again.

"Candor," I called after him, and when he stopped again, I asked, "What do you think is going to happen?"

Candor didn't even turn around before he answered, "Something is definitely off about this. So we're going to need to be very careful," He said those words loud enough so everyone could hear before continuing.

Our dark angel companion watched us intently through that exchange, I knew, because he actually had a clue where we were going.

Whatever happened now, all bets were officially off because we were down here of our own free will and volition. For some reason, knowing that made me more nervous than I would have been if we had been brought here by force.

I suppressed a slight shiver that had nothing to do with the temperature and followed Candor closely, determined not to let my anxiety show.

The underworld, when we arrived there, was nothing short of a bleak, desolate wasteland.

We had to tread an extremely careful path or risk getting engulfed by the acidic flames spurting out of the jagged rocks which served as the ground.

It didn't help either that we didn't know where we were headed and Therrian was behind us, but neither I nor Candor wanted to be the one to ask him to lead us.

Luckily, we were saved the trouble because he chose that moment to clear his throat pointedly.

"Being that I am the only one who has been on the other side of the gate before, shouldn't I be leading?" he suggested mockingly, faking confusion.

Candor and I stopped for a second time and I held out a gloved hand in front of me. "Be my guest,"

Therrian took me at my word and took his place at the front of the queue, heading off in a different direction than Candor and I had been.

Though I still didn't know exactly where we were going, I followed the silent dark angel without question, trusting that he would lead us where we needed to go and not into a trap.

As we ventured deeper into the deadly abyss, I began to notice a slight shifting in the dense air around us. It became noticeably heavier with smoke-and something else I couldn't identify.

But it felt vaguely like...despair. Despair from the dead souls who never had a chance, I realized with a slight jolt; the ones who had been killed by people like Niral.

People like Candor....and like me.

I was suddenly very grateful that all the others were facing the opposite direction because I had to bite my lip in order to keep from yelling out loud at the impact this heaviness in the air was having on me.

This was what it had been like my entire life, suffering in silence, thanks to all those things I did while I was a member of the assassin's guild; but things should have been different, now that I was no longer affiliated with the guild in any way, shape or form.

They weren't, though. And I didn't think they would be until this was finally over.

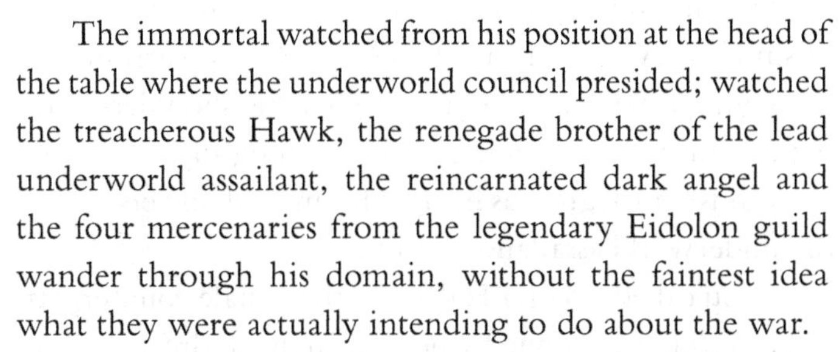

The immortal watched from his position at the head of the table where the underworld council presided; watched the treacherous Hawk, the renegade brother of the lead underworld assailant, the reincarnated dark angel and the four mercenaries from the legendary Eidolon guild wander through his domain, without the faintest idea what they were actually intending to do about the war.

They must be really keen on saving the guild from their well-deserved fate if they're planning to challenge the council and my army of assailants. he observed, tapping his chin in a somehow simultaneously thoughtful and absentminded way.

However misguided the group's intentions were, they did present the leader of the underworld council with a bit of a problem; because the way they were going, they would be standing in the way of his massacre.

So what to do about them, Hawk in particular? Now that was the question.

And he knew whatever answer he came up with, the rest of the council was not going to approve of.

This presented him with a very vexing dilemma indeed.

Involuntarily, a cold smirk spread slowly over his transparent lips as he realized that this wasn't a problem. No, this was an opportunity-albeit, one in disguise, but an opportunity, nevertheless.

He could take this chance to play out his massacre and make Hawk suffer for his crimes at the same time with one action.

Killing two birds with one stone, as it were.

He turned away from his watching, conjuring a sort of slinky grey cloak from the blackness that surrounded the council hall and drawing it over his shoulders; this opportunity was not going to be taken lightly.

Caius' smirk grew as he used his mental powers to call the underworld assailants to him.

"You called, Master Halcott?" the female counterpart of Hawk's lover quipped when she arrived, dressed all in leather and with a very unbecoming sneer on her dark lips.

Caius took a moment, assessing her short, lithe form appreciatively and silently congratulating himself on the plan of turning her into the lead underworld assailant, before responding evenly, "Yes. It is time for you and my army to follow me into battle. The assassins are arriving."

Nyle's upper lip curled even further, a malicious glint in her olive eyes, so like her brother's.

"Excellent, Master. We will follow you outside the second you give the order," she inclined her ebony head in deference to the blank-faced immortal.

Caius nodded, apparently satisfied with her answer. "Good, and then maybe I'll let you perform an even more honourable...*service* for me," his torpid lips quirked suggestively and Nyle's sneer grew.

With those words, Caius dismissed his army and returned to his musing, allowing his smirk to return and widen.

Yes, for now, Hawk would be spared his vengeful wrath.

But soon enough, he *would* pay.

At last, the doors to the underworld council's hideout loomed before Niral's rock-hard eyes, in which the acid green flames surrounding him were eerily reflected.

"This is it," he declared aloud, his silky voice amplified in the deathly silence and taking on a whole new, unfamiliar tone: one of thinly veiled excitement.

All the plans he'd had for so many years were finally going to reach their peak. The destruction he had envisioned for so long was coming.

"Niral Lione," a familiar drawling male voice sighed from behind him, sounding almost regretful.

The assassin's guild leader turned slowly and found himself looking at the all but transparent form of the immortal who lead the underworld council; Caius Halcott.

"Halcott," Niral greeted him, oozing mock politeness. "Where is your army?"

Caius' thin lips twisted into what could only be described as a smirk, "Awaiting my orders, of course, just as your guild behind you is doing."

The guild was, of course, doing exactly that: standing behind their leader, awaiting his orders to begin the final onslaught they'd been preparing to make for years.

But Niral didn't really feel like playing the diminutive today. So he allowed his lipless mouth to curl into a mocking sneer.

"I don't suppose you would consider peaceful surrender from this far?" he questioned with feigned innocence.

The immortal snorted and that was all the answer Niral needed.

"No, I suppose not," he pretended to sigh before hissing out of the corner of his mouth, "Everyone into positions."

He kept his vapid eyes dead set on the leader of the underworld council, who didn't seem concerned in the slightest that his immortal existence was about to end.

The response from the guild was instantaneous and fluid: every member spread out in a different direction to flank him, their gloved hands moving, almost casually, to their weapons' holsters.

There was a resounding gunshot…

And the war began.

When we reached the council's headquarters, I knew immediately that we were too late.

Because the war had already begun.

And it was like nothing I had ever seen before.

Blood was spattered red over the ground like puddles of crimson rain, most of it from members of the guild, very little from the underworld assailants, who were tearing through their opponents with a savagery that I could never have imagined except in my worst nightmares.

People were being cut down in front of me like trees and the worst part was I just. *Couldn't. Look. Away.*

Even more so because one of those sadistic monsters was someone I knew, had known in life as a person: Nyle.

The girl I had known to be tender, sweet, caring and, above all, painstakingly idolizing of her elder brother, was ripping into everyone and everything that crossed her path and devouring their mangled bodies with what could only be described as satisfaction.

It was like seeing someone not even human anymore; it was like seeing something else entirely.

It was then I felt a claw-like grip on my arm and I turned around.

Candor was standing there behind me, olive eyes transfixed on the grisly tableau in front of us, jaw working furiously to contain his horror-and I knew why.

This had to be torture for him, watching his precious little sister slaughtering countless people brutally, without the faintest hint of remorse, only twisted happiness. It must have been ripping him apart inside, especially since he had been the one to turn her into this.

Almost subconsciously, I reached for his hand, unclenched it and threaded my fingers through his, forcing him to meet my eyes.

The grip on my arm loosened and he looked into my face petulantly, guiltily, like a child seeking assurance.

It was only then that I fully understood just how much of an impact this was having on him and I felt a very uncharacteristic wave of sympathy for my lover.

My lover. That was what I thought of Candor as now and it felt right.

I stared straight into his eyes and gave his hand a squeeze. "I know, Jarl," I whispered reassuringly. "I know. But we're here to stop this and I think it's time to start."

I gave an almost imperceptible nod to the four Eidolons and single dark angel standing behind us and they all tensed into striking stances to show that they had seen my go-ahead.

If I was honest with myself, the five did look pretty terrifying, Therrian especially.

I couldn't help but watch as he discarded his dark cloak and glasses, and I almost gasped when I saw the entirety of his fallen angel guise.

Those sable, thorn-covered wings were both nearly twenty feet long, adding up to a full wingspan of nearly half a meter; adding to this threatening, frightening image, razor-sharp thorns, identical to the ones covering his wings, jutted menacingly out of the dark angel's bare coffee-coloured torso.

And to top it all off, there were his eyes: pupiless and whiter than the palest ivory, whiter than the moon itself, yet blazing with...electricity? Power? Or strength?

My mind was utterly blank now, save for a single thought: I was glad that this...*enigma* was on our side.

Hawk. A sibilant voice in my head jolted me out of my slightly stunned stupor. And it was one I recognized-Uronis. He was giving me a sharp look from beneath his hood out of the corner of his scaly amber eyes.

I sent him a well-aimed glare, communicating my response clearly without actually saying anything: "What?"

There was a swift flicker of disapproval across the drakkhon's tanned features before they fell impassive once again. *If you're going to drift off, I suggest you warn your friend there* beforehand, *so he doesn't do something...stupid.*

His tone was cool, laced with sarcasm and somehow still totally void of emotion.

I shook myself, determined not to let my concentration slip again, and deigned not to dignify Uronis' suggestion with an answer, instead clenching my jaw in anticipation for what I knew the seven of us were going to have to do next.

We were going to have to enter the fray and do this from the inside out.

"Jarl, you're going to have to make a choice now," I told Candor out of the corner of my mouth, my voice harsh as I once again faced the deadly battle being fought three feet away from me.

Candor looked at me, a solitary blue-ebony eyebrow cocked in question. "And that is?"

His voice was low and toneless, but I could sense the apprehension and trepidation behind his words, like he was actually scared of what I might say.

Though this unsettled me quite a bit, I didn't hesitate before I spoke again, "How far are you willing to go for this?"

Silence fell.

Whatever Candor had expected me to say, it certainly wasn't that.

"As far as I'd go for you and for my sister," was Candor's fierce reply and I could hear the steel now inserted into his tone; a sharp contrast to the voice he'd used previously.

I nodded in acceptance of his honest response. "Good. Because, to be quite frank, it's going to take nothing short of a miracle just for us to come out of this alive,"

There was one thing left to do: I drew both my guns.

And entered the battle that gave "war" a whole new meaning.

As soon as Varros set off into the fray, the six other members of their motley group separated and began to fight, each using their own characteristic skills like the others.

Candor went after the members of the assassin's guild, bronze submachine guns flashing as he shot down everyone who got in his way.

The others had no such limitations in victims; the three anonymous Eidolons and Therrian were destroying anyone in sight-anyone who got too close.

Of all the attacks, Therrian's had to be the most astounding, because it didn't even appear to be a visible attack.

All it took for him to summarily execute an opponent was a single glance from those blank, soul-less eyes; one glance, and the one on the receiving end would crumple to the ground, lifeless-even if that one was an underworld assailant.

To say he was inhumanly strong would be an understatement.

And then there was Uronis, coolly indulging in his bloodlust by feeding on the members of the assassin's guild.

He would grab one of them around the throat, shift their prostrate bodies into a submissive position and sink his white fangs into their pulse points.

Time itself seemed to stand still as those razor-like appendages pierced flesh, and blood came streaming down into the drakkhon's waiting mouth.

That first warm gush of blood was like an aphrodisiac to the drakkhon's senses, enhancing his powers beyond comprehension. His jaws clamped tighter to his victim's exposed throat, tearing skin and bone in his haste to consume more of the crimson liquid, to get sustenance like he hadn't been able to in the decades since the original assassin's guild had surfaced and cut down his supply of victims.

Uronis felt his senses whirling, spiralling out of control as he absorbed more of the dark red liquid into his system. But he didn't stop, wouldn't stop until his victim was completely drained.

When the well of blood had dried up, Uronis withdrew his fangs from the man's throat with a slight spattering and a thud as the man hit the ground, empty of any fluids to sustain his life for a second longer.

The drakkhon's amber eyes glowed through the darkness as he methodically cleaned the blood from his lips with his tongue, licking every last vestige of blood from there and his teeth before moving on to his next opponent.

Or maybe we should just say victim.

But the ultimate carnage didn't come until Niral and Nyle, the leaders of the guild and assailants, came to face-to-face at last.

They stood, on opposite ends of a sea of mangled corpses, Niral's snakelike face cold and indifferent, Nyle's haunted features alight with malice and bloodlust-or flesh lust, no one could tell which.

There were no other survivors, bar for the council and Varros' group, and now, one of these two leaders were going to meet their end.

For Candor, since he'd quit the assassin's guild, all that mattered was his sister's life. If the choice was his sister or Niral, the choice was obvious now he was no longer Niral's "puppet" and was with Varros in all senses of the phrase.

The two opponents circled each other, never taking their eyes off of one another, even for a second.

Silence filled every ear for miles around until Niral spoke.

"It figures that Candor's little sister would be the final thing for me to eliminate," he sneered, "Cruel, cruel irony. So cruel, in fact, it's almost poetic."

"Your demise is indeed poetic, Niral Lione, for it was your organization that turned me into this!" Nyle snarled, launching for Niral without any further hesitation.

Her dagger-like claws shot forward, aiming, not for his throat or any other vital points, but for his eyes.

At the last second, Niral's hand shot up and closed around her wrist, flinging her in the opposite direction with no visible effort.

When Nyle hit the bloodstained ground, Candor surged forward, prepared to pay Niral back in kind, but Varros held him back firmly.

"She's not done," he assured his lover in an undertone, gripping his arm in case he still needed to hold him back. He needn't have worried, though, because as soon as the dark-skinned youth saw his sister getting back to her feet, seemingly unhurt, he instantly relaxed.

"That wasn't the best you could do, was it?" Niral taunted coldly, eyes gleaming with ill-concealed mirth. "I've had greater challenges fighting humans."

The female underworld assailant let out a feral growl and tore after him, bloody pools livid; but this time, Niral was ready for her.

As soon as she was near enough, he drew a knife with a speed that should have been impossible and she ran right into it, driving it into her chest all the way to the hilt.

Silence blanketed over them all as Nyle fell backward, recoiling off of the knife

Down..

Down...

Down...

Thud.

"NYLE!"

CHAPTER 14

Desperate Times Call For Desperate Measures

The silence shattered with Candor's cry of anguish once his sister hit the ground, mouth still open and eyes wide and glassy.

Her body seemed to shrink as it changed out of its underworld assailant form back to a human girl, and then finally, into dust.

That was when Niral turned back to us, stowing the knife back into his belt as he did so.

My grip on Candor's arm tightened. I knew he wanted to go after Niral; I could feel it in the way he was shaking-whether it was with grief or anger, that was what I couldn't tell.

I myself wasn't feeling so great; how could I be? I had just watched someone I knew get brutally murdered right in front of me.

Not that my face showed anything of the sort, of course.

"You see, Hawk?" Niral spoke in a clear, taunting voice, his ever-present sneer still pasted revoltingly across his olive-skinned features. "Emotions are such fragile things-which is why it's better not to have them at all."

I cocked a slate eyebrow at him, curling the gloved fingers of my free hand over the handle of the service pistol I had holstered in my belt. "Is that so?" I drawled, my lip curling upward ever so slightly in a cynical smirk.

Niral didn't seem fazed, but I could tell I was getting to him, if only a little.

"You have seen what burdens people who let their emotions rule them carry. A prime example would be this, ah...little inconvenience for your friend there. That was his sister, was it not?" he clicked his tongue with feigned regret. "Shame that."

"You fucking bastard!" Candor burst out savagely, wrenching free of my hand and launching himself at the laughing snake.

"Candor, no!" I shouted at him valiantly, but it was no use. He was too wrapped up in his anger to hear me as he went charging straight for Niral, who didn't look the slightest bit worried. I knew why, too. It had slipped my mind for quite some time, but it was coming back now: Niral had fixed our training so that he couldn't be killed by any renegade assassins.

Nothing bad would happen to those who tried-they just wouldn't be able to kill him.

My mask would have cracked completely at remembering this if I hadn't seen something else at that exact instant: Therrian advancing lethargically toward

Niral next to Candor, but with his killing intent clear in those pupil-less white eyes of his.

Maybe that would tip the scales? I didn't have the faintest clue.

With a roar of pure fury, Candor hurled his clenched fist at Niral's stomach and nailed him dead-on.

The hit didn't even seem to rock the guild leader, though; it was like he was simply hitting a brick wall. I hoped Therrian would have better luck at fighting him.

The dark angel moved to Niral's side and snapped his ebony wings, dislodging what looked like a hail of thorns that came raining down on the snake, embedding themselves in every inch of exposed skin.

I distinctly heard Niral curse as he wrenched one of the thorns out of his eyelid, which had been punctured and was now bleeding rather profusely.

"It seems you still haven't come to your senses, Therrian," he stated with an almost resigned shake of his head.

Therrian didn't even bother with a response, choosing instead to rocket off of the ground and drive himself higher until he was above Niral, looking uncannily like the angel of death in the blackness.

I could quite literally feel my heart beating in my ears, racing with anxiety as I continued to watch. I wanted to help, but for some reason, I couldn't seem to get myself to move.

Luckily, the dark angel wasn't having the same handicap.

I saw him circle in the sky, inverting his body in midair, then inverting it again and spinning a kick at an angle that defied the laws of physics into Niral's jaw, knocking him to the ground.

While the snake was picking himself off of the ground, Therrian shot me a look that said quite clearly, "Don't let your friend interfere with this."

I looked over at Candor, who looked ready to start swinging again and I knew I had to stop him so Therrian could take care of Niral. I went to stand next to my lover and put a hand on his shoulder to calm him down.

Unfortunately, this gesture had the complete opposite effect. Candor jumped about a foot in the air when he felt my touch and spun his head around to face me.

"He killed her, Hawk," Candor hissed, olive eyes flashing angrily even once he realized who it was, "That asshole killed my sister-I'm going to kill him, no matter the cost."

And he wouldn't even let me get a word in edgewise before he went tearing back into the battle.

"Shit," I swore under my breath before drawing my twin service revolvers, finally shaking myself out of my stupor and preparing to enter the fight.

Though Candor was no doubt determined to kill Niral, Therrian seemed to be the only one out of the two of them who was able to actually hurt him, whereas Candor's attacks just seemed to bounce off.

It was a little strange, to be quite honest, but I knew this was only the beginning.

The dark angel shot off another one of his thorn storms and again, Niral was pelted with thousands of knife-like projectiles that ended up tearing every bit of skin they made contact with.

Small rivulets of blood were running all over Niral's uncharacteristically battered visage and I could see him getting frustrated by it.

No doubt this had never happened before; then again, I don't think he had ever had to face a reincarnated dark angel before.

Therrian's attacks were smooth, quick, and almost unnaturally precise-as if he knew every one of them off by heart. His precision and fluidity surpassed even mine.

Boy, was my confidence ever taken down a few pegs from watching him; but as one-sided as the battle looked, nothing could have prepared me for what happened next.

Niral used his transporting powers to avoid a third shower of thorns and reappeared behind me.

He gripped me expertly by the throat and pressed a cold metal something to my temple.

"It's such a shame I've had to resort to this, Hawk, "he crooned in my ear, causing shivers to run down my spine, "We could have been so good together,"

"There was next to zero chance of that ever happening," I retorted in a deceptively calm tone, despite there being a gun to my head.

"So here we are," Niral finished almost regretfully.

Then he raised his voice, addressing Candor and Therrian with his next words. "If either of you attacks me again, Hawk dies."

As if just to prove his threat, I heard him undoing the safety catch on his gun and then he pressed the barrel harder into my skin.

My crimson eyes shot forward to see what my lover and the dark angel's reactions would be.

Both were completely unexpected; Candor dropped his livid stance, dejected, and backed off, olive eyes wide with evident concern.

The reaction that really surprised me, though, was Therrian's; he whipped his wings around, giving himself more height and folded his arms across his thorn-covered chest.

That shocked me because I never thought he would try to stop Niral killing me, no matter where his loyalties lay. Did he actually care? I didn't think I was going to get the chance to find out.

Niral chuckled at the two's retreat. "I expected this from Candor, but not from you, Therrian," he commented slyly, applying more pressure to the hold he had on my throat, "Do you care for Hawk, or is this somehow serving your ends?"

I had to repress the urge to vomit as I felt Niral's rough hand caress the side of my face tauntingly, no doubt looking to get a rise out of the dark angel.

Therrian didn't even react, although Candor looked ready to spit nails at the sight of Niral touching me. "Don't touch him," he snarled[see?], baring his teeth.

All he got was another mirthless chuckle in response.

"You are in no position to be making threats, Candor," Niral pointed out coolly, "Especially since I now hold all the cards."

That was when the world twisted and Candor and Therrian's images were replaced with spiralling oblivion.

INTERLUDE

The Guardians of the Border

In the time when Vanadis and Earth were still one, thousands of years ago, a great cataclysm occurred: the Holy war between Heaven above and Hell beneath our feet.

The underworld did not pass judgement on those who died because it did not diversify between the good and the bad and all were cast into the pits by the ones who controlled the gate of Souls.

There was no salvation for the dead on Vanadis and hardly any punishment for the dead on Earth.

But the ruler of the true Hell wanted to change that and take away salvation from all, living and dead. That was when the mighty masters, Egan Cyle, Elyseum Morningstar, Yyx Halidith and Croft Ankin, decided it was time to separate the worlds, and thus erected the border.

But their spells had a fatal flaw: the moment the border was created, it began to wear thinner and thinner with every passing year. The masters were scandalized and, unfortunately, at a loss of what to do in order to rectify this flaw.

It was Egan Cyle who finally came up with the solution.

Prophecies were written by the masters to give the people on both worlds hope that when problems arose, they were meant to be solved.

And so, master Cyle spoke and transcribed a prophecy that foretold of three men, who, when the border was at its lowest point, would be created with the power to seal it permanently, so that the worlds would remain separate and the ruler of Hell would not be able to return to the land of the living.

"The border is now at its lowest point, Iove," the master of the Destiny Tower declared softly and bluntly.

The prophecy-keeper nodded sombrely. "I have been watching both worlds," he informed his master.

The master's mouth twitched slightly, as if to suppress a smile.

"I know you have." he paused, frowning as if in concentration. "Read me the Guardians prophecy. Remind me what its precise wording is."

Without preamble, Iove acquiesced with the master's request and set about finding the prophecy in question within his many scrolls and records of other such prophecies.

When he was finally able to produce it from his library, he held it up to eye-level, cleared his throat and began to read it aloud.

"When the border between the two worlds is created, so, too, will three powerful men who will be needed when the border begins to fail.

They will be the Guardians of the border; the Guardians of blood, darkness and finally, ice,"

The master sighed as Iove fell silent, re-furling the scroll and setting it carefully down.

"That couldn't possibly be clearer. We know that those three men have been created. Now it's just a matter of discovering who they are. We know the blood and darkness guardian's identities already. Find the ice guardian, Iove, or we're all doomed."

It wasn't until after the master had left, though, that Iove was struck by a sudden unexpected premonition that sent him reeling on his feet.

Images began to pour into his subconscious like nothing he had ever seen before. How was this happening? He was human; nothing like this had ever happened until now.

Flashes of glaciers and crystalline rivers danced before his eyes, intertwining with a multitude of shockingly bright colours and Cyrillic symbols. A cacophony of voices rose up above the jumbled scenes, filling the prophecy-keeper's ears with a maelstrom of white noise.

The voices were, each and every one of them, as different as day and night-and the way they chorused together, it was impossible to distinguish what they were saying; that is, assuming they were actually saying something and not just making noise. They grew louder and louder until it felt as if Iove's head was about to split open.

Fingers of ice pressed against his spine, causing him to have to suppress a violent shiver. This shouldn't have been happening; prophecy-keepers weren't supposed to have any powers. As far as Iove knew, he didn't *have any-which made this, ah,* vision, *all the more startling.*

He couldn't close his eyes-because, even when he did, the images remained, swirling and cycling like some sort of bizarre slideshow. Truth be told, it was really starting to make his head ache.

Minutes passed in what seemed like hours before the voices and chaos faded to reveal what it had all been leading up to. Iove felt a frown crease his forehead when he discovered exactly what that was.

A very tall, dual-haired male stood alone atop a precarious cliff, eyes partially hidden by his cobalt bangs and dressed in a grey biker jacket, stonewashed jeans, silver gloves, and dark blue motorcycle boots. The most striking thing about him, though? The way the surrounding ice clung to him like a kind of glacial shroud.

Wind rippled through the man's two-toned hair so Iove only caught minute glimpses of his face; but from what he did see, the man was almost unnaturally pale. His flawless skin was the colour of pure, white snow.

The prophecy-keeper instinctively knew that this man wasn't human; he couldn't possibly be, not with the way he looked and the way he carried himself, like he was a king amongst commoners. The question was, then, if he wasn't human, what the hell was he?

As if to answer his thought, time itself seemed to freeze so that the strange male's hair was blown aside and his eyes were finally fully unveiled.

It wasn't the eyes themselves that made Iove give a sharp intake of breath-although, they were definitely an astonishing sight in and of themselves. No, it was what the prophecy-keeper saw in *those unearthly cold, blue eyes that really jarred him-and actually gave him an inkling of what this guy was.*

Because when he looked into those frigid azure orbs, all he could see was ice.

They say the eyes are the windows to the soul-and in this case, those words couldn't have been truer. This man's soul was a virtual glacier, which could only mean one thing.

This was the Ice guardian he had been searching for.

Iove felt his heart rate increase substantially. After all these years, all of this time, he finally had a face for who just might have been the most important man in the world. Unfortunately, he still didn't have a name.

With a strangled yell, he was thrown from the vision and back into reality, the impact making his knees buckle. He took a moment to regain his bearings, keeping his head in his hands until it ceased its incessant pounding.

When he had finally salvaged some semblance of composure, he straightened up and instantly began to draw out the likeness of the man who was currently occupying all of his thoughts. Luckily, he was a pretty good artist, so the drawing came out quite similar to the reality.

After finishing, he put his pencil down on the marble desk and held up the drawing to his face, committing every line and contour to memory. Those startlingly blue eyes were seared permanently into his memory; there was no way he could ever forget that man's face, even if he wanted to.

Who was this man? Iove found himself staring at the picture, unable to look away. The Ice guardian, even just as a drawing, had the most hypnotic stare-and it was pulling him in like a magnet.

Out of nowhere, a haunting voice came, unbidden into his head, and it uttered only two words in an ominous whisper:

"Sehto Howl."

Oddly, the exact same words then appeared on Iove's drawing in glowing silver ink. The prophecy-keeper blinked, dumbfounded; obviously, someone-or something- was trying to send him a message.

Struck by a sudden idea, he pulled out a laptop from one of the many shelves lining the walls of the Destiny Tower and searched the name "Sehto Howl".

It, apparently, wasn't a very common name because only a single result came up: "HOWLtd". And when Iove clicked on it, the first thing he saw was a digital rendering of the man he had just seen in his vision.

Iove smiled with satisfaction. At last, he had a face-and a name to go with the final person he needed to save the worlds.

Sehto Howl.

Best of all, now he had a location, too. It was time he paid a visit to Russia, on Earth.

CHAPTER 15

The Ice Wolf

"Master Howl, you have a visitor," a male voice stated tentatively from outside the steel door.

Sehto looked up from his stack of papers and called back effortlessly, "Send them in."

"Right away, sir," came the stuttered reply, accompanied by a quieter, and slightly more assured, "Come this way. The boss will see you."

Sehto let the papers slide out of his pale hand and rested his azure eyes on the man now walking through his office door.

He looked to be about 20 years old, of average height and build, but the authority with which he carried himself would make you think he was a lot older; his sandy hair hung past his chin, though it was neatly, and obviously deliberately, spiked and silver-tinted at the ends, giving the impression that its length was desired and not detested.

In a drab contrast to his white, but lightly tanned skin, the man was dressed all in grey. Grey gloves, grey cloak, grey pants, and dark grey boots that began just below his knees with the only non-grey material in his attire: a ruby-red buckle.

The man's liquid-looking eyes appraised Sehto carefully as he came to stand in front of his desk, gloved hands still and resting against his hips.

"Is there something I can help you with?" Sehto asked smoothly, leaning back in his chair to consider the man in front of him.

The man fixed him with a deadly serious expression before responding, "You don't know me, Master Howl, but my name is Iove. And I've been trying to find you for a very, very long time; almost half my life, in fact."

Sehto arched a cobalt eyebrow.

"And why, exactly, is that?" he questioned Iove without emotion, his diamond face completely deadpan-except for his eyes, which had hardened into icicles.

Iove wasn't deterred by the intensity of his gaze, however, and answered without hesitation. "Because you are a guardian of the border. The ice guardian, to be exact."

The only reply to this news that Iove got was Sehto's other eyebrow cocking up to join the first. There was silence for several minutes until Sehto spoke again.

"A guardian of the border," he repeated in a voice of almost deadly calm. His ice chips were the only sign of life on his figure; he was totally still and expressionless, but those slanted, frozen voids were burning cold fire in their sockets, freezing Iove to his current spot.

As if to add to the suspense, the sky outside Sehto's window darkened and the moonlight now illuminating the dimly lit room threw Sehto's diamond-like features into sharp relief.

The outline of his tall, broad figure glowed a sharp, bluish shade, like the colour of ice.

"Exactly what game do you think you're playing?"

"I am playing no games, Master Howl," Iove stated truthfully and patiently, "Everything I tell you is the absolute truth."

He pulled a roll of paper from inside his cloak and placed it on top of Sehto's cherry wood desk.

"What is that?" Sehto demanded, his voice even more deadly than before, pointing his chin at the roll of paper.

Iove picked it back up off the desk and unrolled it. "This," he said, "is the reason I am here, and the reason why you were created."

He cleared his throat and began to read from the piece of paper.

"When the border between the two worlds is created, so, too, will three powerful men, who will be needed when the border begins to fail. They will be the guardians of the border; the guardians of blood, darkness and finally, ice."

Iove looked up at Sehto, whose eyes were now virtually reduced to slivers of ice. Other than that, though, nothing about his expression, or lack thereof, had changed.

"That time, when the border will fail, has come," Iove declared, "The border has been, and is, growing weaker as we speak. That is why I have dedicated the last 17 years of my life to discovering the identity of and tracking down the three guardians. But the other two, as well as the battle, are on the opposite side of the border: Vanadis, the world of the assassins."

"Assassins?" Sehto repeated dully, eyebrows rising higher.

"The first guardian used to be an elite assassin, but he quit and was in hiding until his former boss decided to go after the only person he cared about," Iove clarified calmly, "The second was working for that boss until very recently and is not at all what you'd expect."

"The guardian of darkness is not what I'd expect?" Sehto repeated fluidly, adopting an expression for the first time, albeit an immensely sardonic one, "What is that supposed to mean?"

Iove looked back into those frigid infernos and said, "Quid pro quo. I will tell you everything you want to know, but in exchange, you will come back to Vanadis with me and help save the border."

The ice guardian appeared to consider a moment before saying, "And if I refuse? There is still the matter of 1.you still haven't convinced me you're telling the truth and 2.I have a company to run."

Iove had great difficulty not rolling his eyes.

"Time between the worlds isn't relative," he explained, "If you manage to succeed in sealing the border, you could return here at the exact time you left, down to the very second. As for me not convincing you yet, I assure you, any further convincing I need to do will be taken care of the second you set foot on Vanadis. So do we have a deal?"

Sehto's still blazing eyes fixed him with a stare so penetrating he had to repress a shiver.

"We do," Sehto finally conceded. "But know this: I am not a vengeful man unless crossed. If you are lying to me, or lie to me about anything, this deal will be null and void and you won't be around to make the same mistake twice. Now let's go, if we're going."

He swept his silver Armani jacket over the dark blue turtleneck that was strained against his toned chest in a single, fluid motion and waited. Iove grasped his arm and the office disappeared.

What Sehto saw when they came to a halt was nowhere near what he was expecting of Vanadis.

The air was grey and denser than smoke and it didn't help that it was also damp, presumably from a recent storm or something.

"Homey, isn't it?" Iove commented sarcastically, correctly interpreting Sehto's stony expression, "Really mirrors the fact that it's been overrun by assassins, doesn't it?"

"And that's a good thing?" Sehto quipped, cocking an eyebrow at the grey-black, lightless sky.

"Whether it's good or bad is irrelevant at the present time," Iove said matter-of-factly, "What's really important is the border's condition, which is why it's necessary for us to be here; the border isn't visible on Earth, only on Vanadis,"

Sehto looked back at him skeptically, not saying a word. Iove's grey-gloved hand once again encircled Sehto's silver-clad arm and after they transported for the second time, a seemingly solid, translucent black wall loomed in front of the two men, blinking in and out of visibility at varying intervals.

"Is that the border, then?" Sehto asked, stuffing his hands in his jacket pockets and adopting a casually nonchalant position even while standing ramrod straight.

The storming, moonless sky did such wonders to illuminate the prominence of his sharp features that Iove actually found himself staring.

Outlined by a blurry, ice-blue aura, the crash of thunder highlighted all of the major features of his pale, aristocratic face; the thin, low cobalt eyebrows, the high, chiseled cheekbones, the angular jaw, the perfect and distinctly Greek nose and the smooth chin.

And then there was his body: well over six feet tall and all flawless angles, sinewy, muscled limbs and impeccably toned muscles, visible mostly through his dark blue turtleneck.

The harsh outlines of his torso suggested hard-living and more than one violent encounter. His faded and frayed grey jeans were low-slung and revealed pale hips marked, not only by scars and dark bruises, but also by bite- and burn-marks.

"Yeah, that's the border," Iove confirmed, tearing his eyes off of Sehto's scarred hips with a massive effort.

"It looks...unstable," the wolf commented bluntly, apparently oblivious to the rain pouring down his face and drenching his skin.

"I told you, it's been deteriorating for centuries now and sooner or later, it is destined to fail completely and then, not two, but *three* worlds will be doomed to collide; Earth, Vanadis and the underworld," Iove explained honestly, expression dead serious now.

Sehto reached up to brush hair out of his eyes and at the same time, another clap of thunder rang out and the resultant flash showed a pale blue cross running up the back of his hand from the silver sleeve of his Armani jacket.

"So the guardians are expected to do something about that?" he surmised dully and when Iove nodded, he snorted. "And what makes you think the other two will even go along with this at all, when they were both formerly working for the leader of this assassin's guild?" he wondered, his scepticism growing.

He didn't get a reply for several seconds, but when Iove spoke again, he ignored Sehto's question, "Come on, we have one more destination and then you can decide whether or not I've convinced you to accept your Guardian heritage."

Sehto had difficulty not grumbling in annoyance as Iove grasped his arm for a third time and the border vanished to be replaced by an imposing stone tower with a tall spire that looked to Sehto like a giant lighting rod.

"That is the Destiny Tower," Iove answered Sehto's unspoken question this time, "It's where all prophecies are kept and where I learned to be a prophecy-keeper," He paused, watching his companion carefully.

When Sehto merely stared at the tower impassively, Iove continued, "It's also where I've been keeping track of the other two Guardians ever since I discovered their identities," Sehto turned to him and he broke off abruptly, waiting.

But Sehto didn't get the chance to voice what was on his mind because, the very second he opened his mouth, gun shots suddenly erupted around them, followed instantly by the flash of machine gun fire.

"Get down!" Sehto ordered Iove, yelling to be heard as he drew his ice-coloured revolvers from their holsters.

Closing his eyes, he fired a point-blank shot and a nearby tree came crashing down. Iove stared, wide-eyed, as Sehto managed to somehow dodge the barrage of bullets coming straight at him seemingly effortlessly and fired off several more rounds, lessening the shooters one by one.

That didn't last long, though, because when the clearing fell silent, the final assassin made his move.

And Sehto found himself held by gunpoint, staring down the barrel of a metallic pistol, aimed directly at his forehead.

"One of the three Guardians of the border, I presume?" the man sneered ruthlessly, cocking his pistol. "All these prophecy people seem to think they're invincible, don't they?"

Sehto was silent, mostly because he couldn't understand how this man could be holding a gun when his hand was practically transparent; as was the case with the rest of his tall, lithe form-and yet, he managed to be not only be holding the gun, but threatening someone with it, too,

The man chuckled without humour, a high, cold laugh that Iove, unfortunately, recognized.

"Step away from the ice guardian, Halcott," a new, deeper and also male voice commanded Sehto's would-be assassin softly and very dangerously.

The man turned, but on account of the gun pressed against his forehead, Sehto couldn't see who he was looking at.

"So, and here I thought masters were supposed to remain neutral," the man commented, keeping a tight grip on his gun as he addressed his invisible companion.

"You, of all people, should know that that rule was disregarded two decades ago," the second man stated without emotion, "Now step away from Howl."

There was the sound of a sword unsheathing as the man threatening Sehto retorted coolly, "And if I don't?"

"Then you know as well as I do exactly what will happen, Halcott," was the sober, matter-of-fact answer, emphasized, no doubt, with a sharp prod from the sword Sehto had heard being drawn.

It seemed those words finally succeeded in striking a chord because Halcott lowered his pistol and backed off, palms raised in a gesture of mock surrender.

With a sneer, he tilted his head to face Sehto, who was holstering his twin revolvers nonchalantly.

The ice guardian folded his arms across his chest as Halcott spoke, "You got away this time, Howl. Next time, you won't be so lucky,"

Sehto rolled his ice slivers at the cliched threat and responded calmly, "I'll be waiting."

Halcott snorted and disappeared, giving Sehto a clear view of his saviour.

There was nothing particularly remarkable about this man, other than the indisputable authority his presence held, from his steely hair to his iron, armoured boots and Sehto knew instantly that this was the man who was running this whole show.

But even knowing that, he remained stubbornly stiff, whereas Iove lowered his sandy-haired head in a short bow.

"I take it your mission was a success, Iove?" the master observed tonelessly, surveying the bowed man with no emotion.

Sehto saw Iove shift uncomfortably. "Well, yes *and* no, master, because-"

"Because what?" the other man interrupted sharply.

"Because I'm a lot harder to convince of all this than he was banking on," Sehto cut him off coldly, eyes flashing cold fire, daring the master to reprimand him for interrupting.

The master merely raised an eyebrow at him, as if contemplating his statement. "And what about all this, exactly, are you still not convinced of?" he questioned patiently, staring Sehto down.

Sehto stared back coolly, refusing to be cowed by this man whom he had just met. "What does any of this have to do with me?"

The other man shot him a droll look. "Clearly, it has everything to do with you," the master stated as if it were the most obvious thing in the world, "I would have thought you'd have gathered that from the way Halcott threatened you; you are one of the keys to sealing the border,"

Sehto saw fit to address the matter that both Iove and the master seemed to think was a given; "And why is it so important for the border to be sealed?"

The master sighed. "Because if the three worlds; Earth, Vanadis and the underworld, collide-like is inevitable if we don't seal the border-every inhabitant of both Earth and Vanadis will be annihilated and the lost souls of the underworld will be transported to somewhere where they will be wreaking even bigger havoc on the resulting world; humans, assassins and even immortals will be killed. Of course, there are small pockets of people from both worlds that think they'll somehow survive, or that they'll be able to use the power of the Guardians for their own ends, so they come after the Guardians, or hire assassins to do so. So, you're going to need to harness your powers to get rid of them because not all of them are going to be scared off as easily as Halcott was. Now you have a choice: accept your heritage or go back to Earth, where you will be hunted now that you know your true identity. Which is it going to be, Master Howl?"

Silence descended as Sehto considered his options.

As far as he could see it, he only had two:

One: he could leave and forget about all of this. There would be remorse, though, now that he knew exactly what was at stake-not to mention the fact that there was the possibility that the master was right and he would be hunted, even if he did return to Earth.

Then there was option number two: he could accept all of this as the concrete truth and his heritage and help these two men seal the border. There would be repercussions for that, too, one of which was the possibility that if him and the other two Guardians succeeded in sealing the border, he might never be able to return home to Earth. But he wanted to harness these "powers" he was supposed to have, so that was a risk he would have to take.

"You win," he said bluntly, "I'll accept that I am a guardian of the border."

"Good," the master concluded. "Then, you'll need this."

He held up a metallic-blue disk strung on a thin silver chain to Sehto.

Sehto took it in his pale hand and clasped the chain at the base of his neck. "What is it?" he asked, fingering the disk curiously.

He drew back his finger almost instantly, though, because it was too cold. "It is your ice medallion," Iove answered with quiet reverence.

"And you're going to need it to retrieve the blood guardian," the master added, looking grim.

"Why, what's happened?" Iove questioned in surprise.

"His quitting the assassin's guild has finally come back to haunt him," the elder man stated cryptically.

Iove knew what the master meant by this: Niral had kidnapped the blood guardian and was about to decide his final fate.

Varros Hawk was on trial.

CHAPTER 16

Protector or Destroyer?

I was unceremoniously dragged into a large, dim room that looked uncannily like a courtroom. The only difference was, instead of podiums at the front for the judge, the jury and the witnesses, there was a single steel chair with half-foot long metal spikes rather than legs holding it up.

One of my "guards" caught me glancing at it and chuckled roughly.

"Like it? That's where Lord Niral is going to hold you until you're brought to the execution block," he said with something bordering sickeningly on relish in his gravelly voice.

"And on what grounds, exactly, am I being "brought to the execution block" as you so knowledgeably refer to it as?" I questioned coolly, fixing my "guard" with a piercing stare, daring him not to answer.

He let out another ruthless chuckle. "Well, what do you think we've dragged you here for, then? To *list* the grounds for which we are having you executed, It's your trial, Hawk."

More like it's going to be Niral making a show of flinging any and every accusation he can think of at me. I observed grimly to myself as the "guard" to who I had been speaking tossed me in the direction of the chair, where one of his companions then pushed me onto it.

From that position, I could see better in the dark. Niral entered the room afterwards, clad in his customary emerald green suit and wearing what could only be described as a gloating smirk on his lipless mouth.

"The ever-elusive Varros Hawk has finally fallen into my clutches," he declared in a sneering hiss, "And all because of his precious *friends*."

He pronounced the word "friends" with the same sort of tone someone else might use for saying "scourge of the world".

I merely stared at him as I was effectively bound to the steel chair; he came to stand in front of me, looking as though he was a human child on Christmas morning.

Various members of the guild filed in after him, taking up spectating positions up against the wall and in a row near the room's rear.

Niral turned his back on me to address them, "Tonight, we are going to decide the final fate of one of our least faithful members; Varros Hawk."

His soft, dangerous voice carried throughout the lightless room and I had to suppress a snort.

Sure, when I was no longer even a member, I became a "least faithful". What utter crap.

The snake continued, "Even though he has already proven countless times that he is guilty of insubordination, he shall have a trial, a chance to refute just how guilty he really is. The penalty, should he remain unshriven, is, of course, death-or at the very least, purgatory."

Okay, that was it; I couldn't refrain from making snide comments anymore.

I called out, overriding Niral, "And what's the reward if I am "shriven"? Are you going to pray for me? Give me a gold star, maybe? When did you turn into such a Bible-toting freak?"

Niral, to his credit, managed to ignore me and didn't stop speaking, beginning my so-called "trial" with a single, irrefutable statement; "He sold us out while he was still a member-"

"Yeah, and if you were smarter about keeping things under wraps, I wouldn't have been able to "sell you out' 'I spat out brutally; hey, it was true, "-and then he dares to become a renegade and interferes with our operations, whilst leading another one of our members astray-"

I was definitely going to blow a gasket now.

Aaand here we go: "You're not a fucking convent! You're a bloody assassin's organization, for fuck's sake!"

And....cue Niral's creepy-ass smirk.

"You don't wish to deny these accusations, Hawk?" he said, his lipless mouth curling in a knowing smile.

I, in turn, treated him to my most mocking one. "Why should I? The truth is the truth, after all," I stated indifferently, my mocking smile becoming icy.

I could see Niral fighting to suppress his glee as he responded, "And you've resigned yourself to your fate, then?"

I smirked, "Well, now that's the problem. I seem to have a little thing called a *brain*-and it's telling me to kick your slimy bastard ass, so I gotta say, I don't think that's going to happen."

Niral had a moment of apparent shock and then he recovered himself and flung yet another accusation at me, "Hawk is committing treachery this very moment, you see?! He has threatened me and done nothing to deny it!"

"Maybe because of the ever-present fact that I'm not an assassin anymore!" I exclaimed, hissing with invective.

This was ridiculous! How was threatening him treachery if *I wasn't a bloody assassin anymore?* And while we're on the subject, why was I on "trial" when I was no longer under his command?

God, this is total bullshit. I mentally groaned.

"He convinced another to become a renegade like him-"

"Because I didn't want him to be as morally corrupt as you and the rest of your freaking guild are!" I shouted, seething now at how utterly absurd this whole sham was.

"He's been spying on me left and right since the beginning and carelessly shares all of his "discoveries" with anyone who would ask-"

"That is complete crap and you know it, Lione!"

Why didn't I just shut up and shoot him, you might be wondering? Because, besides the fact that I wouldn't be able to kill him, they'd taken my bloody guns away!

The one time Niral did something smart, it had to be at my expense. Figured, didn't it?

"A more prime example of an insurgent there has never been," the snake concluded with a finality in his tone that I definitely didn't like. "So who shall decide his sentence? The jury, of course-the jury of the assassin's guild,"

Six members of the guild stepped to one side of the room from behind Niral, one of them actually daring to give me a taunting grin.

Niral turned to them and spoke up again, "So, my jury, based on the trial, what is your verdict on the life of Varros Hawk?"

Of course, he would be leaving it up to people who hated me to decide to whether or not I was guilty.

The man who'd grinned at me averted my eyes and faced Niral to voice his opinion, "My verdict is guilty. Who else agrees?"

His peers all smirked.

All except the fifth, who kept his head down underneath his cloak so that I couldn't see his face.

Niral appeared to not even notice him and his own expression changed to mirror the other four's.

"Well, it seems we have a majority," he observed, "which means-"

"I vote not guilty," the hooded man cut him off and my gaze, as well as Niral's, shot instantly in his direction because something about his voice, quiet as it was, just seemed to command the attention of the room.

Out of the corner of my eyes, I saw the confusion on Niral's snake-like face; clearly, he didn't recognize this man.

He stared coolly and called, "And just who might you be?"

The man chuckled-a frigid, Siberian laugh that sent shivers down my spine-and drew an ice-coloured revolver from beneath his cloak, directing its barrel at Niral.

"Your slayer, Lione," he answered coldly, lifting off his black hood and glowering at Niral with his Arctic blue eyes.

Before Niral could say another word, and before anyone could stop him, he clicked the gun and released the trigger.

The bullet hit Niral square in the chest and a brown stain bloomed almost immediately on the front of his dark green suit.

Cocking his revolver a second time, he directed it at the two "guards" who had relieved me of my guns and spoke again, "Give Hawk back his guns. This trial is over and we're *both* leaving,"

I think the unlikelihood of being on the business end of a gun, rather than being the one wielding it, was a shock to their system because they untied me and handed me my guns without question, backing off to let me leave, Niral's "jury" all wearing similarly ugly expressions at, I assume, being cheated out of seeing my death.

My mysterious saviour stowed his revolver out of sight as I re-holstered both of mine beneath my cloak and tossed off the rest of the ropes they'd used to bind me.

Strangely, as I followed my "saviour" out of the room, not a single member of the guild made a move to hinder us.

"Got a penchant for getting into trouble, do you?" the man asked sardonically once we were outside.

I shrugged, "It's a curse. But, if you don't mind me asking, who are you and how do you know who I am?"

"That will have to wait until we are elsewhere," he said. "Now, since I don't think you've been where we're going before, I suggest you take my arm,"

I folded my arms stubbornly, "I'm not going anywhere with you until you at least give me your name,"

I heard him sigh. "Fine, my name is Sehto Howl." Then, he grabbed my arm and we disappeared.

Well, "Sehto" turned out to be right; I *definitely* had not been here before. We landed in front of a tall stone tower topped with a tall spire that seemed to be catching the lightning from the rain storm that I'd forgotten had occurred earlier.

"That is the Destiny Tower," Sehto told me quickly, forestalling my obvious question in a tone that didn't invite any further enquiries on my part.

Just to emphasize this, his eyes slid shut and he crossed his arms over his chest, keeping his head tilted slightly downward so that his black hood covered his cold blue eyes.

"And it's a fitting name, too," a new voice declared as the entrance to the tower swung open to reveal an averagely built man coming toward us, liquid eyes scrutinizing me carefully.

My own crimson eyes were doing the same to him, but much more subtly-or at least, I'd like to think so.

When the man reached us, he held out his hand to me.

"My name is Iove; I work in the Destiny Tower as a prophecy-keeper," he introduced himself cordially. "I sent Sehto here to retrieve you from the guild because the two of you are part of one of the prophecies I keep."

"And what prophecy would that be?" I shot at him tonelessly, not really sure I wanted to know the answer.

"It has many titles, but it is most commonly known as the guardians of the border prophecy, and the two of you and one other are depicted in it," Iove explained, meeting my gaze steadily, a rather momentous feat for someone shorter than me.

"Really?" I drew out the single word into two distinctly sceptical syllables.

Iove must have heard my disbelief because he attempted to placate me with an indulgent smile. "Yes," he confirmed.

I considered this for a minute before asking, "So who's the other one, then?"

Iove hesitated and I had to repress a smirk. "You've already met him," was Iove's matter-of-fact reply, "Who would you consider a candidate of immense power?"

"The dark angel," I said automatically.

There was no discrepancy there; Therrian was the most powerful *being* I had ever met, so much that it seemed almost derogatory to refer to him as a person.

"There's your answer," Iove pointed out. "Now you're going to have to make the same decision that master Howl here did; are you going to accept your heritage as a guardian or not?"

"You haven't even told me about this prophecy yet, so how can I make a decision?" I quipped, raising an eyebrow.

The prophecy-keeper pulled out a long scroll of parchment and wordlessly handed it to me.

I read it and surmised that this was the so-called "guardians of the border" prophecy I was supposed to be a part of.

"That seems to be in order," I finally concluded, giving the prophecy-keeper back the scroll. "But here's the thing: I don't happen to have any special powers, besides the ones I derived from being a member of the assassin's guild."

The prophecy-keeper shook his head, "You have them-they just haven't surfaced yet and you don't know how to control them."

"And I suppose you expect to teach me?" I challenged incredulously, my second eyebrow rising to join the first now.

"Not quite yet. There's still the matter of retrieving the guardian of darkness and I expect you'd like to see your lover again, wouldn't you?" Iove turned his back on me to address Sehto, "You still have another task, although this one won't require won't require any subterfuge as long as Hawk cooperates."

And he said this while I was right behind him, too.

I perceived this as rudeness, but you could think what you liked about it.

Luckily, Sehto seemed to be thinking along the same lines as I was because he stared down at Iove and retorted smoothly, "You shouldn't talk about people like they're not here, especially when they happen to be right behind you."

Iove didn't look remotely abashed, but he did heed Sehto's words and return to facing me before he piped up, "You have to make your decision, Hawk; we won't be able to move on from here until you do,"

So, like nearly always, it came down to my decision. But from there, it sure as hell looked like the choice was obvious; "I'm the guardian of blood; let's go retrieve the guardian of darkness,"

"So you're not going to even bother trying to save Hawk after you just stopped attacking Niral for him?" Candor spit at Therrian venomously, crossing his arms over his bare, dark-skinned chest in frustration.

The dark angel let out a long, heavily exaggerated breath and answered with the air of trying to explain something to a very slow child, "Look, Candor, if Lione didn't kill Hawk here and he kidnapped him, odds are that you can bet that he's killed him by now."

Candor clenched his jaw and threw himself irritably onto a nearby rock.

Even though they were out of the underworld now, his anxiety levels were still flying off of the charts because Varros wasn't around to calm him down since Niral had kidnapped him.

"Well, I can't just sit here!" he exclaimed, his deep voice raw with emotion. "And we've already effectively put a stop to Niral's war against the underworld council, so what are you still doing here, anyways?"

"Same reason why the Eidolon over there hasn't moved since we left the underworld," Therrian supplied dully, pointing his chin in Uronis' direction, where the drakkhon had remained completely stationary since he had gotten there.

"Which is what, exactly?" Candor quipped, his contravention finally starting to really get the better of him at this point.

Therrian turned his shielded eyes to Uronis expectantly.

Said Eidolon actually noticed this and deigned to speak, "I've actually invested quite a bit more in this operation than you'd think because I know something about Hawk that no one else does-except for the people who raised him and the dark angel, of course."

"And what would that be?" Candor demanded to know, now turning to face Uronis as well, confusion written on his face.

"I expect it's what I just found out, Jarl," Varros' familiar voice cut in, forcing Candor to whip his head around and jump up in shock.

The person he'd been worrying was dead or worse stood in front of him, unharmed and wearing a sober expression over his folded arms. Behind him, though, were two male profiles that Candor didn't recognize in the slightest.

He didn't waste time with relief and instead just asked, "Who are they?"

"This one's a prophecy-keeper," Varros tilted his head at the shorter of the two, "and the other one is the only reason I'm here at all, Sehto Howl,"

Candor raised an eyebrow at his lover, but Varros simply shrugged wordlessly, unfolding his arms and putting his hands in his cloak pockets.

"So what is this thing you've just found out about yourself?" he wondered curiously, re-folding his own leather-clad arms and leaning against the rock he'd been previously sitting on.

Varros shot a look at the "prophecy-keeper", who gave him the slightest of nods, before replying, "That I am a guardian of the border, just like Howl, and Therrian over there."

Therrian didn't look the slightest bit surprised at this piece of information and just continued to focus his gaze on Uronis, who didn't appear to notice.

"Border?" Candor repeated dubiously, his confusion evidently increasing by the second.

"The border between the two worlds: Earth and Vanadis," the prophecy-keeper explained calmly for Varros.

Candor blinked. "Why exactly does the border require guarding?" he questioned.

"Because it's failing," Sehto declared baldly, "And it has been doing so for long enough that, if we don't do something about it soon, the two worlds above and the underworld below will merge and then subsequently end."

"Well, that's a bust," Candor commented frankly, sounding a lot less confused now and more like he was taking this much too fatalistically for it being about the end of all life.

"That's an understatement," Varros muttered, rolling his red eyes expressively.

"So what, exactly, are we supposed to do about the border failing?" Therrian asked critically.

All eyes turned to Iove, who, in turn, cleared his throat.

"Using your guardian powers, you are supposed to seal it," he told them truthfully with a slight shrug.

"In essence, this whole plan hinges on whether or not all three of us decide to go along with the guardians prophecy and work together," Sehto summarized dryly, sounding bored. "I've already accepted. So now it's down to the other two,"

"Give up the chance to actually do something good for once? As if," Varros snorted, "Of course I accept. Therrian?"

The dark angel lifted his dark glasses off of his eyes, revealing them in all their glowing white, pupil-less glory. "The way to solve the problem of the failing border after we've harnessed our guardian powers lies in the underworld, which means that I will have another chance to settle my score with the council, so, I, too, accept."

Varros swivelled his body around to face Iove and added, "My acceptance comes with a price, however; wherever you take us next, Candor comes with me-or I don't come at all,"

Iove bowed his head in a wordless accord. "Our next destination happens to be the border and then your new lodgings. Well, the border is Hawk and Shalis' destination at any rate; Howl's already been. You know where to return, master Howl."

Sehto acquiesced with a flick of his fingers and vanished on the spot.

For the second time that night, Varros was transported to an unfamiliar destination, only this time, he had Candor, Therrian and oddly, Uronis tagging along.

"Do you vouch for the Eidolon as well?" Iove asked, arching a sand-coloured eyebrow when they landed and he noticed the drakkhon's presence.

"He's a mercenary and we've bargained with him, but if he wants to stay, I don't think there's really anything you can do about it," Varros replied as Candor came to stand beside him and draped an arm casually over his shoulders.

Uronis, meanwhile, seemed completely immune to Iove's glowering and bore it with a cool nonchalance.

"Fine," Iove surrendered, tearing his eyes away from the Eidolon to look over at the border; the black, smoky wall that seemed to be flickering in and out of the visible spectrum.

Uronis swept his hood back over his blue-streaked hair so no one could see him smirking.

"There is the border," Iove declared, pointing at the blinking black wall of smoke in front of him with a grim expression.

"I'm surprised it hasn't already failed completely, being that unstable," Candor commented, sounding faintly bemused as he jammed his free hand into his jacket pocket.

Varros cast a sideways glance at him, clearly telling him to shut up. With a shrug, the ex-assassin fell silent, leather-clad arm relaxing across Varros' back.

"That border is being sustained by the slimmest of threads and will not hold out for very much longer," Therrian said fluidly. "Although it is unclear exactly when its collapse will occur."

"If the three of you harness your powers quickly and effectively, hopefully never," Iove put in determinedly. "Now that you've grasped just how serious our predicament is, I think we can trust you to try and do what is required of you. So, I can show you your new temporary homes, if you like."

Arms were grabbed and the five men were transported to a series of medium-sized, hut-like buildings that appeared to all be attached in some way.

"You can choose whichever one you wish, although essentially, they are all identical. Master Howl has already claimed the one on the left end and has requested to be left alone, so that one is off-limits. Sleep well."

With those polite words, the prophecy-keeper exited the scene, leaving them to their own devices.

"Dark angel, you and I are taking this one," Uronis spoke up quietly, indicating the building directly in front of him.

Therrian gave him a barely perceptible nod and the two of them disappeared into their house, for lack of a better word.

Candor cleared his throat to get Varros' attention and when his lover looked over at him, he jerked his head in the direction of the house on the far right, virtually next to Uronis and Therrian's.

Varros rolled his eyes and followed the dark-skinned renegade inside.

Once Candor and I were inside our house, Candor took a long look around and let out an appreciative whistle.

"Not bad," he observed soberly, dropping himself into a wine-coloured armchair, "Not bad at all."

I had to agree. At least, it was far better than the conditions I had been living in for the last few years.

The house had smooth, whitewashed walls that surrounded the large sitting room and adjoining kitchen/

dining room with space to spare-quite a stretch from what I was used to.

Everything in the living room, all of the various chairs and the one couch, were a dark, brownish red leather that contrasted the rest of the brightness well.

Discarding my cloak over the back of the two-seater couch, I sat down on it, slinging one of my legs over the other and resting my gloved hands on my knees, staring straight ahead.

"So once again, you're a legend and I'm your tag-along," Candor stated out loud in a toneless drawl.

"Is there some sort of problem with that?" I asked calmly, turning my blood-red eyes on him.

Candor shrugged. "I don't know. It was just a statement. It's the truth, isn't it?"

"No, actually, it isn't," I refuted emotionlessly, "You aren't a tag-along-you're here because I want you to be."

"And this is supposed to make me feel better?" Candor quipped.

"No, it's supposed to make you shut up," I retorted seriously, getting to my feet and passing through the doorway of the nearest room, kicking the door shut behind me.

Once inside, I pulled off my gloves and headed for the window, which was already ajar. It looked out on a barren land, accompanied by a pathway that lead down to a beach.

I smirked. Ah, memories. And I had no idea that there was an actual beach on Vanadis.

"So do you really want me around after everything, Hawk?" I heard Candor's quiet voice ask tentatively from behind me.

I sighed and turn around, resting my elbows on the windowsill to address Candor where he stood, leaning his shoulder against the door frame with his hands jammed, like always, deep in the pockets of his leather jacket.

"We've already been through this, Candor," I said in a matter-of-fact tone, "I've forgiven you for all that and we're together now, so of course I want you with me while I'm saving the worlds from certain destruction,"

The corners of Candor's mouth twitched as if to suppress a smile, "I knew that; I just wanted to hear you say it."

He was about to leave, but I grabbed his arm to stop him and pulled his head down for a kiss.

I think he was surprised by that, but he responded eagerly, nevertheless, pinning me by my waist up against the wall. I grabbed a handful of his dark hair and pulled him down lower to make up for our height advantage.

His hands clamped down on my hips, pushing me back into the wall while his tongue parted my lips and went to explore my mouth.

This is definitely one of the main reasons why I keep Candor around, I thought, opening my mouth under his in order to give him better access.

CHAPTER 17

Dangerous

Mist clung to every corner of the haunted moor as a lone figure made its way to the very centre of the deserted terrain.

"You're late," was the greeting he received from the drakkhon known as Uronis.

"I think being dead for nearly a thousand years excuses a few minutes' lateness," the figure retorted in his smooth, velvet-like baritone.

Uronis inclined his head slightly before speaking again, "So I expect you know everything that has been going on since your return?"

His companion's dark eyes flashed slightly in the blackness; the only part of the figure's face not shielded by their black cowl.

"Yes, of course; the war between the assassin's guild and the underworld council, renegade assassins turning up left and right, and the guardians of the border finally learning their true identities. I picked an extremely convenient time to come back to life, especially now that the spell I cast to weaken the border is reaching its peak," the figure summarized with what sounded oddly like satisfaction.

Uronis' scaled amber orbs glittered in faint amusement.

"So why choose now to return, Lord Xaliden?" he questioned in a cold tone, as if he didn't actually care about the answer.

Xaliden Cyle let out a singularly humourless chuckle.

"Come now, Uronis, I thought you had complete mastery of your mind-reading abilities and would be able to know the answer to that without asking," he mock chided, "What with all of the wars and a showdown on the way, I think it's the perfect time for the lord of the drakkhons to rise,"

`*Darkness.*

Death.

Despair.

Betrayal.

Disaster.

That is what lies in the future for the Guardians.'

Iove frowned.

That couldn't be right.

Everything in the prophecies he'd read pointed toward the guardians' success in sealing the border.

But this one apparently begged to differ. Nothing was written on this scroll, save for those five words and the sentiment.

What did it mean? the prophecy-keeper wondered fervently, staring hard at the scroll in his hands, as if doing so might wring some more meaning from it.

Needless to say, that didn't happen and Iove ended up tossing the scroll of parchment to the floor in evident frustration before throwing himself against the wall and closing his eyes.

Maybe it wasn't even a real prophecy and Halcott had just left it there as a sick joke because of his grudge against Hawk.

Because that *couldn't* be right.

Not with the hell the worlds were going to be plunged into if it was.

Coincidentally, a certain dark angel was seeing something that mirrored exactly what that dismal scroll was saying.

His electric-white eyes were staring out at a cast wasteland, divided in half. Two worlds, ripped asunder and no border in sight.

Therefore, it had to be the future, because the border still existed in the present. What wasn't clear was exactly *how* far in the future it was.

There was not a trace of life in either of the worlds, but Therrian could detect billions of souls burning on the outer edges of the map.

A voice spoke then, echoing out in the deathly silence.

"This is what we've waited for."

Out of the virtually impenetrable darkness came a man.

Or more accurately, a male drakkhon with the characteristic tanned skin and scaled eyes, his the colour of burnt coal underneath immaculate tendrils of purest obsidian hair and thick, black lashes.

Add that to his menacing aura and the fact that he was nearly seven feet tall and you had a force to be reckoned with.

Said force was followed by another drakkhon, this one a familiar face: Uronis.

But he was different because there was actually some emotion on his face. To be specific, one emotion: triumph.

The unfamiliar of the two Eidolons spoke again in a quiet, yet carrying baritone, fluid as flowing water.

"The Guardians have failed and the border has been destroyed. And with the rest of the races annihilated, both worlds will fall once again under our control. It is time to begin anew," he declared fiercely, his statement making Uronis crack a faint smile. "And the future now belongs to us."

With that elegant sentence, Therrian was torn from the vision.

The dark angel's coffee-coloured eyelids snapped open, taking in the familiar grayness of his room in the house he now shared with Uronis whilst trying to regain some semblance of stability in his current location.

Generally, he prided himself on being able to handle anything Fate had to throw at him and so far, had made good with that pride, but this was something completely alien.

How *did* one deal with the end of not just one world, but two, and, not to mention, the complete obliteration of every race that inhabited both, bar for Eidolons?

Therrian suppressed a shudder with difficulty; he didn't have the answer to that.

That vision definitely meant something, though; if that was the future, he wasn't going to be there to see it. None of the Guardians would-because they would all be dead. And that prospect did not sit well with him in the slightest.

His door opened at that moment, interrupting his thoughts, and causing him to face one of their subjects.

Uronis' scaled ambers surveyed him impassively from the doorway for several seconds before he dropped the pretence and stated flatly, "I know what you saw, dark angel."

Therrian didn't even blink. He wasn't surprised: the drakkhon could read minds, after all.

"Should I care?" he questioned smoothly, cocking a steel-white eyebrow and pushing his dark glasses further up his nose.

Uronis stared at him, as if trying to peel him apart, "It depends; are you planning on selling me out for being a double-agent?"

"Not if you tell me who it is you're spying on us for," Therrian responded evenly, daring Uronis to decline.

The drakkhon, surprisingly, complied without complaint. "His name is Xaliden Cyle," he began to explain, "And he is my ancestor, the drakkhon ruler, and, above all, the ultimate reason why the border separating Earth and Vanadis has been failing all this time. Hawk was wrong, you see; I am no mercenary. My loyalties, along with loyalties of the rest of the Eidolon guild, lie with him, and him alone."

"And he intends for the Guardians to fail at sealing the border, thus allowing it to dissolve completely, and in turn, destroying every single race on both worlds, save for his own," Therrian concluded effectively, electric-white eyes glittering behind his dark glasses.

"Precisely," Uronis confirmed, inclining his hooded head slightly.

Therrian appeared to consider this for a moment before getting to his feet.

"I want you to take me to this...Xaliden Cyle," he decided, throwing the hood of his black cloak back over his head and pulling up the cowl.

"Why?" Uronis asked suspiciously, scaled amber eyes flashing in the dark.

The dark angel turned to face him. "Read my mind and find out."

Uronis did so and, afterwards, he made his decision. "Very well," he conceded, grasping Therrian's arm tightly and transporting them both to the moor Therrian had seen in his vision.

Standing in front of them when they arrived was the very person they had come there to see, an appraising look in his coal black eyes.

"And what business could a reincarnated dark angel have here?" the drakkhon lord said, his velvet voice soft and silky as he gazed unwaveringly down at the two males.

"I assume that you are the drakkhon ruler?" Therrian quipped, deliberately ignoring Xaliden's question for the time being.

Xaliden inclined his raven-head, "That I am, dark angel. And why are you here?"

"It just so happens that I have a proposition for you," Therrian replied fluidly.

Xaliden arched one of his thin black eyebrows. "I'm listening."

Therrian lowered his dark glasses, offering Xaliden a full view of his electric-white orbs before he spoke, "I have no loyalty to the other guardians, only a desire never to return to the underworld. Since you no doubt intend that the ice and blood guardians will be killed in their endeavour to seal the border, I've decided that my interests are best served if I ally myself with you."

"How do I know I can rely on you, dark angel?" the drakkhon ruler challenged, "After all, you abandoned Niral Lione when he needed you the most and he was the one who resurrected you."

The dark angel stared him down. "Lione was a dunce. I abandoned him because his plan was not the way to settle my score with the underworld council, that being the only reason why I allowed him to resurrect me in the first place. He was right about one thing, though; I am treacherous. But only against those who I deem unworthy of my loyalty," Therrian finished in a coldly matter-of-fact tone.

The Eidolon's dark coals surveyed him carefully over the cowl of his cloak and Therrian bore it steadily from behind his steel-white mane of hair.

"So am I to understand that you have deemed myself as worthy, then?" the drakkhon ruler quipped, his second eyebrow arching up to join the first in a single, fluid motion.

Therrian smiled, showing his silvery canines, "Exactly,"

"In that case, I accept your proposal," Xaliden said. He held out a clawed hand to Therrian, eyes glittering malevolently. "Welcome to the Merging-bringers,"

Therrian took the hand with a sly grin, "The pleasure is all mine,"

Knock. Knock. Knock.

Sehto mentally groaned and pushed himself out of bed, pulling his dark blue turtleneck back over his head. Who the *hell* was knocking on the door at this hour?

His answer came in the form of a familiar slate-haired man standing outside in the rain and yet somehow completely dry.

"Did you want something, Hawk?" the wolf asked placidly, leaning his shoulder against the steel door frame.

Varros shrugged. "This might just be my own personal superstition," he started, "but I get the feeling that something bad is about to happen."

Sehto raised his twin cobalt eyebrows appraisingly. "Well, even if there is, what do you think you're going to do about it?" he asked.

Again, Varros shrugged his black-clad shoulders before replying, "I have no idea. But I'm going to talk to the prophecy-keeper about it. I'd think you want to know as well, though, because I get the feeling it has something to do with you."

"Fine, let's go, then," Sehto agreed tersely, yanking his silver jacket off of the metal hook beside the door and replacing it over his shoulders.

The blood guardian led the way to the tower at the centre of all the houses. While they were walking, Sehto decided to take the opportunity to ask Varros a couple of questions.

"So you're a renegade assassin, am I correct?" he piped up, seemingly unperturbed by the pounding rain that was currently drenching every inch of his diamond-like skin.

Varros hesitated slightly for a fraction of a second before he answered, "Being a renegade implies that I'm still affiliated with the profession, which I'm not. I don't do assassinations anymore; I only kill people now if it's absolutely necessary. Candor isn't a renegade, either, and everything else you heard at my "trial"," he spat the word out derisively, "Was complete crap,"

"I thought you said it was the truth?" Sehto quipped dubiously, kicking absentmindedly at a stone with the toes of his spiked, dark blue boots.

"In essence, it was, but the way Lione put it was bullshit," Varros clarified, stuffing his black-gloved hands in the pockets of his dark cloak almost subconsciously.

"Right," Sehto said, for lack of anything better to say.

Varros shot him a quick sideways glance but didn't comment, deciding to ask Sehto a question of his own, "Why did you come to my rescue at the "trial", anyways?"

Sehto's words stopped him dead in his tracks; "Don't think it's because I care about you; I don't even know you. But you're the blood guardian and the prophecy-keeper sent me to retrieve you and I would think that would have been a lot more difficult if Lione had killed you. So, don't expect the same courtesy *ever* again. From now on, you take care of yourself."

And the ice guardian marched ahead, apparently unconcerned that he had just struck Varros dumb.

Shaking himself slightly, the hawk followed after him, intending to get to the bottom of his statement. But when he caught up with Sehto in front of the tower, Sehto held up a hand to forestall him, most likely because of the voices Varros could hear emitting from inside the tower.

Sehto recognized the voice of Iove's master, clearly addressing the latter inside, "We're keeping a closer watch on Caius Halcott from now on. Iove, don't your family ties hold any sway over Halcott making attempts on the Guardians' lives?"

Both of the men listening outside the door froze because each of them recognized the name "Halcott". Sehto recognized it as the name of the man who had threatened him earlier that night.

Varros recognized it as the name of his surrogate father all those years ago; the one who was now the leader of the underworld council-and the one he'd *killed*.

He was so immersed in his shock that he almost missed Iove's response; "It might interest you to know, master, that this conversation is no longer private."

The door separating Sehto and the very distressed Varros from Iove swung open, revealing the prophecy-keeper standing in the centre of the room and the master retreating down one of the back corridors in silence.

"How much did you hear?" the prophecy-keeper addressed them, attempting to keep the nervousness out of his voice.

Sehto deigned to take the initiative and spoke for both of them, "Everything. What did the master mean about your "family ties" holding sway over Halcott threatening our lives?"

Iove shifted his feet uncomfortably like a guilty child before taking a deep breath and declaring, "My full name is Iove Halcott. Caius Halcott, the leader of the underworld council and the one who threatened you, master Howl, earlier this evening......is my brother."

Some sort of flash streaked through Sehto's azure eyes and when he spoke again, his tone was colder than Arctic pack ice.

"I warned you, prophecy-keeper, of the consequences of lying to me, but it looks like they were just empty words to you," he said in a quiet, dangerous tone just barely above a whisper.

Then he smirked, sending shivers down Iove's spine, "So be it. It looks like I'll just have to show you that I *never* make empty threats. Oh, and if you were wondering about what my company back on Earth did, HOWLtd is just a smokescreen for a branch of the Russian mafia."

With that ominous revelation, the ice guardian turned on his heel and exited the Destiny Tower soundlessly.

"What are you doing here, Candor?" Uronis enquired of the dark-skinned youth standing in the sitting room of the house he shared with Therrian.

Candor turned to face him, leather-clad arms crossed over his bare chest.

"Where's the dark angel? I thought you and he were sharing a house," he asked a question of his own, instead of answering Uronis'.

"The dark angel is out, obviously," Uronis stated evasively, scaled ambers becoming the sole source of light in the dim room. "What are you doing here?"

Candor's arms dropped, as did his gaze. Not to be averted, then.

"I, I had something I wanted to ask you," he stuttered flatly, olive eyes fixed on the house's wooden floor.

The drakkhon cocked a querying eyebrow at him and quipped coolly, "Such as?"

Candor inhaled deeply and tilted his blue-ebony head up to meet the Eidolon's razor-sharp gaze, "I want you to make me an Eidolon."

Uronis stared at him, "And why, pray tell, would you want to become an Eidolon?"

Candor sighed and answered in complete honesty, "Because out of the two of us, Hawk has always been the stronger one. Because now that we're together and, even though I know he can protect himself, I still want, I still *need* a way so that if the time comes when he *can't* protect himself, I can do it for him."

Uronis looked deep into the olive eyes in front of him and found that Candor was telling him the truth. He truly had no ulterior motives for wanting to be turned other than a genuine desire to defend his lover.

"Very well," he decided. "Give me your left wrist."

Candor looked taken aback, but complied, allowing Uronis to take his wrist into his gloved hands.

A single claw protruded out of the index finger of his glove and the drakkhon inserted it into the vein in Candor's wrist, holding the limb tightly to keep it still.

As soon as he retracted the claw, it was replaced almost instantly with his pointed, white fangs. The ex-assassin had to force himself not to cry out in pain as he felt the venom from Uronis' fangs entering his system. Uronis pulled back and pressed his gloved finger over the steadily growing dot of blood.

Minutes passed in silence until Uronis finally lifted his finger and saw that the wound beneath it had stopped bleeding.

"The change will overtake you in minutes, but first, there is one last thing to do."

Faster than Candor could blink, the drakkhon put his hands on either side of the renegade's head and snapped his neck.

Xaliden interlinked his fingers over his desk before addressing the stationary dark angel in the corner. "Therrian, I have your first task under my service,"

Said dark angel tilted his head downward in a silent accord, prompting Xaliden to continue. "I want you to resurrect Nyle Candor in her human form," he stated clearly, "She'll make a fitting blood consort and one I can use as ammunition against the blood guardian and his lover."

He got to his feet and his servant, because that, in essence, was what Therrian was, followed close behind.

They walked out into the underworld, acidic flames spurting out of the ground in their wake until Xaliden halted.

"You saw the place where she died, I gather?" he asked, facing his servant expectantly.

"Yes," Therrian confirmed tonelessly, his expression carefully neutral under his black hood and, knowing what Xaliden wanted, he took up the lead and made his way to the centre of the land of the dead.

The acid green glow reflecting off of the flames eerily illuminated Therrian's slightly haunted features, and it gave him the look of some sort of demon.

They reached the very heart of the underworld and when they did so, Therrian stopped.

A thin and barely noticeable layer of dust covered about five feet of the bloody ground in front of him.

"These are the remnants of Nyle Candor's body," he said offhandedly, pushing off his hood and shedding his dark glasses, baring his electric eyes to the steadily dying light.

"Do you need anything to perform this?" Xaliden asked him, folding black-clad arms across his chest.

Therrian shook his mass of spiked steel-white hair in a negative, "No. My eyes and considerable quiet are all I need for this task."

"Very well, then," Xaliden inclined his head, "Begin."

Therrian turned his ivory orbs on the dust below and they began to glow.

Electric strobes of light hit the dust covering the bloodstained ground, and it began to rise into the air.

It mixed with the acid flames surrounding it and the combination black and green filled Therrian's smooth, pupil-less eyes.

"*Corpus anastasis,*" the dark angel breathed in a soft, melodious voice, gaze transfixed on the swirling mass of dust, light and fire.

As he watched it, it appeared to take on a distinct shape and form; one that he recognized.

The white light from his eyes escalated in luminosity, bathing the dark terrain in its electric glow, throwing the cracked ground into sharp focus.

BANG.

With a single, ground-breaking explosion, the smoke, flames, dust, and light cleared and in their place stood the shape of a teenage girl with olive eyes and ebony hair.

Nyle Candor.

The glow from Therrian's eyes began to fade as Xaliden advanced toward the previously dead ex-underworld assailant.

"You are Nyle Candor?" he said to her, adopting a polite questioning tone, helped along by his velvet-like undercurrent.

The dark-skinned woman nodded, "Yes, I am. What's it to you?"

Xaliden chuckled, a deep, musical sound before responding. "I have the means for you to finally take revenge on your larcenous brother. But nothing is free. In order for me to educate you in this method, you will need to do something for me."

"Such as?" Nyle quipped suspiciously, olive eyes blazing with determination.

Xaliden smiled, a smile that sent shivers crackling down the length of the former underworld assailant's spine, "Surrender to me. You will become my consort, in all possible meanings of the phrase."

Therrian hid a smile as he replaced his dark hood and glasses over his eyes, from which the glow had now completely disappeared.

Nyle considered a moment; then she smirked. "Anything for revenge," was her firm response.

Xaliden didn't bother to suppress his satisfied grin. "Excellent," he commented, black eyes glittering.

CHAPTER 18

Deception and Grudges

Candor blinked feebly up at the unfamiliar surroundings. He felt...cold. And thirsty.

"Open your eyes, renegade," a familiar voice commanded dully from the other side of the room.

Dark brown eyelids snapped open and Candor nearly cried out in pain, shutting his eyes again instantly.

Everything had been unbelievably sharp and the light in the room had been like a thousand tiny needles stabbing at his retinas.

"Did it hurt?" the voice from before asked without emotion, somehow much louder than it had sounded previously, sounding as if the speaker were right next to him, instead of across the room. "You don't have to speak-just nod."

Slowly, Candor nodded, keeping his hands clamped tightly over his eyes to block out the light.

"Good, that means that the change took and you have your night vision abilities," the voice commented, "Keep your eyes closed; I'll turn the lights off so you can see."

When Candor sensed the dimness through his closed eyes, he carefully and gradually opened them again. It was like the first time he'd opened them-only now that the lights were off, it was less painful.

Even in the total darkness, Candor could now see every detail of the room, right down to the convoluted knots in the wooden walls that had escaped his notice before. He could hear the wind blowing outside and clouds moving overhead.

Uronis watched the new half-drakkhon revelling in his newly elevated senses and powers, leaning against the wall casually.

After letting his scaled olive eyes roam freely over everything around him for several minutes, Candor found that the feeling of cold hadn't gone and the thirst had grown.

He turned to Uronis and reeled back in shock.

He could hear the drakkhon's thoughts as clearly as if they were being spoken to him aloud.

"It's something, isn't it?" Uronis said to him quietly, reading Candor's mind(literally);his voice was somehow still inherently loud and Candor flinched.

"It'll pass," Uronis reassured him, "Once you drink blood for the first time, the sense development stage will be over."

"And where am I supposed to get blood? I refuse to go preying on innocent people," Candor declared firmly, keeping his own voice just barely above a whisper while trying to shut out Uronis' constant thoughts.

Uronis cocked a single teal eyebrow at him, "Isn't that what you assassins do? Kill innocent people?"

Candor just barely restrained himself from rolling his eyes.

"In case you haven't noticed, Eidolon, I don't happen to be an assassin anymore," he stated impatiently, "And at any rate, not all of our victims were innocent people,"

"Well, if you don't want to prey on innocent people, get your lover to become your blood consort and drink from him and no one else," Uronis suggested indifferently, crossing his arms over his chest.

Candor looked at him appraisingly, but found no evidence that he was joking. "Are you serious?" he questioned incredulously, not believing what he was hearing.

Uronis faced him fully, "Do I look like the type to joke?" Candor shook his head, "What makes you think Varros will even accept being my blood consort?"

"Look, either you drink from him or other 'innocent' people-it's your choice. Now kindly get out of my house," Uronis ordered in a bored, final tone.

Recognizing his dismissal, Candor turned around and left the Eidolon's house without another word.

When he reached the house he was sharing with Varros, he found the younger man waiting for him outside the front door.

I stood outside my front door, leaning against it with my eyes closed, mulling over what had happened in the Destiny Tower.

To say it had been an eventful night would have been a gross understatement.

And it was about to get even more so.

"Hawk," I heard Candor's familiar deep voice call out to me. My pale eyelids opened and I looked at him.

Something was different about him; his eyes had taken on a distinctly scaly appearance and were a lot brighter than usual. His skin was now more tanned than dark and he was giving off a strangely cold aura.

"What happened to you?" I asked him curiously, stuffing my gloved hands in my cloak pockets.

He shifted uncomfortably under my piercing gaze. "I've become an Eidolon," he admitted in an undertone.

I froze, sure I had heard him wrong. "Excuse me?" I said, my crimson pools hardening into garnets in their sockets.

Candor looked at the ground and repeated his previous statement, only slightly louder this time, "I've become an Eidolon."

Are. You. Shitting. Me? was all I wanted to say, but this wasn't really the time to get angry. So instead, I just closed my eyes again and suppressed a sigh.

I shouldn't have been surprised; Candor always was the king of rash decisions. "Have you had blood yet?" I asked him, struggling to keep my voice even.

"Well, no, because I told Uronis I wasn't going to feed off of innocent people," Candor confessed hesitantly.

I opened my eyes again and stared at him.

"And I suppose you expect me to be your blood consort?" I quipped, raising my slate eyebrows in his direction.

Candor still wouldn't meet my eyes when he shrugged and answered, "Not if you don't want to. I won't force you-or feed on you without your permission."

I couldn't suppress my sigh this time and beckoned my lover to follow me inside.

He did so without question, hands stuffed deep in the pockets of his leather jacket.

Once we were inside, I faced Candor again, mirroring his position with my gloved hands in the pockets of my cloak. "I'm going to let you feed on me," I said before he could say anything, "And I will consent to being your blood consort-but only because I don't want you feeding on random people, either,"

Candor snapped his mouth closed and nodded gratefully, "Thanks, Hawk. So are we going to do this now? I mean..." He trailed off uncertainly and I rolled my eyes.

"How do you want to do this?" I asked him, pulling off my cloak and gloves and tossing them both on the couch while watching him expectantly.

Candor sat down on the couch and patted the space beside him.

I took it and let him put his arm around me. "Well, unless you feel like arguing with the classics, I might as well feed from your neck," he suggested, watching me out of the corner of his eye for my reaction.

When I merely shrugged, he edged closer to me, pushing the collar of my coat away. Before the fangs, I felt his lips touch the nape of my neck tentatively and he whispered against my skin, "Are you sure about this?"

By way of an answer, I tilted my head back and rested it on his arm, baring the full expanse of flesh that was my neck to him. I heard him chuckle before planting a light kiss on my neck, "I'll take that as a yes, then,"

He opened his mouth and I felt the point of his fangs graze my skin lightly, creating a small puncture wound. I closed my eyes again before Candor's hand cradled the back of my head and his pointed teeth completely pierced my skin.

His arm wrapped itself loosely around my waist, pulling me closer to him and my own hands grasped at his leather-clad shoulders while the pain slowly eased.

After another few minutes, it didn't hurt anymore and all I could feel was Candor's cold hand rubbing the back of my neck soothingly, prompting me to relax.

When he withdrew his fangs from my pulse point, I felt his tongue licking away any remaining traces of blood and sealing the cut he'd made.

"Are you okay?" were the first words out of his mouth as he licked the red liquid from the points of his incisors, scaled olive eyes considering me carefully.

I slid my hands off of his shoulders and met his eyes evenly, "I'm fine, Candor,"

I made to stand up, but he caught my wrist. "Varros," he said quietly, turning me back to face him again.

"What-" I barely got the whole word out before he was pressing our lips together.

His hand was once again at the back of my head, deepening the kiss and tangling in my slate hair. I let him kiss me, but didn't reciprocate it, preferring to have him work my lips with his own.

I allowed him a few minutes before I broke away for lack of air.

"You sure you're fine?" Candor questioned sceptically, releasing my wrist and dropping both of his hands to his sides.

"Yes," I told him emphatically, licking my lips without conscious thought and stuffing my own hands back in my pockets, only in the pockets of my trenchcoat.

"Right then," Candor mumbled awkwardly, turning away and disappearing into the bedroom.

The ground was becoming steadily covered in blood and dead bodies as Therrian summarily executed one unlucky hindrance after another without emotion.

When the last of them fell to the ground, Therrian turned to his observer, whose black eyes were surveying the carnage remorselessly over folded, black-clad arms.

"How long do you think it'll take someone to recognize this as your work and not the work of the assassin's guild?" he said, nodding his chin toward the pile of bloody corpses.

Therrian appeared to consider the question as he methodically cleaned the blood from his cloak with a quick spell.

"Long enough," was his confident response as he replaced his dark glasses over his electric-white eyes.

He cast a final look at the macabre compilation of his victims lying prone on the ground before following Xaliden back to their base.

It was noticeably empty when they arrived and the dark angel was surprised.

"Where are all your other precious minions?" he questioned tonelessly, smoothly raising one of his immaculate steel-white eyebrows.

His companion deigned not to reply, instead placing a greying sheet of paper on top of his desk and resting his hand on top of it.

"I've come up with a few more plans to bring the border to its final stages and they require you to carry them out," the drakkhon ruler informed his servant matter-of-factly, black coals glimmering with unrestrained malice beneath his tanned eyelids and obsidian bangs.

Therrian deftly lifted the sheet of paper out from underneath Xaliden's hand and scanned it subtly from behind the black lenses of his glasses, committing the content to his memory.

"You do realize that the majority of those plans requires me revealing my identity as a double-agent?" he quipped, setting the paper back down on the wooden surface of Xaliden's desk and staring at the Eidolon sitting behind it.

Xaliden rolled his eyes expressively, "No, really? I hadn't realized that; I mean, it's not like they're my plans or anything,"

It was Therrian's turn to roll his eyes and he scoffed, "Be serious, if you don't mind. Do you really want me to do that, when exposing myself means exposing Uronis as well?"

"It is necessary, dark angel, and without this course of action being taken, it will take longer for the border to fail completely," Xaliden stated bluntly.

Therrian nodded towards the paper, "Very well, then. What would you like me to do first?"

By way of an answer, Xaliden steepled his fingers together and gave him a pointed look, eyes shining in their sockets.

"Right," Therrian said tersely, turning to leave the drakkhon's office as Nyle, his blood consort, was just coming in. Once out of the room, shadows enveloped the dark angel and he disappeared from within them.

When the black tendrils withdrew from around him, he was standing in front of the translucent, smoky wall that was the border separating Earth and Vanadis.

It looked like it had become more transparent in the last twenty-four hours, since he'd last seen it. It was almost a shame that he had to make it deteriorate even further.

He raised his dark glasses for the second time that night and turned around at the tell-tale sounds of his accompaniment's arrival. "I almost expected you not to come," he informed the newcomer offhandedly, ivory eyes glittering under the obsidian sky.

Dark clouds shifted overhead as Uronis spoke in a colourless tone; "You think I have more important things to attend to than this?"

Therrian chuckled without humour. "Hardly," he supplied dully, "After all, what could possibly be more important than the destruction of all manner of civilization?"

"You tell me," the drakkhon said without emotion, gloved fingers flicking themselves in Therrian's direction. "Are we doing this or not?"

Therrian directed his razor-sharp gaze back at the border and the pale irises dominating his eye sockets began to glow explosively, the only sources of light underneath the shadow-covered sky above, illuminating Therrian's inhuman features and throwing them into sharp focus.

From one of the pockets of his black pants, he withdrew what looked like a glass sphere full of wine; but the liquid inside looked far too dense to be wine, so Uronis surmised that it was blood.

"You're going to need this, aren't you?" Therrian stated knowingly, holding out the blood-filled sphere to his companion without moving his gaze from the border.

Uronis took it from his gloved hand wordlessly, popping the stopper at the top and pouring the viscous red liquid into his open mouth, somehow managing not to spill a single drop.

As soon as he had drained the glass completely, he threw it on to the ground, where it smashed, and tilted his head back as his scaled amber orbs mimicked Therrian's eyes and lit up the night immensely, filling their sockets entirely, eviscerating the corneas and pupils from existence.

"Let's do this, then," he declared in a slightly magnified voice, tilting his hooded head forward, so that he, like his companion, was looking directly at the border.

Both pairs of glowing eyes focused on the flickering border, gaining more unnatural luminosity by the second.

Shadows trailed out of Therrian's dark form, this time surrounding the border instead of him, spreading blackness all around the two otherworldly beings, effectively shielding them from view.

"*And now you break*," Therrian hissed, enunciating each word clearly and whiteness from his pale eyes overcame the blackness from the summoned shadows, causing it to glow as well.

When the glow had fully consumed the blackness, the rumbling began beneath the ground.

Slowly but surely, a hole began to take shape in the far from solid wall that continued to flicker in and out of sight even as the aforementioned hole tore into it.

The aperture steadily grew in size until it was the size, and roughly the same shape of a large boulder.

The night fell again into total darkness with this development as the glow emitting from Therrian and Uronis' eyes vanished.

Therrian's dark glasses were replaced over his eyes and he grinned. "Let's see what the remaining Guardians will say about this."

Uronis grinned back and both of them vanished on the spot in a whirl of shadows as the first clap of thunder shook the ground.

There is no way in hell *that this is happening again.* I thought mutinously as I heard the omnipresent sound of someone knocking on the door of the house Candor and I shared.

I disentangled my black-clad arms from around Candor's sleeping form and slid out of our bed, grumbling under my breath as I exited the bedroom to go open the front door.

The wooden door swung open to reveal Therrian's dark, cloaked shape standing in the doorway with the most serious expression I have ever seen him wear since we met.

I cocked a slate eyebrow at him curiously and asked, "Is something the matter, dark angel?" "I've just been to see the border and there is a hole in it," Therrian informed me flatly.

I cursed mentally.

God, why couldn't someone wake me up with *good* news for a change?

"Are you sure?" I questioned, folding my arms across my chest.

Therrian tossed me a withering glance. "I wouldn't have bothered telling you if I wasn't absolutely certain, Hawk. See for yourself if you still don't believe me."

I sighed and gestured to Therrian to lead the way before stepping out of the house and silently closing the door behind me. I would have woken up Candor, but I thought at least one of us should be able to get some sleep tonight.

Before heading for the border, we stopped at Howl's house, but it didn't look as though anyone was there, so we just transported straight to the border.

The first thought that went through my mind was that this was going to be a huge problem.

Actually, my first thought was *Shit,* my *second* thought was that this was going to be a huge problem.

Because staring me right in the face, was a hole the size of Arterran ripped right through the centre of the border separating Earth and Vanadis.

"Not very pretty, is it?" a familiar smooth voice commented from somewhere to my left.

I looked over my shoulder and my eyes settled on the tall form of Sehto, angled across a tree and twirling an unlit cigarette between his slender fingers.

When he saw the surprise on my face, his pale lips creased in a slight smile, "The dark angel must have neglected to mention that I was already here,"

Therrian didn't look remotely abashed when I turned to look at him accusingly.

"Did I now? Well, that's annoying," he stated vapidly, and even though he was still wearing those ever-present dark glasses, I could see his electric-white orbs flashing from behind them as if daring Sehto to make another comment.

Sehto shrugged his broad shoulders before repeating his earlier quip, "Like I said, it's not very pretty, is it?"

I had to agree with him; this hole wasn't the slightest bit pretty-and *that* was putting it nicely, too. It was simply gaping and just overall, completely unpleasant.

The question was, what did this mean? It looked like the border was in its final stages and I had no idea what to do about it at this early on. There was going to be hell to pay when this all blew over, especially if the border ended up failing completely.

All at once, I began to feel the first drops of rain seeping down the back of my neck and with them came an eerie coldness that reminded me somewhat of the aura following Candor around now that he was an Eidolon-only much colder, like a clammy frost.

It crept over my neck, but Sehto was the first one to notice it and to call out its source.

"Why don't you stop skulking back there and tell us what you want, drakkhon?" he declared swiftly, tossing the still unlit cigarette onto the ground and swapping it for one of his ice-blue revolvers.

From behind the tree Sehto was leaning against, an unnaturally tall figure came sidling, dressed entirely in black clothes that covered the majority of his tanned body.

Scaled black eyes glimmered maliciously from beneath similarly-coloured bangs and a low hood.

"I must be getting old if a human is able to detect my presence so easily and identify it," the figure spoke, revealing that it was a male with a voice like flowing water.

He spent a minute looking Sehto over critically before amending his statement, "Ah, not a normal human, then. I should have known: you're one of the guardians of the border."

It wasn't a question, but Sehto's upper lip curled in a cocky sneer as he turned his liquid azure eyes on the speaker.

"That's right, I am one of the guardians of the border and you are the cause of all this," Sehto surmised without emotion, managing to stare the other down even being the shorter between them.

The taller man gave him a mock bow.

"Well-guessed, master Howl," he grinned crookedly, "Xaliden Cyle, drakkhon ruler, at your service."

My slate eyebrows shot up so high I think they were in danger of disappearing into my hair. "Drakkhon ruler?" I quoted dubiously, crossing my arms over my chest.

Sehto shot me a dangerous glance over his shoulder before riveting his gaze once again on the "drakkhon ruler".

"Yes. Did you not think that the Eidolons had a social hierarchy like every other race?" Xaliden said effortlessly, throwing back his hood and simultaneously lightly tousling his raven-black hair.

I didn't answer, mostly because I didn't have a retort for that.

Xaliden smirked. "It seems you 'guardians' don't know your history very well," he observed mockingly, "Since the border started failing, I have been helping it along," His smirk grew wider, "In fact, I cast the spell that made it start failing in the first place,"

After that declaration, there was silence except for the sound of Sehto undoing the safety on his revolver.

He directed it straight at Xaliden's chest.

"Let's put the history of the Eidolons to the test," he hissed out savagely, finger poised on the trigger of his gun.

I couldn't do anything except stare at Sehto blankly.

What the hell did he think he was doing? Guns had no effect on regular Eidolons, much less the most powerful type of Eidolon. I didn't even hear what Sehto said about putting the history of Eidolons to the test.

Xaliden merely continued to smirk in the face of Sehto's apparent fury.

"Like I said, you 'guardians' really don't know your history, do you?" he shook his head almost pityingly at us. "We Eidolons can't be harmed by human weapons, except for swords."

"Well, it's a damn shame that no one even bothers to use swords anymore now that we have these, but they do happen to be just as effective," Sehto all but snarled, his grip on the ice-blue gun turning his knuckles white; well, whiter than usual.

Xaliden lifted a black eyebrow at his would-be killer and just stared wordlessly, clearly unfazed by the prospect of being shot.

Sehto gave him an artificial smile before firing his revolver point-blank at the drakkhon's unprotected chest.

And like we all expected, nothing happened and when the shot cleared, Xaliden remained standing in front of us, tanned face completely expressionless.

"I told you," he deadpanned blandly, black coals boring into Sehto seemingly without conscious instruction, "Now if you'll excuse me, I have other matters to attend to; places to go, civilizations to topple, the like. ***Dosvidanya,*** master Howl,"

With a conspiratorial wink in Sehto's direction, Xaliden walked off, a clap of thunder rapidly succeeding his exit.

I was stunned and turned to Therrian, but he was as metronomic-looking as ever and Sehto was stowing his gun back in the holster strapped to his calf.

"Let's get the hell out of here," Sehto growled, flicking rain-drenched cobalt bangs off of his diamond-pale forehead, somehow still managing to look regal, even soaked to his skin.

Without waiting for our responses, he disappeared on the spot, leaving Therrian and I alone.

The dark angel gave me a significant glance out of the corner of his eyes before he, too, transported away from the border, bone-dry even after standing in the pouring rain for the last forty-five minutes.

Casting the border a cursory glance over my black-clad shoulder, I copied the other two guardians and transported myself back to my house without another word.

When I arrived in front of it, Candor was awake and waiting for me by the door.

"Where did you go?" he asked me, scaled olive eyes questioning.

"Tell you inside," I told him, unlocking the door and beckoning for him to follow me.

Once we had both sat down on the wine-coloured leather, I faced Candor so I could explain.

"There's a hole in the border," I told him without preamble, slinging one of my legs over the other and leaning back against the couch.

Candor raised his blue-ebony eyebrows at me. "And you've seen this?" he questioned curiously, sounding as though he was having trouble keeping his voice even.

I nodded, "You were blooded by Uronis, weren't you? So you should be able to read my mind and know without me telling you,"

"Yeah, but I would think you wouldn't want me reading your mind on a regular basis," Candor shrugged defensively.

It was all I could do at that point not roll my eyes. "That's your ability and you can use it on me as much as you like," I said indifferently, "It's not like I'm hiding anything you don't already know,"

"That's true," Candor conceded, looking me in the eyes and I knew he was taking me at my word and just reading my mind instead of asking any more questions.

I didn't fight, mostly because I had just given Candor permission to do exactly what he was doing, but also because I didn't really feel like answering more questions tonight.

When he had apparently read everything pertinent to what he wanted to know, he sat back, a frown creasing his broad, tan forehead.

"So all this time, the one behind the border separating the two worlds failing has been this 'drakkhon ruler' character," he stated, looking thoroughly discomfited.

I couldn't blame him, either; he had just become a half-drakkhon and was technically related to this 'drakkhon ruler' character.

"That pretty much sums it up," I confirmed without emotion, letting my pale eyelids fall shut as I rested my head on the back of the couch.

"I'm guessing, along with sealing the border, you're now planning to kill him as well?"

I replied without opening my eyes, "What do you think, Candor?

The former leader of the underworld assailants, known to humans as Nyle Candor, entered Xaliden's office as Therrian was making his way out, kicking the door shut behind her.

"You summoned me, Lord Xaliden?" she quipped, coming to stand in front of Xaliden's wooden desk and sinking into a formal bow.

Xaliden rose from his chair and walked around Nyle to lock the door before speaking, "Indeed, I did. I know of a way to set up the perfect conditions for your revenge on your older brother,"

Nyle cocked a curious eyebrow, intrigued. "I'm listening," she intoned smoothly, giving Xaliden her full attention.

The drakkhon ruler cleared his throat and laid out his plan for her. "Your brother is now a half-drakkhon, so when I feed on you, I can broadcast an image of it into his mind; he'll come running and you can take your revenge."

Nyle sat back on the spiked heels of her grey combat boots, considering.

Then she sneered sinisterly.

"That's a good plan; let's do it," she accepted, her sneer full of malevolence.

Xaliden didn't bother concealing his smirk and he tilted Nyle's head back, exposing her dark neck with a swift motion of his gloved hands.

His pointed fangs traced her jawline, stopping at her pulse point and sinking into the flesh there. Nyle bit her lip to keep from screaming out when she felt those razor-sharp appendages pierce her skin.

Warm blood flowed directly from the open wound into Xaliden's waiting mouth, streaming past his lips and down his throat.

The result was a powerful shock to the drakkhon ruler's system and he knew he couldn't waste the power that with it.

While his fangs were still embedded in Nyle's throat, he used the power spike to quickly send the mental image to her brother via the connection they shared as Eidolons.

In his mind's eye, he could almost see the half-drakkhon's fury at seeing his late little sister *allowing* an enemy Eidolon to feed on her.

With literally no warning, Candor leaped up out of his seat, clutching his head and crying out in what I assume was anguish.

My eyes flew open at his agonized yell and I went over to him, placing a tentative hand on his hunched shoulder. He didn't move at the contact, keeping his head in his hands, pressed against the wooden floor.

"Candor, what's going on?" I asked in a low voice, even though there was no one around except for the two of us.

He shook his head; clearly, he wasn't ready for words yet.

"Candor," I repeated forcefully, my crimson pools boring holes in the back of his head; patiently waiting for a response was not my strong suit.

Finally, Candor spoke, and although his words were muffled, they sent my world spinning on its axis; "I saw *her,* Hawk,"

Speechless, that was the only word that could accurately describe my reaction to that; because there was no question in my mind of who the "her" he was referring to was.

"Nyle's dead, Candor," I said cautiously when I found my voice again, "You saw it with your own eyes: there was no way anyone could have resurrected her from that state,"

Candor made a strangled noise at the back of his throat by way of a response, digging his nails into his scalp, like he was ready to tear his blue-ebony hair out in grief. And I knew why, too: he'd already had to go through the pain of his little sister's death twice now, and twice was most likely two times too many.

"Candor, talk to me," I pleaded with him, kneeling next to him on the floor, opting for the gentler approach.

"I saw her being *fed on* by that drakkhon ruler person," he hissed aloud, "And she was *letting* him feed on her."

"You don't know that," I told him in a stern, matter-of-fact tone, "Mental images can be deceiving,"

Again, Candor shook his head as if trying to rid himself of the mental assault of images I assumed he was seeing. I didn't know what to do, especially since that if I weren't so intent on pretending like I didn't have emotions, I would most likely have been going to pieces just like him right about now.

This was actually physically painful for me, seeing someone I cared about going through so much agony and not being able to do anything about it.

"I have to get out of here and see this for myself," Candor decided abruptly, getting to his feet.

"Candor, you don't even know where she is," I called as he exited the door, but he ignored me and disappeared.

"Candor!" I shouted after him, but he was gone.

Fuck. I swore in my head, staring at Candor's vacated spot and clenching my gloved fists in my pockets.

Once again, my brainless lover was making a stupid decision because of his sister, and once again, I was going to have to chase after him.

Suppressing a groan, I gritted my teeth and walked out of the front door to transport, thinking I wanted to go wherever Candor was and trusting my powers to take me there.

When the spinning stopped, I found Candor's tall, leather-clad form standing, shaking, in front of the gate of Souls-which was, oddly enough, still wide open, thanks to the previous onslaught of what lay beyond it.

"So he's set up his base in the underworld; I can't say I'm surprised," I stated dully, voicing my thoughts and making Candor jump about a foot in the air.

He twisted his head around to face me.

"You're not stopping me from doing this, Hawk; I *have* to know if what I saw is the truth," he all but growled, jaw clenched stubbornly.

I raised my palms at him in a gesture of surrender, "I'm not here to stop you, Jarl; I want to know the truth, too and I'm also here to keep you out of trouble,"

Candor just stared for several minutes, before sagging and turning away from me, heaving a deep, shaky breath. I walked up to his side and put a hand on his arm, attempting to calm him down. "You don't have to do this, you know," I whispered, slipping my hand off of his arm and into his hand.

He gripped my hand tightly and replied just as quietly, "Yes, I do, Varros," And he marched through the open gate with me following silently beside him.

The underworld itself no longer unnerved me. What could happen while we were in it this time most certainly did.

Was I going to have to watch Nyle's death a third time? I didn't think I could handle that again.

Never mind me, I didn't think *Candor* was going to be able to even remotely handle it, especially when you considered how he'd taken it the last time.

And this time, he wasn't going to have Therrian to help him out of whatever scrape he got himself into against this Xaliden character.

I was pretty much useless because I didn't have a clue how to fight an Eidolon so powerful. At least, not yet; I definitely intended to find out.

The two of us marched ahead, Candor seeming to be following some sort of mental compass and me quickly doing a mental inventory of what I was and wasn't prepared for.

But before I got very far with that, the voice of the 'drakkhon ruler' rang out across the barren ground, "Hmmm, you responded to that mental image even quicker than I expected, Master Candor,"

Both of us snapped around to see the Eidolon coming toward us languidly, a smirk playing onto his dark lips. But what my eyes were drawn to was the person following behind him.

That short, dark-skinned female profile was all too familiar.

I could see Candor's jaw working furiously out of the corner of my eyes to conceal his anguish and pain at seeing his formerly dead sister again. I gave his hand a furtive squeeze and said out of the corner of my mouth, "Don't rise; it's what he wants."

Xaliden brought his gloved hands together in a round of mocking applause. "Bravo, master Hawk, you've successfully assessed my intentions," he drawled smoothly, "The question is, I think, what do you plan on doing about them?"

"I plan on stopping you, obviously," I retorted coldly, keeping a firm grip on Candor's hand so he wouldn't get any ideas. And by ideas, I mean violent urges.

Nyle, from behind the drakkhon ruler, creased her lips in an artificial smile. "I told you they were tough bastards," she commented, folding her arms across her chest.

"And you weren't lying, darling," Xaliden concurred in that cold baritone of his. Candor actually snarled and I had to twist his wrist backward to keep him from launching himself at Xaliden.

"Nyle, what the *hell* are you doing here? You're supposed to be dead," I demanded, further locking Candor's wrist to keep him from saying anything.

Nyle turned her ebony head around to face me, her fake smile widening fractionally, "I knew you'd come along, Hawk; you were always the brains to my brother's brawn, so surely you can figure out what's going on here."

It took me a minute to process her words and then the answer to my question became obvious: "Cyle resurrected you to be his blood consort."

The dark-skinned former underworld assailant grinned, exposing her canines.

"Well, that's only half of it, but congratulations on getting that far. Perhaps my dear ***sandres*** can provide you with the rest of your answer?" she cocked her head in Candor's direction, olive eyes alight with barely concealed mirth.

"You made a bargain with him; your blood in exchange for a second chance at revenge on me," Candor mumbled in a low, flat tone, looking at the ground as his shoulders went limp with guilt.

This was killing him, I could tell. This was serious.

I could feel myself getting angry now.

I turned my livid crimson pools on Xaliden, who was watching our exchange with mild amusement.

"I suppose you're enjoying this, aren't you?" I spat at him scathingly, unable to suppress my ire and disgust, "After all, no doubt this was your plan all along, am I correct? What gives you the right to cause people so much pain? Candor never hurt you; why are you hurting him like this?"

Xaliden faced me fully, obsidian eyes glittering with pure malevolence. "Because I can," was his simple, colourless answer.

My anger at this point was so immense, I could barely form whole words.

"*Because you can?!*" I spluttered indignantly, too pissed to even care that I was never inarticulate. "You're plotting to destroy two worlds, annihilate all races besides your own and basically torturing my boyfriend *because you can?*"

"Did I stutter?" Xaliden said, arching a dark eyebrow. "Yes, I'm planning to do all these things simply because I have the ability to,"

"That is ridiculous!" I exploded, losing all of my composure in a split-second, "Just because you *can* do something, doesn't mean that you *should*."

"On the contrary, actually," Xaliden cut me off effortlessly, "If you *can* do something, I think you not only *should* do it, but you will have the duty to,"

"So if I could kill you right now, I should?" I questioned acidly, abruptly recovering my sense of cynicism.

Even despite his evident misery, I heard Candor hastily stifle a chuckle at my sardonic quip; but I was not in the frame of mind to be amused.

"In essence, yes," Xaliden conceded, "But you can't kill me, so you're not going to."

I rolled my eyes, releasing Candor's hand to fold my arms across my chest irritably. "Yeah, no shit," I snapped.

Candor turned his head in the opposite direction so I couldn't see him laughing, but I could hear him attempting to muffle it.

"So what now, then?" Xaliden quipped curiously, cocking both of his eyebrows this time expectantly, "Are we two immortals to argue the ins and outs of necessity until you end up dead and I end up ruling the worlds?"

"Or you could surrender and save yourself the trouble of fighting me," I suggested innocently, keeping my arms crossed stubbornly.

Xaliden let out a single, humourless laugh and stared me down coolly without wavering.

I didn't flinch, however, not only bearing his stare, but matching it.

Nyle, however, chose that moment to interrupt our 'staring contest' and spoke aloud, "Lord Xaliden, don't you have other, more important matters to attend to, other than arguing with Hawk?"

"This, my dear, is philosophical debating at its finest; it doesn't get any better than this," Xaliden stated incredulously, as if daring Nyle to contradict him. Nyle rolled her eyes expressively at him and leaned against a nearby tree to wait for us to finish.

I bet anything that Candor was glowering at someone behind me, most likely the drakkhon.

"It's not usually considered a debate if there's the prospect of someone dying," I pointed out without emotion, still as stone.

Xaliden gave me a mocking grin, showing his pointed fangs before turning his back on me. "Debate or not, this will continue," he declared, beckoning Nyle to his side, "Be prepared," And he left.

"Nyle!" Candor shouted after his little sister, but she was already gone. He made to chase after her, but my gloved hand closed around his arm before he could transport.

"Let her go, Jarl," I told him firmly.

Candor looked scandalized.

"But, Varros, "he began to protest, but I cut him off, "We'll go after her again another time. Right now, she's out of our reach."

My boyfriend sagged hopelessly and his arm went slack in my grip.

"Good," I said, retracting the hand around his arm, "Now let's get out of here,"

Candor nodded silently and surrendered, and the two of us transported back to our house.

CHAPTER 19

Shifting Loyalties

Visions are usually considered a way to look into the future; but when you are a legend-like one of the guardians of the border-the future isn't the only thing you can look into.

Some are able to look into the past and even...the present.

Voices. Pounding relentlessly at his head and then....

Blinding white light.

Sehto lifted his diamond-pale eyelids to the same dark, desolate moor he had glimpsed when he had looked into the mocking eyes of the drakkhon ruler, Xaliden Cyle.

Only when he'd seen it then, it had been totally deserted. It still was-save for three people, all of whom he recognized.

One was Uronis, the lead drakkhon, presumably; the dark angel was easily identifiable as the other; and the third was, of course, Xaliden himself.

Xaliden was the first out of the three to speak, before Sehto could fully process exactly what he was seeing, addressing the dark angel, "Despite your arguments that my plans would have exposed you as a double-agent, you seem to have maintained your disguise quite nicely,"

Therrian rolled his ivory eyes, a visible action since they currently weren't covered by the usual dark glasses.

"That is because weakening the border was, all things considered, the least treacherous thing you wanted me to do. When I complete the rest of them, there is no doubt in my mind that I will no longer be able to fulfil my role as a double-agent because the Guardians, despite what you think, aren't stupid," he drawled in an almost metronomic tone.

"Maybe you aren't, dark angel, but I don't think I can say the same for your companions," Xaliden snorted and Sehto inwardly seethed.

He knew this was actually happening, but if the three of the men hadn't noticed him yet, this was obviously some sort of vision of what was currently happening.

"I mean," Xaliden continued, apparently oblivious to Sehto's anger, "Howl tried to shoot me and if he wasn't stupid, he would have known that guns don't kill Eidolons,"

For the second time, Therrian rolled his eyes at the drakkhon ruler, almost pityingly shaking his hooded head.

"That doesn't make him stupid, just uneducated. After all, there are no Eidolon breeds on Earth, only humans and animals," Therrian reasoned dispassionately, "And that is beside the point, actually. My role as a double-agent remaining secret does not hinge on their level of intelligence,"

"Then what does it hinge on, exactly?" Xaliden queried curiously, cocking a black eyebrow at the dark angel.

Therrian turned those blank, merciless white orbs on the very spot where Sehto was watching and said, "It depends on their seeing powers,"

Sehto cursed loudly as the white light consumed his vision once again and he was brought back to reality by the cold press of steel against his exposed throat.

"So," Therrian's emotionless voice hissed into his ear, the pressure of the knife against his throat increasing slightly, "Your present-seeing powers have picked now to develop,"

"Yeah, what's it to you?" Sehto snarled defiantly, keeping his head tilted back, away from the deadly blade.

He felt its tip tap his lips to shut him up.

"Don't speak, listen," the dark angel admonished coldly, his voice taking on a decidedly hard edge. "I'm not going to kill you, but I am going to tell you some things that the prophecy-keeper most certainly won't. Now, like I said before, your power to see what is happening elsewhere in the present seems to have chosen now to develop, which means the final power is going to develop soon as well. Mine has already developed and I already have full use of it; I can see the future. And in case you hadn't guessed yet, Hawk can see the past-but his power hasn't developed yet. This also means that your other powers are going to come along rather quickly, which might become a problem. Not for you, obviously, but for Lord Xaliden, Uronis and myself,"

Therrian paused, as if thinking of what to say next, "So, strictly speaking, I *should* kill you, but I have a feeling you are no longer intending on using those powers to help seal the border, are you? I will now allow you to answer me."

"*No,*" Sehto hissed as soon as the knife was lifted from his lips, but before he could say anything else, it was back in place.

"Because of the prophecy-keeper lying to you," Therrian surmised tonelessly. He waited a beat before asking his next question. "So, what do you plan on doing now?"

"Showing him what happens when someone crosses me, even after I've warned them not to."

"Strong words from a man that is subdued by the threat of a mere knife," the dark angel mocked, adopting an actual tone for the first time since they'd met. "How do you plan on making good on that threat when you can't even stand up to me, even though I have no intention of killing you?"

"Who says that I don't just choose not to stand up to you?" Sehto sneered and, without warning, he launched himself backward, wrenched the knife away from his throat and twisted Therrian's wrist so that it clattered to the floor.

As a final move, he spun out a kick that knocked Therrian's head back, giving Sehto time to retrieve the fallen knife and direct it at the dark angel's chest. "Still think I won't be able to deliver on my threat to take down the prophecy-keeper?" he commented, a crooked grin splitting his pale lips tauntingly.

Therrian just stared, calmly pushing the knife away from his chest and pulling it out of Sehto's unresisting hand.

"Why are you working for that drakkhon ruler, anyways? He can't be more powerful than you," Sehto asked, not missing the knife.

"Like I said, I can see the future and I saw one where we all died; I refuse to return to the underworld," Therrian stated with a rather unnerving return to his usual emotionless tone.

Sehto blinked, "So the border ends up failing, anyways?"

Therrian nodded and the ice guardian snorted. "So then there really is no point in sticking around; better things can be done with my powers while I'm in this world."

He turned to leave, but Therrian called out to him, "Feel free to oust myself and Uronis to Halcott. We have no qualms with not hiding it any longer."

And he vanished as Sehto was pulling his silver jacket back on. Once it had been replaced over his blue turtleneck, he kicked his door open and wasted no time transporting himself to the front of the Destiny Tower, kicking that door open as well.

Iove was standing behind one of the dozen or so tables when he entered, eyes staring hard at one of his scrolls, but he looked up as Sehto came storming toward him.

"Is there something I can help you with, master Howl?" he asked, attempting a mild tone, but actually feeling rather apprehensive.

"I warned you, prophecy-keeper, of the consequences of crossing me, and now they're going to take effect," Sehto ripped his ice medallion from around his neck and slammed it down on the table in front of him, "You'll have to find yourself another ice guardian. Because I'm done,"

Before Iove could say a word, the wolf turned on his heel and marched back toward the door.

When he reached it, he stopped and added over his shoulder, "Oh, yeah, and now that I'm leaving, you only have *one* of the Guardians left under your thumb because the dark angel is a double-agent."

And with that, he stormed out of the open door and into the night.

I usually prided myself on being very on top of things, especially when they involved me. But lately, that pride had been taken down quite a few notches because of me having no idea about this Guardians prophecy I was a part of.

And even more so for it describing powers I didn't even know actually existed, let alone were possessed by someone, or someones. But one of those powers turned out to belong to me.

I could tell because what I was witnessing right now had definitely already happened.

Standing directly in front of me, colourless eyes uncharacteristically wide and fearful, was a familiar face, one I never thought I'd see again; the face of my late surrogate father, Caius Halcott.

Inwardly, I froze; Caius was alive and solid here, and the only time I had ever seen him look that afraid was when I had killed him.

I tried to shut my eyes-I didn't want to see this-but the scene still obscured my vision.

The sound of a dagger being drawn interrupted my inner turmoil and I swivelled my head around in the direction of the noise.

There was me, a child of only eight, and all too prepared to murder the only two people who ever took care of me, who ever loved me, even despite my occupation.

"Varros dear, what are you doing with that knife?" an airy female voice echoed as the speaker entered the room.

No. I swore mentally; I *really* didn't want to see myself killing my parents *again.*

My surrogate mother's big brown eyes widened in confusion as my eight-year-old self turned the dagger on her. "What's going on?" she asked nervously, eyes flicking back and forth between Caius and me.

"Varros, don't do this," Caius intoned imploringly, determined to get me to see sense.

The younger me turned his crimson eyes below the dark hood onto the floor, glittering coldly.

"I have to, "he whispered without emotion.

Caius stepped forward, perhaps intent on attempting to reason with me some more, but he never got the chance because the second he was within arm's reach, my younger self coolly slashed the dagger across his unprotected chest, tearing his white shirt and drawing a stream of blood.

The older man fell to the floor, clutching his bleeding chest and watching helplessly as his adopted son did the same to his wife that was done to him.

"No!" I cried out pointlessly as my adoptive mother slumped down next to Caius, blood draining steadily from the wound in her chest.

Simultaneously, me and my younger self's knees hit the floor as well as the room quickly filled with the stench of death.

The difference was, though, as soon as my knees collided with the floor, I was transported back to the present, where I repeated the same action in the house I shared with Candor, this time clutching my head to hold in the scream I so badly wanted to let out.

Curse it, why did my power have to be looking into the past?

"Hawk, are you alright?" I heard Candor's voice question me worriedly from the direction of our bedroom.

I dropped my hands onto the floor and hung my head, attempting to resist the urge to throw up from having to relive that murder yet again.

I felt Candor tentatively place his hand on my back to offer me support. "What happened?" he wondered quietly, keeping his voice as even as possible.

I swallowed hard and lifted my head to look at Candor before I answered, "I think I just found out what one of my Guardians powers is; I have visions of the past."

I saw understanding immediately come into those scaled olive eyes.

"You saw yourself killing your parents again, didn't you?" he said sympathetically, hand now rubbing small circles in my back.

I nodded wordlessly and took a deep breath to try and calm myself down, actually taking some solace from Candor's touch.

This had to have something to do with Sehto, Therrian and Uronis leaving and going off on their own to do who knows what. "Something is about to happen," I said, voicing my thoughts aloud and getting to my feet.

Candor tucked his hands into the pockets of his dark green camouflage jacket and waited for me to continue.

I ran a gloved hand through my hair before doing so, "I think I need to talk to the prophecy-keeper about this, see what he thinks we should do about it,"

"Did you want me to come?" Candor asked, leaning back against the wall and crossing his brown-clad legs at the ankles.

"I don't think that's necessary; I'll be back in a minute," I told him, buttoning up my black jacket over the red turtleneck underneath and walking out of the door, toward the Destiny Tower.

My five-minute journey to the Destiny Tower was spent in complete silence because I was too consumed in my thoughts to make even the slightest sound. I could have just transported and gotten there in half the time, but walking gave me more time to think and sort out my thoughts before arriving at my destination.

Speaking of destinations, I'd just reached mine of the moment.

I raised my black-gloved hand and knocked on the metal door, not curious as to if someone would actually answer at this hour. The door opened about a minute later, revealing Iove's sleep-deprived face looking faintly bemused.

"Yes, master Hawk?" he queried with forced politeness, doing his best to hide the exhaustion I could see he was feeling.

"I want to talk to you," I told him seriously, doing *my* best to keep a straight face.

Iove stepped aside to let me in in silent acquiescence and I entered the Destiny tower before turning to face him again.

"I have visions of things that have already happened," I stated without preamble.

Iove didn't blink.

"So the 'seeing' powers are starting to develop," he mumbled, flicking a strand of sandy hair out of his face with two of his fingers.

I pursed my lips together thoughtfully at that. "Could that be why Howl quit, maybe? Because he saw something he didn't like?" I wondered.

The prophecy-keeper shrugged. "I don't see how because his power is 'seeing' the present," he revealed, a crease appearing between his brows.

I cocked an eyebrow of my own, but didn't say anything more on the subject.

Unfortunately, Iove chose to continue with it and asked, "What was your first vision of?"

At that, I turned away with a sigh, not wanting to meet his eyes. "The night I murdered my adoptive parents," I replied tonelessly, striving to keep my eyes focused on the curved stone wall.

Silence met my declaration and I didn't dare turn around because I didn't want to see Iove's expression.

"That probably has something to do with the fact that my brother was your surrogate father and is now trying to kill you and the other two Guardians, no doubt," Iove commented soberly from behind me, but I still continued to face the wall, mostly because I didn't have a suitable response.

"I do wonder why it came now, though; it doesn't really stay with traditional terms of visions since Caius has been after you ever since you forced him to become the leader of the underworld council," he wondered aloud; I wasn't sure if he was talking to me or himself, but I remained silent.

Before he got any further with that train of thought, there was a loud, sycophantic crash that knocked him off of his feet and finally prompted me to turn around.

"What the hell was that?" I exclaimed, my slate eyebrows shooting probably up to my hairline.

Almost as if in answer, the smell of burning paper filled my nostrils at a rapid pace.

Jet black flames began to appear in the air, licking at the walls and catching on all of the various scrolls and prophecies scattered throughout the room.

My first thought was to just get out, but it did strike me as odd that that 'the master' character wasn't doing something about this. "Can't your master do something to stop this?" I said, staring Iove down with my bloody crimson pools.

Iove shook his head. "The master is out, so we're going to have to stop this ourselves," he declared honestly.

The Destiny Tower was on fire. And we had to stop it.

The dark angel watched the Destiny Tower being engulfed by black flames from behind his dark glasses, a satisfied smirk quirking the corners of his black-tinged lips.

Soon that place would be reduced to nothing but stone, ash and mortar.

He let out a slight breath of laughter that condensed in the night air as frost crept over the edges of his black wings.

His smirk grew and he took off higher into the air to get a better view of the ground below; so Howl's crusade was beginning now, too. Excellent.

The flames were speeding up now, melting the metal front door and offering Therrian a full view of the prophecy-keeper trying frantically to save his precious prophecies and the dark angel had to resist a second laugh at the sight of Hawk struggling to decide what to do.

Obviously, the urge to do something good for once was having to fight down the urge to save his own skin. And the best part of this pyrotechnic display was there was no way to douse those flames once they got going.

Unfortunately, Hawk and Halcott did manage to get out of the Tower before it burned to the ground; but that didn't mean Therrian couldn't still have some fun with them.

He cast a sideways glance at both of his wings, sliding his dark glasses off of his nose and they were instantly transformed into twin masses of dark fire jutting out of either side of the thin black t-shirt that stretched across his broad, muscled chest.

With a snap of those flaming wings, Therrian dropped altitude and his black knee-boots hit the surface of a frosted tree branch that was directly in the path of Varros and Iove's exit.

The second the two men caught sight of the treacherous dark angel, Iove was immediately on the defensive. "I didn't believe it when Howl said you were a double-agent, but-"

"But that was your mistake," Therrian finished for him smoothly, offering the prophecy-keeper a sly smirk that showed off the points of his almost fang-like incisors, "You'll find that one of the most common traits found in successful double-agents is that they're the ones you least expect,"

Hawk's reaction was all too predictable. "I've been on the lookout for something like this from the beginning, but I never anticipated it would be from you, dark angel," the ex-assassin snarled coldly, his gloved hands clenching over the handles of his twin service pistols.

"And that is *your* mistake, Hawk; placing your faith in me when I have a long history of being an insurgent, except to those who are worthy of my loyalty,"

Varros' slate eyebrows shot up so high they were in danger of disappearing into his hairline. "And Xaliden Cyle is worthy of your loyalty?" he spat out scathingly, "When he's planning on decimating every race on both worlds, bar for his own?"

Therrian's smirk widened, "You forget that warlords need powerful troops and I am more powerful than the strongest Eidolon; even the drakkhon you lot still trust admits it,"

Varros gave him an icy look. "Are you saying that Uronis is an insurgent as well?" he asked.

Therrian inclined his steel-white head in an affirmative, but Varros remained sceptical. "If that's true, then why did he blood Candor?" he demanded, crossing his black-clad arms over his chest.

Therrian pretended to think about it for a minute; truly, he didn't know why Uronis had turned Hawk's boyfriend at all-but Hawk didn't need to know that.

"So tell me, how is dear Candor now that his little sister is Lord Xaliden's blood consort of her own free will and volition?" he quipped mockingly, changing the subject instead of answering.

The bloodless face of the hawk contorted into a look of raw fury.

"I'll bet you brought her back to life and put her into that position just to mess with Candor's head," he growled furiously, drawing one of his guns and aiming it at Therrian.

Therrian, though, characteristically didn't even flinch at once again being on the business end of a gun.

"It's quite the contrary, actually, Hawk; I *did* bring her back to life, but we gave her a choice and she complied with becoming Lord Xaliden's blood consort without complaint," the darkness guardian contradicted him coolly, folding his tattoo-covered arms over his chest.

"Because you swindled her into it somehow, no doubt!" Varros hissed indignantly, looking just about ready to tear his hair out in anger.

The silver chains hanging from the left pocket of Therrian's leather pants gleamed in the absence of the moon as he spoke again in a coldly nonchalant tone, as per usual, "Swindling, I assure you, was nowhere on the agenda. Lord Xaliden merely offered her a genuine deal and the lovely Nyle took it."

Varros just spluttered, his rage apparently so immense it prevented him from forming words.

Therrian gave him an artificial smile and waited patiently for Varros to come up with a suitable response, turning to address Iove a second time, "While we're on the subject of siblings, Caius Halcott is your brother, is he not, prophecy-keeper?" Then he grinned crookedly, "Or are you going to try and hide that from me as well?"

The prophecy-keeper tossed him a withering glance before replying defensively, "What's it to you?"

Therrian's grin grew, exposing his knife-like teeth and a black tongue. "Oh, nothing, I'm just wondering how that affects your job to protect the person that he wants to kill," he said offhandedly, acting as if it didn't really matter, "Anyway, you *can't* hide it from me; I already know,"

Iove blew out a lot of air and just glared, deigning not to answer.

Therrian clicked his tongue with mock disapproval at Iove's lack of reply. "I expected so much more. How do you expect to defeat the drakkhon lord as well as myself and the entire race of Eidolons when you can't even win an argument against me?" he chided, shaking his head with fake disappointment.

"Look, why don't you just fuck off?" Varros blew a gasket, "You're not accomplishing anything by toying with us; you've succeeded in burning down the Destiny Tower, congratulations. Now get the hell out of here before I *make* you,"

"And how exactly do you plan on 'making' me do anything?" the dark angel retorted calmly, his grin morphing into a fully-fledged smirk.

By way of an answer, Varros transported behind Therrian and held his drawn gun to the dark angel's head.

"That enough of an answer for you?" he snarled savagely, undoing the safety catch on his service pistol.

Therrian, however, just laughed humorlessly and kept his cocky sneer fixed effortlessly on his kohl-lined lips.

"It seems that everyone's solution to my treachery is always to simply shoot me," he stated, apparently unfazed by this fact, "But unfortunately, the threat of death by a gun doesn't scare me, so just go ahead and try to pull that trigger, Hawk,"

"With pleasure," Varros replied and he did exactly what Therrian told him to.

Or tried to, rather.

Before he could release the trigger, Therrian's gloved hand closed around his throat and the dark angel vaulted him overhead and slammed him into the tree trunk, pinning him there by his throat.

"You're not even worth toying with, Hawk," he hissed, "You're weak, weaker than when you belonged to the assassin's guild and you, you will never be able to stand up to me,"

Disgustedly, Therrian threw the defenceless ex-assassin to the ground from the branch he was standing on.

Varros slumped pitifully on the frozen grass, the impact from the fall causing him to lose consciousness; and Iove immediately rushed to his side.

"Attacking another Guardian? That's just low," he spat at the darkness guardian venomously, cradling the unconscious man's head in his gloved hands.

"People always perceive the 'villains' of every story to be 'just low', but what they fail to realize is that we play by a whole different set of rules than everyone else. Now then, I think that's enough fun for one night."

With a taunting wave, Therrian turned around, unfurled his twin masses of black fire and took to the frosty air, looking uncannily like the angel of death in the blackness.

When I finally came to, the first thing that registered in my body was how freaking *cold* it was. I mean, had it suddenly started snowing while I was out of it or something?

Bizarrely, when I opened my eyes, I saw that that actually wasn't too far off the mark; the entire expanse of land around the remains of the now decimated Destiny Tower was completely covered in what looked exactly like ice.

"Shit, how long was I out for? Has Vanadis entered the Ice Age?" I mumbled; yes, I did know what the Ice Age is-I had cracked open an Earth book before.

"Good, you're finally awake," Iove's voice spoke from my side, uncharacteristically tense, "And to answer your question, no, Vanadis has not entered the Ice Age,"

I sat up and cast another look around, taking in all of the ice and frost blanketing over everything and making sure I wasn't just seeing things. "Sure as hell looks like it to me," I commented skeptically, cracking my neck to get rid of the stiffness.

Iove sighed, forcing me to face him before he spoke up a second time. "This is part of Howl's crusade to make me pay for not telling him that Caius Halcott is my brother even after he was threatened by him," he explained solemnly, looking shamefacedly at me.

I looked at the frozen land third time and found that it made sense; after all, Howl *was* the ice guardian, but who knew he had the power to do something like this? And just because of a stupid grudge, too.

"Damn," was all I could think of to say to that.

Iove gave me a fleeting, small smile, then his face fell again into lines of unease. "You told me last night that you thought bad things were going to happen soon. Well, bad things are happening now and we need to do something about them," he declared.

"I agree. What do you want us to do?" I quipped seriously, deciding it was time to put my game face back on.

"There is something you and your lover should both do," Iove took a deep breath, "If you want to be able to defend yourselves against not only the drakkhon lord and his minions, but also Howl's crusade, find the catacombs."

CHAPTER 20

Truth

My boyfriend was waiting for me like I had told him to when I returned to our house and, when I came through the door, his blue-ebony head looked up expectantly.

"What took you so long? I thought you said it would only take a minute or two," he asked, raising an eyebrow furtively.

I stuffed my hands down the pockets of my black jacket and answered calmly, "Things didn't go exactly as planned; some complications forced me to stay there longer than I had to,"

"Such as?" Candor wondered, his second eyebrow rising to join the first.

"The tower caught fire, the prophecy-keeper and I ran into the dark angel on our way out, I attacked him and got knocked unconscious and only just woke up," I listed tersely, mentally counting off the "complications" inside my head.

Candor sniffed the air lightly when I said the Destiny Tower caught on fire and grimaced.

"No wonder you smell like sulphur," he commented with a slight frown, trying to be flip. When he saw my stony expression, he hastily added, "But seriously, are you okay? You didn't get like burned or smoke inhalation or anything?"

"No, I'm fine," I assured him, "but do you know where my laptop is?"

"It's in the bedroom. Why?" Candor said curiously, jabbing his thumb in the direction of our bedroom.

I beckoned him to follow me as I withdrew my hands from my pockets and headed for our bedroom.

While I set up my laptop, I explained to Candor what I needed it for.

"The prophecy-keeper wants us to find some place called the catacombs. Apparently, something there'll help us be able to withstand all of the things that are happening now," I told him, switching the laptop on.

"I think I've heard of that place," Candor piped up, reaching his arms under mine and clicking on the search window, "I'm pretty sure they're in underground Vanadis-and close, too,"

I lifted my hands from the keyboard and let Candor rest his chin on my shoulder while he scanned the search for information on the "catacombs".

"There," he directed his tan finger at the screen vigorously, "They are in underground Vanadis and the entrance is not too far from here, either,"

I looked at him out of the corner of my eye, "So did you want to go now, then?"

"I think that would probably be smart, yeah," Candor replied honestly, loosely wrapping an arm around my waist and tilting his head slightly to look back at me.

"Okay, so let's get going, then," I prompted, nudging him in the ribs with an elbow.

His dark lips brushed the corner of my mouth before he released me and took a step back. "Bring your laptop with you," he advised me as I turned to leave, "We might need it,"

I turned back and held it under my arm before beginning to walk out of the bedroom again.

"It's fucking freezing out side, just so you know," I informed Candor when we were behind the front door. I had already pulled my cloak and gloves on and used an expanding spell on my pockets so I could fit my laptop in there.

"Yeah, well, in case you haven't noticed, Hawk, I don't happen to have a cloak or anything thicker than this jacket, so I'll just have to deal with it, won't I?" he retorted, attempting to sound nonchalant, but I could see him fighting to suppress a shiver.

I shrugged my shoulders and turned the doorknob, opening the door and re-entering what I was now referring to as "Vanadis' Ice Age". It was kind of plagiarism, I knew, but who was gonna bust me on it?

We walked in relative silence until we reached the edge of the secluded piece of land that accommodated our houses and then I spoke.

"Where are we actually going, Candor?" I asked, swivelling my head around to face the man next to me.

"Brigaden Mountain," Candor responded truthfully.

"Right, so let's just transport, shall we? It'll be much quicker that way," I suggested reasonably.

Candor shrugged. "Okay, I'll meet you there, then," he agreed, pecking me on the cheek before disappearing on the spot.

I inhaled deeply before mimicking him and transporting to Brigaden mountain where, hopefully, the entrance to the "catacombs" lay.

Now there was a fortunately and an *un*fortunately of what happened when I arrived at the mountain after Candor and turned my eyes forward;

The fortunate part was that the entrance to the "catacombs" was indeed within the mountain.

The unfortunate part was that it was being blocked.

By a wolf.

"What the fuck?" I exclaimed in a hiss, turning to Candor to see if he could come up with an explanation for this, but he was simply gaping, open-mouthed, at the snow-white wolf that was standing in our way.

Obviously, he had about as much a clue of what was going on as I did; which happened to be none whatsoever.

I turned back to the wolf and lasered in my blood-red eyes on it. This didn't look like an ordinary wolf; it was much too...*still.*

I decided to throw caution to the wind and took a step forward.

The second I did, there was an explosion of white light and I was blasted off my feet and knocked about a foot across the frozen ground.

I felt a hand on my back, but couldn't tear my eyes away from in front of me.

Because of that white wolf; I could see its outline through the light and its silhouette was growing and turning into that of a very tall, very well-built human.

When the light cleared and I saw who it was, I absolutely could not restrain a gasp from slipping from my lips.

It was Howl.

But he was completely different than the last time I had seen him, which was long before he quit being a Guardian.

He no longer looked even the slightest bit regal; now he just looked...cold. And that impression was only added to by his new clothes.

Instead of what I had only recently become used to him wearing, he now donned a dark navy trenchcoat covered in frost with grey bands encircling the forearms over a grey muscle shirt and low-slung faded black jeans.

The grey bands around his forearms matched the ones around his ankles and sharply complimented his silver-studded, steel-toed boots and similarly coloured fingerless gloves.

A timely gust of wind that blew back a few locks of his dual-toned hair and the side of his trenchcoat showed the silver hoop he now had in his left ear and the large, razor-like swords gleaming at his waist beside his twin ice-blue revolvers.

Before I could speak, he drew two of those swords and pointed one at me and the other at Candor.

"Don't bother getting up, Hawk; you won't be able to stop me from killing you and your lover," he said in a voice so cold, it actually sent shivers down my spine.

I swore my insides just froze at that ominous statement.

"You-what are you doing here? I thought you returned to Earth," I demanded, futilely fighting down my astonishment.

Howl's glowing icicles of eyes virtually cut into me as he responded effortlessly, "Did I not just tell you that? I'm here to kill you, Hawk, as well as your dear lover there,"

I didn't dare roll my eyes, but instead spoke up a second time.

"Yes, I believe we've established that, but why?" I pressed, one eye watching Howl while the other was focused on the sword he had aimed at my noticeably unprotected throat.

My threatener smiled frostily at my impatient quip, "I decided these powers I have are better served by using them to gain more; so in essence, I've become a mercenarial assassin and I'm quite good at it, if I do say so myself,"

"So you've been hired to kill me," I surmised dully, "By who?"

"That's on a need-to-know basis. Which means, you don't need to know."

And then without warning, the blade of the sword he had pressed against Candor's windpipe came down on my lover's forehead, eliciting a loud curse from him before he hit the ground, bleeding from the spot where the sword had cut him.

I had to fight down the instinct to rush over to him, namely because Howl still had his other sword pressed against *my* windpipe.

Oh shit, now he was pointing *both* swords at me. I thought I'd better do something about this situation before Candor and I ended up dead.

My solution came by way of me snapping my head backward and attempting to spin a kick into Howl's jaw, but he blocked it with his still-drawn sword and nearly sliced my foot off in the process.

I tried to follow up with a roundhouse kick into his throat, but that, too, was deflected and I heard the crunch of bones that told me Howl had just broken my ankle. With his *hand,* no less.

Fuck. I mentally cursed, trying to ignore the arrows of pain now shooting up my leg.

And in a split-second, I was back on the ground, this time with Howl's boot crushing the air out of my lungs.

One of his swords' points was positioned under my chin, tilting it up and forcing me to look my killer in the eyes.

Even while gradually losing consciousness for the second time tonight, I couldn't help thinking that never before in my life have I seen eyes as cold as the ones I am currently staring into.

Seriously, if they were square and you took them out of their sockets, you could stick them in a glass and use them as ice cubes.

Macabre thought? Just plain gross thought? You tell me. I just thought of it. I think the lack of oxygen was starting to get to me.

Howl was currently staring at me lying defenceless on the ground with absolutely no emotion and his eyes literally were freezing me in this position.

And I was powerless to do anything about it.

"Give the prophecy-keeper a message from me; the underworld is waiting for him," he hissed icily and those six words were enough for me to figure out who his employer was before I blacked out completely from the lack of oxygen.

After my disastrous episode of getting knocked unconscious twice in one night last night, I decided to take on the task of keeping an eye on the border so I could have some time to sort out my thoughts. Namely the recent revelation of finding out that my late surrogate father had hired the former ice guardian to murder Candor and I, and Howl had accepted.

How wrong was that?

I mentally grumbled while keeping my crimson pools trained on the translucent, smoky black wall that no longer deserved to be called the border between Earth and Vanadis now that it was so unstable, not to mention had a gaping hole in the middle of it.

But more about that some other time. Right now, I was still focusing on the fact that Halcott had hired a mercenarial assassin to do away with me and my lover; and that assassin was someone who was supposed to be on my side in stopping the border from failing, too.

Almost as if in answer to my distressed contemplation, the heavy scent of grave soil filled the icy air and I recognized the transparent form of my thoughts' subject: Caius Halcott.

He was standing on the edge of the roof I was watching the border from, a mirthless smirk playing knowingly across his colourless lips.

"Hello, *son,*" he greeted me with a mocking inflection on the last word.

I was so angry at him right now that I couldn't even respond, so instead, I settled for just glaring.

He probably picked up on my anger because his smirk grew wider and he filled the silence by speaking again, "I take it by your silence that you have found out that I hired Howl to kill you. It was quite the genius move, I think,"

"Genius?" I spluttered indignantly, gripping the dagger beneath my jacket instinctively, "You think it's genius to turn one of the Guardians against the other?"

"Actually, yes," Caius confessed, "but in any case, you seem to have forgotten that Howl is no longer a Guardian. He quit, did he not?"

"In *his* mind, he's quit, but something I've learned is you can't quit being who you are, or in this case, *what* you are," I retorted firmly, repeating something I heard Iove say after Howl "quit" being the ice guardian.

"Strong words, coming from someone who insists he's no longer an assassin, even though that happens to be "what you are"," Caius commented caustically, toying with a metallic gun I hadn't ever noticed before.

"I don't commit murders for money anymore; that is the definition of an assassin, and it's not what I am," I argued without emotion, still keeping a white-knuckled hold on the handle of my dagger to keep from lashing out.

I was having to master my violent impulses and this was a good way to train myself to do that.

Caius laughed without humour, "You may not be killing for money, but you are still the obedient puppet of people who are lying devoutly to you. The prophecy-keeper being my brother? That was just one of the more minor secrets he is hiding. He may not be great at keeping prophecies, but he is definitely an expert at keeping secrets."

"And I expect you know what these other things he's keeping from me are?" I quipped scathingly, narrowing my crimson pools at him in evident suspicion.

Caius smirked again. "Well, that is one of the advantages of being not only his brother, but an immortal to boot," he confirmed cockily, "I suppose you'd like an example, so, the "master" he serves? His real name is Egan Cyle and his *son* happens to be the only reason why the border is failing at all,"

God, how many unpleasant revelations was I going to have to go through before I finally knew everything about this screwed-up situation? Because it seemed like things just kept getting shittier and shittier with every new thing I learned.

"If that's true, then why is he intent on getting me to foil his son's plan to destroy the border?" I challenged sceptically, unwilling to believe what I was hearing.

"The mind of a master works in mysterious ways," Caius told me, his smirk turning crooked, "Masters were supposed to remain neutral, no matter the plight the two worlds were facing, but master Cyle chose to disregard that rule and fought. When his son chose to fight opposite him, I imagine master Cyle disowned him and now intends to stop his plan from succeeding,"

"My God, does *everyone* on Vanadis have a fucked-up family life?" I exclaimed loudly, turning away from the smirking immortal to mull this over.

Everything was getting turned upside down and everyone I thought I could trust was turning out to be connected to someone who wanted to kill me or wanted to decimate the worlds.

What was reality and what was fiction? Who could I place my trust in when everyone was turning out to be something other than what I thought?

"Iove doesn't even know that his precious Guardians prophecy is incomplete and there is a fourth Guardian he still hasn't found," Caius continued, now sounding as if he were speaking more to himself than to me.

I whirled around at hearing that, dropping the dagger I had had concealed under my jacket in the process.

"If this is a trick, Halcott, I swear to God," I warned him dangerously, retrieving my dagger from the ground when he wasn't looking and pointing it at him once he was.

"You won't be able to kill me, Hawk; I, unlike you, am a true immortal, not a selective one," Caius sneered disdainfully, "And anyways, what could I possibly have to gain by lying to you about something like this?"

He had me there, I had to admit. He wanted me to suffer and was making me do so by telling me the truth.

"So, what about this fourth Guardian? Who is he? *Where* is he?" I wondered pressingly, daring Caius not to answer. "You know, it's a shame you no longer have Howl on your side because it would have been much simpler to find the fourth Guardian if he was," Caius 'tsk'-ed ruefully.

"And why is that?" I questioned suspiciously.

"Because he was and still is a contract killer for Howl's company," he stated matter-of-factly.

I couldn't suppress a groan at that news. "Yeah, the Guardians needed another murderer like we need ten years of bad luck," I grumbled irritably.

Caius let out yet another humourless chuckle. "You're going to have to deal with it, unless you intend to just sit back and let the drakkhon ruler destroy the border," he sneered mockingly before leaving me to my moody thoughts.

Once he was gone, I stuffed my dagger back into my coat and turned away from the border with a huff.

Yeah, this was exactly what I needed, for the fourth Guardian to be *another* hired killer. Like two wasn't enough? Well, three now, if you counted Howl becoming a mercenary as him being a hired killer. This was just *perfect.*

Okay, I should really stop with the sarcasm now.

The question was what could I do with this information now that I had it? I wasn't telling the prophecy-keeper, that was for sure. At least, not until I knew I could trust him, which I definitely didn't at the moment; same with his 'master', Egan Cyle, who was apparently the father of the drakkhon ruler.

Getting to Earth and attempting to find this fourth Guardian seemed like a good idea; but before I did that, I should probably find out some more information on him.

I pulled my laptop out of my pocket and sat down on the surface of the roof, placing the portable computer on top of my crossed legs and leaning forward to switch it on.

I clicked on the search window. Now what was Howl's company called again? It had something to do with his name...Oh, come on, I'd heard him say it after he found that Caius was Iove's brother...Oh, HOWLtd, that was it.

I typed in "HOWLtd" in the search bar and hit the enter key.

Clicking on the first result, a security bar came up. Looks like this website was on a private level. Guess I'd just have to hack it since I didn't happen to have the actual password. I input a few choice numbers and hit enter again. The website came up.

Like I suspected upon hearing that the company was one of the branches of the Russian mafia, the website was a shady one, devoted to all sorts of forms of death and destruction.

I bypassed everything else and clicked on the headline "employees".

A list of forms of employees came up next and of course, I was looking for hired killers.

Four names, two male and two female, appeared on the screen, along with a summary of their contracts. If I thought about this, I was probably looking for the best out of the four.

I typed in "highest rated" and a single name was left: Ash Kiernan, the phoenix.

"You can't hide from death,"

The man this sentiment was directed at turned slowly around to face the speaker.

The one they'd sent to kill him was unlike any other person he had ever encountered before in his life.

He was standing, no, *leaning*, against one of the far walls, an almost unnaturally tall, streamlined figure, clad in a red and black trenchcoat that covered the grey jeans he wore with random rips all over them and the dark red sleeveless shirt. Below that, the rims of his 'destroyed' jeans disappeared into metallic black boots beginning at his ankles.

The dominant red of his attire matched the crimson sunglasses that covered his eyes perfectly. Hanging from a copper chain, positioned between the bones of his neck was a flat, phoenix-shaped ruby medallion.

The man's eyes followed the copper chain to his killer's throat, which was gruesomely and heavily adorned with angry white scars.

"So you must be the famous Phoenix, the mafia's most talented killer," the man surmised calmly in his rough Russian accent.

The taller of the two men smiled without humour and curled a pale hand over the rims of his crimson sunglasses, allowing his victim a fleeting glance of the auburn flame tattoos encircling his slender fingers before the hand was lowered along with the sunglasses.

Sweat beaded down the Russian's forehead as his gaze was drawn into the molten ember orbs staring down at him.

The intensity of those eyes knocked his feet out from under him and he was on the floor before the other man had yet to utter a single word.

"Like I said, you can't hide from death," the possessor of those burning orbs intoned softly, his voice like crackling flames with a distinct German lilt to it, as the rooms was filled with his victim's screams.

Once the screams faded, they were replaced with the sound of slow clapping.

"Not one of your more difficult assignments, I'd wager," a harsh male voice commented airily from behind him.

The assassin faced away from his victim and stared coolly down at the new arrival. "Varros Hawk, I'm assuming?" he said swiftly, slipping his crimson sunglasses back up his nose.

When Varros nodded, he continued, "And you already know me as Ash Kiernan, so let's get straight to the point: what do you want?"

"Straight to the point, eh, Kiernan?" Varros repeated coolly, "Very well, what I want is simple; if you know of your identity as the fourth Guardian of the border, embrace it and come with me to Vanadis to stop the border from failing."

Ash raised a single brow above the rim of his sunglasses, "And if I refuse?"

As if to add to the statement, two enormous masses of fire rose out of the back of his trenchcoat, almost explosively illuminating the dim room.

"Well, really, what are you getting by using your powers here on Earth, where no one really appreciates them?" Varros reasoned matter-of-factly, folding his arms across his black-clad chest and surveying Ash critically over them.

"Hn," was Ash's only response as he mimicked his primary position and leaned against the concrete wall effortlessly, angling his legs across it and leaving his arms hanging at his sides.

Varros just smirked at his non-committal answer and rose to his feet, "I surmised as much; whereas on Vanadis, everyone would truly appreciate your exceptionalness and commend you for being a Guardian. Does that not appeal to you?"

Ash looked at him briefly before vanishing and Varros shook his slate head before doing the same.

The two of us landed in an underground corridor, away from prying eyes.

I brushed myself off and beckoned the fourth Guardian to follow me, "I'm going to tell you right now that, at the moment, the only people who know about you being the fourth Guardian, besides you, are myself and my friend, who you're about to meet in just a minute,"

I led the silent phoenix down the corridor and stopped in front of a metal door, which was barred by a single steel plank.

"Candor, open the door," I called to the person on the other side, not bothering with subtlety.

The door swung inwards and the steel plank fell off, allowing us to enter. Without speaking, I walked through the open door with Kiernan following close behind me.

"Took you long enough," Candor commented caustically from his position standing against the stone wall, thumbs hooked in the front buckles of his dark brown jeans.

"Yeah, well, no one told me I'd be walking into the middle of an assassination," I retorted acidly, rolling my eyes.

Candor rolled his own eyes before focusing his attention on the man behind me, "So who's this guy again?"

"Ash Kiernan, the fire Guardian, meet Jarl Candor, my half-drakkhon best friend and permanent hanger-on," I supplied dully, introducing the two.

While Candor actually endeavoured to at least nod in Kiernan's direction, the phoenix didn't even acknowledge his presence and adopted a nonchalant stance, much like the one he'd displayed when committing that murder on Earth.

The room lapsed into total silence.

I raised an eyebrow at Kiernan's deliberate rudeness before turning to Candor, whose expression mirrored mine.

"Beautiful attitude, that," Candor observed dryly. I suppressed a snort with difficulty before Candor added, "So what are we doing with him now?"

Kiernan cleared his throat pointedly. "I *am* right here, you know."

I looked over at him. "Well, what do you think we should do with you now? Because the prophecy-keeper doesn't know about you and I intend to keep it that way until I know he can be trusted,"

Kiernan tilted his head downward so that his metallic-blue bangs fell over the top of his crimson sunglasses and said, "If you were planning on keeping me down here until you thought it the right time to reveal my identity to the prophecy-keeper, then why not seek me out then, rather than now?"

"Because I needed an ally; currently, I'm the only Guardian who hasn't turned in one way or another and. strong as I am, I can't fight everyone who's against me with only Candor here as my back-up," I explained without emotion, shrugging offhandedly.

"The ones who have turned, what are they doing now?" Kiernan questioned, listening, I hoped, now.

"The darkness Guardian is working with Xaliden Cyle, the cause of the border failing in the first place, and the ice Guardian is now a mercenary, whom my adoptive father has hired to kill Candor and I,"I summarized shortly, unwilling to go into too much detail on this subject.

Kiernan elegantly raised a metallic-blue eyebrow, but didn't offer an opinion on my summary of the treachery of the other two Guardians, nor did he ask why my adoptive father would want to kill me in the first place.

"So you chose me to be your ally?" he asked instead, raising his second eyebrow to join the first.

"You were the only person I could think of once I found out your identity," I admitted, carelessly waving a hand in his direction.

"It never occurred to you that I might not be willing to help you?" Kiernan quipped, his expression unreadable from behind those crimson sunglasses.

"Are you?" I retorted sharply, staring daggers at him from across the room.

His pale lips curved in a slow smirk and he didn't supply a response.

I heaved a frustrated sigh and let my eyelids drop closed in order to try and alleviate some of the aggravation I was currently feeling.

Honestly, this was like trying to catch an eel; I couldn't get this guy to give me a straight answer. That is, when I got him to give me an answer at all.

"Answer him," I heard Candor command him disapprovingly, no doubt emphasizing his words by drawing one of his submachine guns and pointing it at Kiernan.

"Candor, don't even bother threatening him; he could probably drop you in a heartbeat," I said discouragingly, shaking my head without opening my eyes.

I could practically picture Candor's expression; one of infinite displeasure.

When the fire Guardian finally decided to speak again, that was when I decided to open my eyes to look him in the face.

"You hardly have a future with me as an ally; I'm a hired killer. If someone offered me the right kind of deal, I'd turn on you and your *boyfriend* in a second," he stated with a cool nonchalance that I really didn't like.

Wait a minute, how did he-oh, right, obviously, he could read minds. How had I not guessed that already?

"Well, if you don't want to help me seal the border, what are you going to do with those powers on Earth?" I challenged, thinking I was being clever.

"Same thing I've done with them since they developed; use them to carry out my assignments from whoever has the money to hire me," Kiernan replied effortlessly, crimson sunglasses flashing in the dimness.

"What do you do with the money you get from your jobs, anyways?" I questioned offhandedly, slate eyebrows arching with all-too-obvious curiosity.

"Nothing; money actually means nothing to me, but it means more to the people who have to give it up and I enjoy making people do things they don't want to," Kiernan smirked, crossing his streamlined arms over his chest.

"So even if we had money to offer you, you wouldn't help us?" I surmised dispassionately, contravention starting to pound at my head again.

Kiernan's pale lips parted, allowing me a brief glance of a crimson stud in his tongue, in a wider smirk, "Do you?"

"No," I confessed sullenly, "But there are other things I can pay you with if you agree to help,"

Kiernan's smirk turned ruthless and I could see now why he was renowned as a feared killer when he declared in a silky hiss that filled my head and wouldn't allow me to protest, `*The only payment I will accept from you, Hawk, is the death of your boyfriend by your hand.*'

I couldn't decline; that voice, it was burning through every one of my mental defences like they were nothing and literally scalding my brain until it spoke again, `*You will vow.*`

`*Yes.*` I was unable to stop myself from conceding, `*I vow to kill Candor if you help us.*`

"Well, I guess we've come to an arrangement, then," Kiernan concluded aloud, upper lip curling into a cold sneer, which he directed at me.

I blinked and after that trance, all I could think was *Oh*. Shit.

Candor was looking at me oddly, but I couldn't bring myself to meet his eyes, especially after what I had just vowed to do.

"What arrangement might that be?" I heard Candor ask suspiciously of Kiernan, since I think he could tell I wasn't in the right state of mind to be answering questions.

Though his eyes were still covered by those sunglasses and I wasn't looking at him, I could still see the amusement that was on Kiernan's face when he replied dismissively, "Nothing *you* need to worry about."

I had no trouble picturing him adding in his head, "Yet."

"Right," Candor said uneasily, no doubt shooting me a sideways glance, but I was still determinedly looking anywhere but at him, "So should we get down to business, then?"

"You two go ahead, I'll meet you outside," I told them quietly, my crimson eyes focused on the ground.

I really hoped Candor wasn't reading my mind right now.

"See you outside, Hawk," I heard him mutter as he passed me before he and Kiernan exited the catacombs. But Kiernan left me with his voice filling my head once again; *`There is no escaping your oath, Hawk.'*

The second Candor and Kiernan were out of the room, my knees buckled under me and I hit the floor.

I had just sworn an oath to the Devil.

And that wasn't even the worst part; no, the worst part was that the oath entailed me killing the one person I loved most in this world.

CHAPTER 21

Complete And Utter Catastrophe

"So what happens now? The blood Guardian has found the fourth and struck a deal with him. Now they are heading for our base to find the way to seal the border," Uronis declared soberly, scaled ambers glimmering beneath his teal bangs.

"They won't find it," Therrian assured him confidently.

Uronis arched an eyebrow smoothly in question, "And what, pray tell, makes you so sure of that, dark angel?" he queried.

Therrian grinned, exposing his fang-like incisors. "I can see the future, remember? I know where it is-and I'm going to destroy it," he stated.

Uronis was silent for a second, seeming to ponder that.

"Just what is this way of sealing the border, anyways?" the drakkhon quipped after a long pause, his second eyebrow rising to join the first.

"The border's seal lies at the centre of the underworld and, if it were to be demolished, the border would be demolished right along with it," Therrian summarized swiftly, sweeping his dark cloak over his similarly-coloured clothes and throwing the hood up, "The demolition awaits,"

Without further preamble, the dark angel exited the base with Uronis following close behind him, heading for the heart of the underworld once again.

At the centre of the land of the dead was a white marble stone, on which the key to sealing the border lay, highly conspicuous against the macabre charcoal background.

Along with finding that, the dark angel found something else he was expecting.

"How did I not know that you would be here as well, dark angel?" the voice of the blood Guardian snorted disgustedly as he and his two companions entered the shrine after Therrian and Uronis.

Therrian's gaze, however, was drawn to the red and black-clad figure traipsing about three feet behind Varros and his boyfriend, arms crossed and eyes closed.

He knew this was the fourth Guardian, the guardian of fire-and a more formidable man Therrian had never seen before.

Everything about him, even the relaxed, nonchalant way he stood, just oozed power.

What was more, his eyes were covered by triangular crimson sunglasses and Therrian, being a dark angel, had come to expect that anyone who covered their eyes had some sort of highly dangerous ocular power that could be activated with only a single glance.

This was not someone to be taken lightly, Therrian decided and with an effort, he managed to pull himself back to the present and responded evenly, "I, on the other hand, was fully expecting you and your companions, Hawk,"

Varros cast a quick glance behind him at Kiernan before retorting, "Yeah, what's it to you, traitor?"

Therrian clicked his tongue with mock disapproval, "Hardly complimentary, Hawk, wasting your ire on me. At any rate, it matters nothing to me. You can bring in all the mercenaries you like and we will still succeed in destroying the border,"

"And how's that again?" the blood guardian challenged fiercely, lips curling in an uncharacteristically ugly look.

The dark angel matched his grimace with a cocky sneer and nodded at Uronis before answering, "Simple. You can't seal the border if it's already been destroyed."

He took the matter bomb Uronis was holding out to him and clamped it firmly to the shrine where the border's seal was.

The second the bomb touched the white marble, it exploded.

Fractured marble filled the air and the ground below them literally shook with the impact, knocking nearly everyone off of their feet.

The only three left standing were Therrian and Uronis, who were wearing twin expressions of unconcealed satisfaction, and the fire Guardian, who wore no expression at all.

A second, much more momentous explosion followed the first one as the barriers dividing Earth and Vanadis slowly faded away.

There was no holding back Varros' snarl of rage when Therrian announced coldly, "The border has failed. And so, too, have you, Hawk."

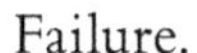

Failure.

Complete and utter failure.

That was something I had never been familiar with.

Even when I had failed to stop the war between the underworld council and the assassin's guild, it hadn't been a total failure because we'd still managed to get rid of all of the underworld assailants, even though the price had been the life of Candor's sister.

But there was no consolation for this; I had failed to seal the border and it was gone. Done, destroyed past the point of no return.

I had failed at my destiny.

I didn't think I'd ever felt more hopeless in my life than I did at that moment.

Because not only had the border been destroyed, but I was stuck down here in the underworld, unable to do a damn thing about it.

"So, Hawk," Therrian spoke up, filling the despondent silence, "What are you intending to now? Your destiny is over and there's nothing you can do to fix it,"

I gritted my teeth and had to dig my nails into the palm of my hand in order to stop myself from lashing out.

My emotions were *not* going to get the better of me again, like the last time we'd met; I was in control-or as in control as I could get.

"Don't listen to him, Varros," Candor intoned out of the corner of his mouth, reaching for my hand and curling his fingers through mine. Though his cold hand was like stone, his touch did offer me at least some form of comfort. "We can come back from this," he assured me, giving my hand a squeeze.

I closed my eyes and concentrated.

What could I possibly do to come back from this? Doing so seemed practically impossible from where I was standing.

And Kiernan wasn't helping, either, standing back there with his arms folded and pale face coolly expressionless, like he didn't even care.

`*Think hard, Varros. There's always a solution.*` Candor's voice echoed through my head and I tried not to shift uncomfortably when memories of when Kiernan's voice had done exactly the same thing surfaced.

But I was coming up short this time. I couldn't think of a way to fix this; as far as I could tell, it was just hopeless.

"I don't know what to do now, Candor," I admitted under my breath, focusing on the ground instead of him because I didn't want to see the look on his face.

My wishes went unheeded, however, because as soon as that confession escaped my lips, Candor's unoccupied hand came under my chin and tilted it up so that I was looking him in the eyes.

"I do, but first, we're getting out of here, understood?" he told me quietly, so that the dark angel and drakkhon wouldn't hear.

I nodded wordlessly, offering him a small smile as a gesture of my confidence in him. He smiled encouragingly in return before turning back to face Therrian.

"We're leaving, dark angel. And you better hope that the one you serve doesn't order you to follow us because the next time I see you, I *will* kill you," he vowed fiercely, gripping my hand.

And then he transported, taking me along with him.

The prophecy-keeper know his time was growing short.

He'd known it ever since he had been forced to reveal to the blood and ice guardians that he was the brother of someone who wanted to kill them both and hadn't told them before; when Howl had threatened he wouldn't be alive to lie to him again.

Iove knew that Howl was not one to make idle threats and in quitting the Guardians and becoming a mercenary, he had proved that.

In ousting the dark angel and drakkhon as double-agents, he had proved just how little regard he had for the immutability of what people referred to as destiny.

All that was left was the end; Iove's death at the hands of one of the people he was committed to protect. And it was here.

In a split-second, a dull frost crept over the room, covering everything from the floor to the ceiling as a white wolf entered, liquid ice eyes glowing in the darkness.

"The time has come, Iove Halcott," the wolf spoke silkily, "For you to die,"

And then, steadily, the wolf began to transform before Iove's very eyes.

The hunched form grew until it was nearing seven feet and perfectly streamlined. The white fur around its torso morphed into a long, leather trenchcoat the colour of a thunderstorm, covering a grey muscle shirt and jeans; the hunched back straightened and became a toned chest that tapered into a broad, yet slim waist and hips, both adorned with a gruesome compilation of scars, bruises, and bite marks; and the paws transformed into slender hands inside silver fingerless gloves with wolf-like claws protruding out of the tips.

One thing remained the same, however; the eyes stayed burning cold fire so intense, it literally froze Iove to his spot.

Slender, diamond-pale fingers hypnotically spun a surgical scalpel between them, the silver blade flashing in the darkness.

"I don't suppose you would accept an apology at this point?" Iove asked hopefully. Truth be told, he didn't want to die; he had been prepared to do so in order to protect the Guardians, but it galled him to do so at the *hands* of one of the Guardians.

Sehto chuckled without humour, a cold, ruthless laugh that sent shivers down the prophecy-keeper's spine.

"I've been commissioned to kill you now, so even if I *were* prepared to accept your apology- which I'm not, by the way-I don't think my employer would be as generous," he said, a smirk fluidly crossing over his frosted lips.

As if to answer Iove's unspoken question, a second, taller male materialized beside Sehto, and it was one Iove recognized all too well: Xaliden Cyle.

"I would introduce you, but I do believe you already know each other," Sehto commented, his voice colder and smoother than a flowing glacier, smirk turning frigid.

"Drakkhon," Iove all but snarled, liquid eyes darkening with hatred.

"Prophecy-keeper," the drakkhon lord responded evenly, a cruel sneer mirroring Sehto's smirk curling his bloodless lips.

"So you're taking assignments from someone who should be your worst enemy," the prophecy-keeper spat at Sehto, unable to suppress his ire at this discovery.

"I take assignments from anyone who has the means to compensate hiring me," Sehto countered effortlessly, still spinning that scalpel between his thumb and forefinger; and that was all Iove's eyes were focused on at that moment.

"And what means might those be?" he questioned, still keeping an eye on that razor-sharp blade.

"Power," Sehto stated matter-of-factly, ice slivers filling his eye sockets, "Disposable power. After all, you can never be too powerful, can you?"

"Hardly," Xaliden scoffed dismissively as if disgusted by the mere thought.

"Living proof would be this *fourth* guardian, correct, Lord Xaliden?" he queried pointedly, turning to his companion with a crooked grin.

Xaliden nodded and Iove's jaw dropped.

"What 'fourth Guardian'? There are only three," he said, aghast.

"How sad. He claims to be a prophecy-keeper and he doesn't even know the full extent of the prophecies he keeps," Sehto drawled disdainfully. He switched his gaze to Iove. "The fourth Guardian has already come to Vanadis and is working with Hawk,"

Xaliden's sneer grew at Iove's shocked expression. "It seems that your prophecy was incomplete, Halcott. What a major oversight on your part," he said, shaking his head.

CRACK.

Iove crushed the object nearest him in his shaking hand.

"Do *not* address me by my last name, drakkhon," he hissed emphatically, knuckles turning white as he clenched his hands into fists.

Xaliden clicked his tongue in mock disapproval. "Denying your family ties? Well, I do suppose that is understandable-especially when your only living relative is someone who intends to kill the very people you were intending to protect," he mused, "Caius Halcott, the evil leader of the underworld council."

"'Evil' is a matter of perspective," Halcott's voice corrected as he, too, appeared to witness the murder of his brother.

Sehto's grin was practically chill-inducing at this point.

"Ready to die, *Halcott?*" he sneered, putting a deliberate emphasis on Iove's surname and halting the spinning of the scalpel to direct the blade at the prophecy-keeper.

He vanished and reappeared behind Iove, pressing the scalpel blade against the prophecy-keeper's white neck.

Icy breath rushed past his ear. "You will never be able to atone for your lies, or your sins; the underworld does not forgive," Sehto whispered coldly. Then, there was a mocking chuckle. "But first, I think there's someone else here who wants a little revenge."

Sehto nodded to Caius, who stepped forward, drawing out a rusty, blackened razor blade as he did so.

"No one will mourn your death, brother," he taunted softly, "Our family is dead and the Guardians and your 'master', they merely use you. Your life was a waste; all you did was pave the way for this apocalypse to become a reality,"

Before Iove had a chance to retort, the razor was stabbed underneath his arm, and he collapsed to his knees.

"For all the efforts to create Guardians to save the worlds, we really have done more to destroy them; and that is what I will help with. Screw destiny; I make my own fate," Sehto declared fiercely as he moved in front of Iove, tilting the shorter man's head up to look in his eyes, "Your fate, however, is sealed," he hissed before ramming the scalpel into the prophecy-keeper's eye.

Stowing the scalpel back beneath his trenchcoat, Sehto coldly kicked aside the bloodstained corpse and turned to face Xaliden and Caius, who had both watched the murder with cool satisfaction.

"I think it's high time we truly took the matter of this prophecy into our own hands," Xaliden stated thoughtfully, "One of you see if you can summon the fourth Guardian and then meet me at the dual crossing,"

Both Sehto and the underworld council leader inclined their heads in understanding and the drakkhon ruler dematerialized, leaving the two remaining to their task.

"I believe this falls to you, Master Howl," Caius observed, focusing his colourless eyes on his stone-still companion.

The ice Guardian inclined his dual-toned head a second time and Caius mimicked Xaliden and disappeared.

Sehto activated his earpiece [yes, he has an earpiece now]and used his wolf powers to track down the fourth Guardian.

"Yes, Howl, what is it? "Ash's smooth, accented voice crackled over the speaker.

"You're still under contract by my company and I have a proposition for you. Or, rather, my current employers have a proposition for you. Busy?" Sehto asked.

"Not at the moment," Ash replied. "Where would you like me to meet you and these employers?"

"The crossing of Earth and Vanadis," Sehto told him.

There was a pause, then Ash responded. "I'll be there in a minute." And the connection was cut, signalling Sehto's time to transport as well.

Every bargain made with someone of the underworld is a bargain dishonoured.

The sanctity of deals was never something the leader of the underworld council truly understood. Any oath sworn with someone like him could never be trusted. At least, not until now.

"I bet you're wondering why I called you here," the former human's voice rang out within the deathly cold grand hall as he stepped out from behind the granite round table. He materialized as if he were made of smoke-which wasn't all that far from the truth, actually.

The ice guardian opened his eyes to direct his freezing stare at the speaker, crossing his arms over his broad chest. "If you're planning to kill me, I would advise you against it," he intoned silkily, tone inhumanly void of emotion. His eyes flashed in the lack of light. "You and I are no longer on even terms."

His former enemy let out a deep, slow chuckle that would have chilled Sehto to the bone, had he still been able to feel anything other than the ice that now permanently encased his heart. As it was, he merely glared, unblinking, until the underworld council leader stopped.

"If I wanted to kill you, I wouldn't have contacted you first," he stated bluntly, a smile quirking the corners of his translucent lips. He slid easily into one of the chairs surrounding the stone table next to him. "I have a proposition for you."

One of the wolf's immaculate cobalt eyebrows arched at those words.

"And what makes you think I would ever make a deal of any sort with you when you tried to kill me?" the taller male shot back coldly, azure eyes now practically glowing with menace.

Caius met his gaze without flinching. "Because I have the means to give you the kind of power that no one else in this world could ever hope for," he said smoothly, smile growing.

Sehto's other eyebrow rose to join the first. The elder knew that he was a mercenary now, on the hunt for power and nothing else. He'd known exactly what to say.

"I'm listening," he said finally in a neutral tone, expression giving nothing away.

Caius's smile grew fractionally. He had the other's attention now; all he had to do was follow through.

"I want you to kill Varros Hawk-and his boyfriend," he declared bluntly, not bothering without any further pretense. His opaque eyes gleamed. "And I want you to make them suffer."

The Russian male actually took a moment to consider it. He had no affection for the blood guardian or the half-drakkhon whom he was currently shacked up with; but he knew the immortal was not someone who he could trust-unless he were bound to honour his part of the agreement.

"If I were to accept, you would have to consent to being blood-bound to honour your part. If you break the bond, your soul will pay the consequences."

Caius inclined his head. "You have my word," he complied.

Sehto took a second to weigh his options; then he nodded as well. "Then it appears we have an agreement," he said with a frigid smirk.

Sehto and Ash arrived at the allotted meeting place at the same time, spotting and recognizing each other immediately.

"Howl," Ash greeted Sehto tonelessly, ember eyes still veiled by those crimson sunglasses, sharply contrasting against the white marble of his almost inhumanly perfect face.

"Kiernan," Sehto replied, voice equally metronomic, yet simultaneously cold as ice.

The two of them had a moment of silent discussion before heading off in the direction of where the border had been when it was still standing.

Sehto's employers were waiting when they arrived, now joined by the dark angel and drakkhon, who were both standing nonchalantly off to the side.

Xaliden was the first to notice them and the first to speak once the distance between their two groups was closed.

"So, this is the fourth Guardian, I take it?" he surmised in that deep, velvet-like baritone of his, looking Ash up and down with a slight gleam in his dark coals.

"Ash Kiernan," Ash introduced himself, lifting off his triangular sunglasses to give the drakkhon lord a full view, "I hear you have a proposition for me?"

"That is correct, Master Kiernan," Xaliden confirmed.

The corners of Ash's pale lips just barely twitched, "And what might that be?"

"You have a penchant for raising destruction, don't you?" the drakkhon lord quipped slyly, dark coals as glimmering as ever.

Ash inclined his metallic-blue head by way of an answer without speaking and Xaliden grinned malevolently. "We have the means to raise the ultimate destruction," he stated, "If you join us in bringing about the Merging."

"You know the only payment I'm accepting at the moment is the death of Hawk's boyfriend by his hand," Ash interceded smoothly, molten embers flickering crimson flames in the dark room.

"By combining powers with Howl, you have the means to make him do just that-and much, much more," Xaliden declared with a swift glance in Sehto's direction.

"Howl already has orders to bring about the death of Jarl Candor," Caius put in, "And as long as Hawk is there to see it, it doesn't matter to me how it happens, so he will still receive his payment from me,"

Sehto leaned back against a tree, awaiting Ash's response patiently.

Said fourth Guardian's gaze focused on him as he appeared to consider the drakkhon lord's proposition carefully.

After a long silence, a slow grin spread across Ash's ivory features and he held out his hand to Xaliden. "I accept," he said.

Xaliden's black eyes flashed with excitement. "Excellent."

It was a rare thing for a meeting like this to take place.

Three of the four guardians in the same room of the mansion where the Merging-bringers had made headquarters was a rare occurrence, indeed.

A fire crackled in the grate, illuminating the ice guardian's ivory face from where he sat on a nearby leather couch with his four swords lying atop a coffee table next to his crossed ankles.

Therrian sat opposite him on the matching black armchair, one of his legs slung casually over the other and gloved hands clasped together in his lap. His eyes remained veiled by the usual pair of dark sunglasses, so his expression was impossible to read.

Last, but not least, was the Phoenix, leaning on the wall behind Sehto. With his arms crossed over his chest and his crimson eyes closed, he was the epitome of bored nonchalance.

"Our plan to kill Hawk and end the worlds has one little snag," Therrian was the one to break the pensive silence without preamble, addressing both his companions in a matter-of-fact tone. "The Blood Guardian's lover will stand in our way."

Sehto scoffed. "I wouldn't call that much of a snag, dark angel. After all, the three of us combined with Uronis and the drakkhon lord are hardly pushovers. We're not going to be defeated by Hawk and a renegade assassin-even if that renegade assassin is a half-drakkhon," he waved away the latter's words cockily, rolling his eyes.

The dark angel had to agree with that statement. The three of them were definitely far more powerful than Hawk and his lover. But there was still one matter that concerned him somewhat.

"My vision dictates that the Blood Guardian and his lover must die. Uronis and I will be taking care of the master, but we all know that Hawk has some insidious abilities trapped inside of him that will come out if we threaten the worlds," the guardian of darkness told the other two with an air of foreboding.

That wasn't a new wrinkle; all four Guardians had a trigger inside of them that was supposed to go off in accordance with their emotions. Each of them had a different one, however; for Sehto, it was vengeance. For Therrian, it was survival-and, well, no one knew yet what Ash's was. But Varros', obviously, was redemption; he was hardwired to protect the border from total destruction.

The rest of Therrian's words was new information, though. "The Merging cannot begin until the Blood Guardian's life ends."

Oddly, it was the Fire Guardian who quelled his concerns. "Varros Hawk carries a ticking time bomb inside of him; a malignant disease festers in his heart that is destined to kill everyone he loves. Jarl Candor will be the first," he paused as his pale lips curved ever so slightly, "I've already made sure of that,"

His former employer arched a cobalt eyebrow, azure eyes appearing vaguely bemused. "How?" he questioned suspiciously, swivelling his head around to face the former contract-killer.

Ash didn't even open his eyes before answering in a careless tone; "I made a deal with Varros: I come back here with him, he kills his lover. And no one breaks deals with me,"

"They were cursed from the start, anyways," Therrian put in bluntly, "Eventually, Hawk's power would have destroyed the half-drakkhon without his volition; it doesn't like Eidolons just on principle."

"Jarl Candor's death will weaken Hawk and he will be vulnerable. He will die-and the worlds will burn," the Phoenix intoned in a low, ominous voice that made the other two's hair stand on end.

That was, by far, one of the longest sentences they had ever heard him utter; a sure sign that the end was imminent.

He was correct, though; Varros would be vulnerable after being forced to kill the only person he loved. And after they killed him, the Merging would come-and both Earth and Vanadis would be turned to ashes.

At the crossing of the two worlds was where the truth became evident: the border had failed.

There was no longer even a translucent, smoky black wall with a hole in it; there was just empty space. Therrian could tell the carnage he was about to wreak on Vanadis would not help matters one bit.

If anything, it would only make them worse.

He and Uronis transported out of the underworld and arrived in front of their destination without a sound; the previous sight of the Destiny Tower, now nothing but ash and charred paper.

The master, in all his regal, master-like glory, stood among the rubble, an uncharacteristically ugly expression on his normally impeccably composed features as he surveyed the wreckage.

"I prefer to think of this as my most momentous achievement; burning down the Destiny Tower. What do you think, *Master* Cyle?" the dark angel commented from behind him, black-tinged lips curving upwards in a mirthless smile.

The master swivelled his body around and when his grey eyes found the source of the voice, he spat out, "You."

"Me," Therrian repeated calmly as Uronis adopted his usual position on his right, folding black-clad arms across his chest in a single, fluid motion.

"You think betraying your destiny is an achievement?" the master snarled.

"Well, yes, actually, I do because destiny truly has no meaning to me," Therrian stated matter-of-factly, "Destinies aren't set in stone; our destinies depend on the decisions we make and I've made the decision to bring about the Merging."

"And how do you plan to do that as long as the other two Guardians still exist?" the master retorted scathingly, not bothering to hide his contempt.

Therrian turned to Uronis, whose pale lips creased in a smile beneath his dark hood.

In the blink of an eye, the drakkhon was in front of the master, pinning him to a nearby tree by his throat.

"Your servant has already been taken care of by one of our back-up plans; two of the Guardians have joined our cause, and the final one will be done away with as soon as I finish with you," he hissed before snapping the master's head sideways and plunging his twin fangs deep into the flesh of his throat.

Blood flowed like water from the ruptured artery down the drakkhon's throat, sparking his nerves.

Nothing, not even human blood was ever this potent.

Therrian watched without emotion as Uronis all but drained the master dry, practically tearing his throat apart in the process.

When Uronis pulled back at last, licking the coating of blood from his lips, his amber eyes met the ivory orbs of the dark angel, which were completely void of emotion.

"He's done," the drakkhon informed his companion dully, using his fingers to clean the remaining vestiges of blood from his pale lips.

"Good," Therrian smirked, exposing his incisors, "Now it's time for the next step,"

The dark angel turned his ivory orbs on the array of houses surrounding the remains of the Destiny Tower and, like with the Destiny Tower, jet black flames rose from the ground and claimed every one of the wooden buildings.

With as little emotion as ever, Therrian's steel-white eyes reflected the houses all burning steadily.

Smoke rose into the air and filled it with the distinct scent of sulphur, overwhelming all other scents instantly.

Wood was reduced in seconds to nothing but matchsticks and the flames consumed everything else in a matter of minutes, leaving bare ground and blackened trees in place of the previous setup.

Inhaling deeply, Therrian took in the toxic acidity of sulphur filling the air before closing his eyes. "I think that's enough destruction for one night, don't you, Uronis?" he commented, opening his eyes to the moonless, pitch-black sky and smiling with barely concealed mirth.

Uronis mirrored his expression with a smile of his own before answering evenly, "Indeed. Tomorrow night, our plans reach their climax and the worlds meet their doom. I suppose we should allow their inhabitants to enjoy this final night of peace."

Therrian nodded in agreement and the two male enigmas were enveloped by shadows, vanishing from within them.

The ground under my high black boots was still adorned with a heavy layer of blue frost; it looked like Howl's crusade was continuing.

What was really bothering me, though, was that I hadn't seen Kiernan since last night, when he left Candor and I in the underworld without telling us anything.

The oath had sworn to him was also on my mind because now that the border had already failed, I had no idea if I was still bound to make good on that oath and it was driving me crazy, to be quite frank.

"Candor?" I spoke up suddenly, breaking the awkward silence.

"Hm?" Candor replied curiously without stopping to look at me.

I grabbed his arm, forcing him to stop and turn around to face me. "Hawk, what is it?" he asked again, sounding more worried than curious this time.

"Do you trust me?" I questioned seriously, staring him straight in the eyes for any signs of misgivings.

Candor looked momentarily taken aback, but when he answered, his voice was firm and unhesitant. "Of course I trust you. Why?" he answered, raising an eyebrow."

I sighed and turned away, continuing our walk, "No reason, I just wanted to hear you say it," I declared, stuffing my hands deep in my pockets. "So what are we doing now? This walk isn't taking us anywhere; what's our plan?"

"Our refuge is over now, so we're doing this the hard way and going straight to the source. I'm thinking if we get in close enough, we might be able to coerce the 'drakkhon lord' into re-erecting the border," Candor explained, taking up the lead again.

I slowed my pace drastically at those words and stared at Candor's retreating back incredulously.

Candor stopped when he realized I was following further behind than he thought and sidled up beside me, taking my hand.

"What?" he quipped, tugging me along with him.

"Do you really think that's going to work?" I asked, raising my slate eyebrows.

"No," Candor confessed. "But it's the only plan we've got, you know."

"Yeah," I said hesitantly. "I think we should see if the border really has failed first and then we can decide what to do from there, how about?"

Candor fell silent for a minute, biting his lower lip while he thought about it.

"That might be a better idea, actually," he mused thoughtfully, the corners of his mouth twitching into a brief smile before his expression was serious again.

I shook my head at him but didn't say anything except, "I'm going to transport to the crossing between Earth and Vanadis now,"

"Okay, we'll do that together, how about?" Candor suggested, pulling us to a stop with a sideways glance at me.

"Whatever," I said with a shrug.

And the two of us disappeared.

When the two of us arrived at the crossing, though, I realized that my plan had been a waste of brain power.

The drakkhon lord was waiting for us; and he wasn't alone, either.

His minions, Howl and, strangely, Kiernan, were all standing there as well, clearly expecting our arrival.

"Ah, Hawk, you two are just in time," Xaliden declared jovially like we were old friends instead of enemies, black eyes flashing in the darkness.

I caught a glimpse of Nyle in the background, being hauled into the fray, flanked on either side by Therrian and Uronis.

At this sight, I turned my now livid crimson eyes on the ruler of the Eidolons and snarled, "In time for what, exactly?"

"Why, in time for the final stage of my apocalypse, of course," Xaliden said with mock incredulity as if it were the most obvious thing in the worlds, grinning and showing the points of his fangs, "And the first step starts now,"

He snapped his fingers at the dark angel and drakkhon, "You know what to do,"

Therrian and Uronis adopted twin malicious smirks and glanced briefly at each other before bringing Nyle to kneel in front of their master.

I had never seen her with so much hatred on her face before, even when she looked at Candor, who had killed her.

"You lied to me!" she spat at the drakkhon lord's feet disgustedly, "You swore I would have my revenge on Jarl in exchange for being your blood consort, not that you would dispose of me as soon as the border reached its final stage,"

Xaliden stared calmly down at her with absolutely no pity in his endless obsidian voids, "You were nothing but a pawn, my dear, and now you have outlived your usefulness; I have your darling brother in my clutches now and he is about to die, so for what do I need you?"

His black head rose to face his servants unwaveringly. "Get rid of her," he commanded.

"No!" Candor burst out furiously, launching forward, but I unconsciously held him back.

"Don't, Candor; if you try and stop this, they'll only kill you, too," I intoned out of the corner of my mouth, eyes riveted on the scene playing out in front of me.

"I don't care, Hawk, I am *not* letting her be killed again," Candor said emphatically, and he wrenched his arm out of my grip and went heading straight for the fray.

And at the same time, Ash's sibilant voice filled my head, effectively paralysing me. `*I think now would be a good time for our bargain to be settled, don't you, Hawk?*` it sneered as I felt an icy coldness entering my mind.

That coldness must be Howl's doing, I realized as I was frozen to my current position.

The worst thing about this mental paralysis was I could still feel everything my body was doing, but I had no control over it whatsoever.

I felt myself draw a knife from my boot and my feet began to move.

My sight showed me chasing after Candor, the knife in my hand pointing directly at him.

*No!*my mind screamed as I steadily caught up to my lover, the distance between him and my knife rapidly growing shorter and shorter.

When the knife was mere centimetres away from the back of Candor's neck, my feet halted and my arm shot out, hand clamping on his shoulder and turning him around to face me.

"Hawk, what-?"he started to say, but before he got the rest of the sentence out, I caught him with a vicious backhand across the side of his face that knocked him to the ground.

I couldn't even open my mouth to tell him I was sorry as my knee was brought down on his windpipe and the knife was plunged brutally into his abdomen. I could hear his every hack of horror as I saw every vicious stab I was forced to inflict on his unprotected torso, splattering blood all over him and me.

And then, in one final ruthless thrust into his chest, it was over and the fog over my brain lifted, allowing me to regain control over my body.

As soon as I could move, I climbed off Candor's prostrate form and tossed the knife away from me distastefully, my knees buckling beneath me as the impact of what I'd just done fully hit me; I had killed Candor.

And I hadn't even done it quickly; I had killed him violently and slowly, choking and stabbing him at the same time.

"I think our bargain has been settled to my satisfaction," Kiernan observed with a cursory glance at the ravaged body next to me, breaking my reverie.

Howl stood beside him and he smirked cockily, folding his arms across his grey-clad chest, completely relaxed.

I could hear the blood pumping furiously in my ears now at those words.

They were treating the slaughter of the only person I'd ever loved as if it were a business transaction! This was bound to spark my easily activated temper and that was exactly what it did.

Without warning, I let out a feral growl, picked up the knife drenched in Candor's blood from the ground and charged straight at Kiernan and Howl, raising the knife and aiming at Kiernan's chest.

There was no stopping me at this point; I had lost everything in the blink of an eye and no one would prevent me from getting my revenge.

Feathered, raven-black masses rose out of my back, ripping slits in my biker jacket and spreading to a span of near thirty feet.

My vision turned far more peripheral than I was used to and I was able to laser in on Nyle's dead body lying in front of Xaliden's feet, utterly drained of all bodily fluids and brutally savaged.

That was just the incentive I needed to allow this transformation to continue. 2-inch talons split the skin at my fingertips and a vicious pain tore through my left hand, as if the flesh was being removed from it.

From the wings, I could tell what I was transforming into: a hawk.

Upon seeing me morphing into the rabid creature, Xaliden took a step back with a little sly smile playing onto his bloodless lips and Therrian, Uronis, Howl and Kiernan moved between me and him, all four looking more than ready for a fight.

"You can't pull the transformation trick on us, Hawk; you're not the only one who has another form to tap into, remember," the dark angel chided mockingly, unfurling his twin wings of dark fire, and turning his head to the side so that he was looking at the other three enigmas standing with him.

My eyes, too, were drawn to them as well, interested to see what they would do next.

Uronis and Sehto backed away from Kiernan, whose slender, flame-adorned ivory fingers curled over the rims of his crimson sunglasses and slid them off of his nose, revealing his auburn eyes, now mirroring livid flames.

Like his eyes, the wings that snapped out of his back were composed entirely out of crimson fire, tapering into razor-sharp tips at a span that overwhelmed even

Therrian's. Fire erupted around him, engulfing him completely and rising from his parted lips.

But that transformation was practically nothing compared to what happened after Howl's.

The ice Guardian, of course, took on his white wolf form and opened his mouth, breathing ice over everything in the vicinity, forcing me to have to suppress a violent shiver.

That wasn't what I was focused on, though; my peripheral vision was centred on the drakkhon at Therrian's side, who looked to be growing.

Teeth beneath his dark lips sharpened into needle-like points and grew until they were all a reflection of his two fangs; dragon-like, leather wings the likes of which I have never seen before in my life ripped out of his back and scaled amber eyes became scalene in shape, glowing more luminously than Kiernan's or Therrian's under the moonless sky.

Claws grew out of his black gloves and the toes of his leather boots, grey in colour and as sharp as his teeth; ridges grew between his wings, jutting down his spine and ending at his waist, where a long, forked tail had grown.

It was obvious to be now where the drakkhons had gotten their name from and I'm not ashamed to admit that it scared the living hell out of me. Because I was now facing down an actual, live dragon.

Compared to the people it was standing between, this dragon was enormous; and I'm not just talking about in size.

It was simply...immense; there was no other word for it.

I was in such shock that I didn't even notice the frost creeping over my skin, clothes and the ground underneath my feet.

Before I knew it, everything around me had become a vast expanse of ice and snow.

No amount of power would keep the cold from penetrating my nerves and I bit down on my lip to keep from shivering; my insides were burning and freezing at the same time and believe you me, it was not a pleasant feeling.

"Can't take the pain, Hawk?" Kiernan sneered tauntingly, garnet eyes flashing with barely concealed amusement.

He turned to Howl, "I think we should give the dark angel and Eidolon the first shot at this, Howl. What do you think?"

"Whatever you like," Howl replied indifferently, sounding bored as he leaned back on his haunches.

Kiernan nodded at Therrian, who smirked. "You see, Hawk, we are all too prepared to fight you to the death-and rest assured, it will be yours," the dark angel declared confidently, staring me down with those steel-white orbs of his.

When he and Uronis, the black dragon, took up almost identical fighting stances, I was jolted out of my subdued state and harshly pulled back to reality.

Never breaking eye contact with my opponents, I took up a fighting stance as well, hand still clenched over the handle of the knife I had been forced to kill Candor with.

And in that moment, I knew that this could potentially be the battle that would finally end my life.

CHAPTER 22 PART I

Guardian vs Apocalypse-Bringers

Darkness.
Death.
Despair.
Betrayal.
Disaster.

Everything, everything the Guardians were supposed to be working for had effectively gone to ground, all thanks to their 'seeing powers'. And now the final stage, disaster, was at hand.

Because two of the Guardians were about to fight.

Varros, despite his fear, lashed out first, determined to make this battle not his last. He swung his grey talons straight at his opponent, the dark angel, without reservation, aiming for his chest; but when the talons made contact, nothing happened.

Instead, they passed right through Therrian's armoured vest and didn't even leave a scratch. Uronis came up behind him and snapped his leathery wings, catching Varros in the torso and knocking him off his feet.

In turn, Therrian snapped his own twin black masses, sending a stream of black flames at the blood Guardian, the whole of which caught on his black biker jacket, clashing against the red beneath it.

"Shit!" he swore loudly, attempting to douse the fire, but nothing he tried to do so would work.

"You can't douse those flames, Hawk," Therrian told him matter-of-factly, "They are made of darkness, not fire,"

Varros had to bite back from yelling out, "Then why the hell do they burn?!"and instead, concentrated his crimson pools behind his back at Uronis.

Blood rushed through his head when he locked gazes with the dragon and his eyes, as well as Uronis', began to glow, both pairs mirroring the other so well, it was almost eerie.

"*Your will, dragon, belongs to me now,*" his voice reverberated through Uronis' head, cold and deceptively calm.

Therrian, watching from the sidelines expressionlessly, let his black-tinged lips curl into an amused smile.

So the blood Guardian was attempting to manipulate Uronis, was he? He was going to get a nasty surprise if he went too deep.

Varros lasered in all his focus on the black dragon, struggling to maintain his control, but Uronis was proving to be a tough bastard.

"*You can't control the mind of a telepath, Hawk.*"

And Varros was pushed out with such force that it nearly blew him off his feet.

"Foolish, trying to manipulate a manipulator," the black dragon spoke in a hiss of ill-concealed amusement.

The hawk didn't even bother with a reply as he struggled to stand back up, clenching his talons over the handle of his knife.

Ice and frost covered everything within ten miles of the battle, behind which the wolf stood watch, utterly relaxed and leaning back on his haunches.

The ice crackled to life out of thin, frost-laced air, freezing the ground, the trees and anything else it could get its icy hands on, so, even shielded by layers of black feathers, Varros still couldn't suppress a shiver as he took up a defensive stance against Therrian and Uronis.

Almost as soon as Varros was fully back on his feet, the ice was joined by fire, which itself froze upon appearance, adding burn to the freeze.

And added even to that, the sky had gone completely dark, so that the only sources of light were those who had glowing eyes and the frozen flames.

It was all too obvious signs of the drakkhon lord's apocalypse coming into inception.

"The Merging has truly begun now," Xaliden declared under his breath, dark coals glimmering beneath similarly-coloured, spiked bangs as he followed the battle between the three men with rapt attention.

A slow smirk was beginning to curve the corners of Sehto's frost-lined, and Therrian's kohl-covered-lips as the mix of ice and fire grew, consuming everything in its path.

Since he was nearing totally frozen, Varros didn't waste time before mounting another attack, spreading his black wings and launching himself through the air at the oblivious dark angel.

Or so he thought.

The second he was barely two inches in the air, he was yanked back down by a dead weight clinging to both of his legs.

Sparing a glance downward, he was soon informed of what that dead weight was: Uronis, clawed hands curled around his lower half, dragging him brutally and forcefully back toward the ground.

It would probably be futile to try and wriggle out of that death grip-but that didn't stop Varros.

He twisted around in midair, inverting his body in an attempt to fling off Uronis' claws-but the attempt was wasted because the drakkhon was over a thousand times stronger than him, as he knew full well.

"Let me go, drakkhon," Varros snarled emphatically, balling his talons into fists and gnashing his teeth.

Uronis' lipless mouth creased in an icy smile, "I think you'll find, Hawk, that I no longer take orders from you and as such, I can do what I want. For example," he squeezed his hands on Varros' legs, digging his claws into the flesh.

The blood Guardian let out a positively bloodcurdling scream when he heard a sickening crunch of bones and a violent snap; it sounded as though Uronis had just severed his leg bones.

Pain instantly shot through both of his legs and he had to bite his lip in an effort to stop himself from screaming a second time.

It was a wasted effort, though, because when his teeth touched his lip, Uronis twisted his legs even harder the wrong way and pushed them backward, causing Varros to bite down on his lip so hard he drew blood.

"You can't win," the black dragon crooned teasingly, yanking him southward and causing him to lose his height.

"Fuck!" Varros yelled out as his body collided with the ground for the second time in as many minutes.

But his torture wasn't over yet; once he hit the ground, his opponent's hands moved from his legs to his wings, wrenching them together and making his claws penetrate the feathers to clamp along the bone.

"You're lucky, Hawk," Uronis hissed, raking a single claw along the joint of Varros' wings.

"Really? And how's that?" the irate hawk growled angrily, straining not to move a muscle, lest the drakkhon snap his wings.

"I take orders from Lord Xaliden now and he has ordered me personally not to kill you, so I can't snap these wings of yours and leave you to suffer the blood loss," the drakkhon said, sounding almost regretful.

Then he grinned. "But that doesn't mean I can't still torture you to the full extent of my abilities," he added sinisterly.

And with those words a lingering threat in the air, Uronis embedded his claw deep in the hawk's wing joint, literally breaking the bone in half and Varros let out a cry of pain as it punctured his flesh.

Uronis didn't even give him a chance to remotely recover before he took hold of the dislocated bone and started to push it through the skin of the wing.

The scream Varros emitted at this action literally echoed off the ice, sounding like a scream of death.

"Now what do you think that's going to do?" Uronis questioned mockingly, pushing the bone in further and further with each word he spoke.

With a satisfied grunt, the drakkhon pushed the bone all the way through and Varros cried out until he was hoarse, slumping to the ice with the bone of his wing protruding through his side.

Backing off with a smug smile, Uronis cocked his head slightly to the side and nodded to Therrian, who then stepped forward, placing his black boot coolly over Varros' throat.

"I, on the other hand, have no such orders not to kill you; I could do it now, in fact," the dark angel spoke calmly as if he were merely talking about the weather or something.

His black-tinged lips curled in a twisted sneer, "However, I have a much more fitting plan in mind."

"And just...what...might...that...be?" his victim choked out, clutching his side in attempt to stem the blood flowing from his torn flesh."

You'll find out, soon enough," Therrian promised.

Then without warning, he hauled off and kicked Varros across the face, hearing the satisfying crack that told him he'd broken Varros' nose.

He kicked at the blood Guardian again, this time aiming for his side and his foot connected with the protruding bone, causing Varros to positively bawl in pure agony.

Remorselessly, Therrian carried on aiming his foot at various vital parts of Varros' anatomy, saving the final kick for his groin; saving the worst for last.

That final kick to his groin elicited such a yell that Therrian closed his eyes, savouring the tortured sound and revelling in the suffering and pain it conveyed.

"This must be like ambrosia for you, hm, dark angel?" Uronis observed knowingly, back in his somewhat human form and cleaning skin out from underneath his fingernails.

Therrian deigned not to respond, instead turning back to the writhing man on the ground, bone now stabbing into his stomach, practically goring the flesh apart. Crimson blood poured from the wound like water, streaming down the front of Varros' red turtleneck.

With absolutely no regard for his pain, Therrian picked up the blood Guardian by the scruff of his collar and threw him into the nearest tree.

Varros slid down the trunk pitifully, still clutching his bleeding side and trying not to move the bone any further.

"That wound could become fatal, you know," Therrian informed him matter-of-factly, sounding as if he didn't actually care.

Varros fought to restrain a derisive snort, "Well, what do you expect me to do about it when you're not even giving me a chance to stand, let alone heal myself?"

The dark angel took a step back. "By all means, stand up," he declared mockingly, his cruel smile firmly in place.

The second Varros was on his feet, however, Therrian kicked his legs out from under him and he was back on the ground before he could speak.

"My mistake, I forgot that I have no mercy whatsoever," he faked confusion, black-tinged lips creased with barely concealed mirth.

Without warning, he followed up with another kick that collided with Varros' sternum, causing him to shoot up off the ground.

"Mercy gets you nowhere, after all," he commented fluidly, aiming a third kick for his opponent's solar plexus and sending him reeling even further across the clear ice, "And compassion gets you even less,"

Varros barely had time to react before a fourth kick collided with his ribs, cracking two of them as effortlessly as if they were made of plastic.

"Love gets you the least of all, which is why you're better off feeling nothing at all," Therrian intoned coldly, ruthlessly continuing his onslaught of kicks to Varros' unprotected body.

The white ground was rapidly becoming stained with red smudges that clashed with the already crimson flames spurting out of it.

Ice and blood were dominating the ground, creating a terribly macabre tableau of red, white and electric-blue.

"Unfortunately, even if you come to your senses and give up, I can't let you live because Lord Xaliden has ordered the death of everyone who doesn't join his cause," Therrian said, sounding more bored than genuinely regretful.

He nudged the bone protruding through Varros' side with the toe of his boot, moving it as far out of place as it would go.

"Arrrrrgh..." Varros groaned agonizingly, trying in vain to fight off his tormentor.

Therrian simply shook his head and continued pushing the dislocated bone further and further until it wouldn't move anymore, eliciting more pained exclamations from his victim.

While all of this torture was going on, the others on Therrian's side merely stood-or in Sehto's case, sat-on the sidelines of the battle, expressions unfathomable. Even Xaliden, for who this was being done, wasn't wearing even a single trace of satisfaction upon his smooth, tan features or in his coal black eyes.

In fact, out of everyone participating in this battle, the only ones wearing any expression at all were Therrian and Varros; the darkness Guardian, one of cruel amusement and the blood Guardian, one of obvious agony.

And no one seemed to be actually paying Varros even the slightest bit of attention; all their focus was riveted on Therrian, who was about to make his next move.

He gave up on kicks and went instead for the knife hooked in his chain belt, tapping the point on the tip of his gloved finger.

"This is all part of your ultimate future, Hawk," the dark angel declared quietly so only Varros could hear, using the toe of his boot to tilt Varros' chin up and force him to look into his pallid, ivory orbs, completely devoid of humanity.

Before Varros knew it, the knife Therrian had been holding was viciously embedded in his shoulder. "And now I think it's time my plan for your fitting death came into play," Therrian mused, then he grinned and twisted his head slightly, "Kiernan?"

When Ash and Sehto stepped forward and Therrian backed off, it was all Varros could do not to start pleading for his life.

"I trusted you, Kiernan," he choked out reproachfully instead, crimson eyes glaring daggers at the tall, blue-haired man languidly advancing toward him at Sehto's side.

Ash just smirked. "I warned you that I would betray you in a split-second if someone offered me the proper incentive-and someone else did. Our bargain has been settled, so everything else is null and void as of now," he said, sounding not the least bit bothered by Varros' ire.

He nodded at Sehto, who took the lead out of the two of them, white-furred face expressionless and pointed teeth bared.

Frost followed him as he took his place directly before the defenceless, injured man laying spread-eagled across the ice.

"Instead of fighting to seal the border, it looks as though the Guardians will be fighting each other," the wolf surmised in a slight growl, voice colder than a glacier and smoother than one, too.

"It's not exactly fighting if one person is constantly on the ground," Varros observed, apparently recovering his sense of sarcasm.

Sehto just smiled icily. "Don't expect mercy from anyone just because they share a destiny with you," he said smoothly, breath fogging in the frigid air in front of him, "I make it a point to defy destiny as much as possible,"

With a slight smile that bared his pointed stark-white teeth, he let out a feral roar, bringing an explosion of icicles exploding out of his maw and hurtling towards Varros.

The icicles hit their mark, embedding themselves in the blood Guardian's unguarded chest and eliciting from him a pained, drawn-out scream.

"I'm not usually one to draw out my kills-but since this kill isn't meant to be mine, I can draw it out to my heart's content," the wolf commented without emotion, liquid azure eyes blazing as he slowly circled his victim.

"What...are you talking about?" Varros just barely managed to wheeze out through the pain.

The corners of Sehto's mouth just barely twitched, "Ah yes, that's right, you aren't the one with the power to see the present. Well, since you can see the past, perhaps you should try and harness your powers and see exactly what the bargain Kiernan and I made with Lord Xaliden was,"

Even being almost completely out of strength, Varros still summoned the strength needed to roll his eyes. "In… case you haven't...noticed, Howl, I'm...not exactly...in the...best condition…to be… doing…anything like... that," he contradicted, inhaling painfully between words, but still forcing himself to carefully follow the wolf with his eyes.

"And you also haven't even learned to harness your powers to show you what you want yet," Sehto finished for him, still continuing to circle his opponent threateningly, leaving behind a trail of ice in the shape of his white paws on the ground.

"And... you…have?" Varros panted, heaving out the words heavily. It was taking him a massive amount of concentration at the moment just to stay conscious, let alone speak, but he forced himself to do so.

"Well, how do you think I was able to see what you were up to in the underworld last night? Or how I was able to locate the prophecy-keeper in order to kill him?" Sehto retorted gloatingly.

Out of everything Sehto said, only one thing really registered in Varros' muddled mind; "You killed the prophecy-keeper?"

"Don't look so surprised, Hawk," the wolf mock chided, "You heard me threaten him and I *never* make idle threats."

Varros bucked suddenly, coughing up blood and the wolf just grinned, showing his canines. "It seems the ice is too much for you," he observed, ice slivers harder than granite.

The blood Guardian couldn't do anything except cough up more blood and clutch painfully at his stomach. "It... doesn't hurt...you that...I'm already...wounded," he groaned.

"You're right, I suppose it doesn't," Sehto mused, finally halting his circling.

His victim covered his bleeding mouth, clearly apprehensive of whatever he was planning to do next. The wolf creased his lipless mouth in a feral smirk, raising one of his ice-lined paws at Varros.

"I think it's much more fitting that you would die at the hands of another Guardian, don't you, Hawk?" he commented before letting out a guttural growl and slashing his poisoned claws across Varros' already bloody face.

Varros exclaimed loudly when the poison entered his veins, forcing another rush of blood to flow out of his mouth.

"You can't take this and you know it," Sehto hissed knowingly, now behind Varros and speaking directly into his ear, "If you just surrender, I might persuade your executioner to give you a painless death, rather than the.... *excruciatingly* painful one we had planned,"

Varros could feel his insides literally freezing and his laboured breath condensed in the air as he asked, "What... plan...might that be?"

An icy chuckle was his response, "Oh, don't tell me you've forgotten about my protocol need-to-know basis, *Varros;* some things, you just aren't supposed to know." A frigid snicker, then. "Although, I do suppose I've already put that plan into action."

Varros screamed as he suddenly felt himself freeze completely. He felt icicles piercing his bloodstream like knives, slowing its flow through his veins and causing his veins to rub together like sandpaper.

Freezing breath rushed past his ear as a single, blue-clad arm encircled his throat and a knife made of ice was pressed against his bare skin.

"It's funny how the prophecy said that your destiny was to seal the border and be hailed as the worlds' saviour, when really, all you're going to do is die, alone and disgraced for killing the only people to whom you ever meant anything," Sehto whispered cruelly, "Your adopted parents, your benefactor, your lover-you murdered every last one of them and now there is no one left to protect or care about you. You have *nothing* and *no one*, Hawk, so I think it's time you grasped that."

The air shifted again as Sehto reappeared directly in front of Varros, back in his human form and twirling the ice knife idly between his blue-tinged thumb and forefinger.

If it were even possible, the air grew even colder around them and Varros' crimson eyes fixed on Sehto.

A swirl of snow erupted around him and two enormous clusters of ice sprouted out of the back of his trenchcoat, surrounding him completely. Ice poured down the surface of those 'wings' and added even more menace to his cold image.

His azure eyes glowed as he declared, "You see, Varros, I am the perfect mercenary."

"And why is that?" Varros challenged without conviction, shivering almost violently now.

Sehto grinned as Ash joined him, fiery pools blazing.

"Because no one can stop me."

The blood Guardian was knocked explosively back as a frigid shower of mixed ice and fire hit him square in the chest and sent him flying into a tree.

He groaned as his body slid limply down the tree's trunk, and he slumped forward in agony.

But the onslaught didn't stop there: as soon as Varros was on the ground, a spurt of flame engulfed the tree he had just collided with and caught on his black biker jacket, burning right through the leather as if it were paper.

Varros cried out hoarsely as the fire touched his wounded side and started to enter his body.

"The fire is now entering your system and, in about ten seconds, it will start to incinerate your insides," Ash stated matter-of-factly, actually sounding like he was enjoying this.

Sehto shot him a swift, calculating glance, which was met with a barely perceptible nod, before he spread his 'wings' and shot another flurry of ice at the defenceless hawk, effectively rooting him to his current position.

And, sure enough, Varros started to feel the cold inside him dissipating and being replaced with a livid burning.

He fell onto his back, virtually writhing in agony, clawing at his body and squeezing his eyes shut.

Sehto didn't hesitate before speeding to Varros' side and snapping a brutal kick into his ribs. Ash gave him a second nod and he followed up by stabbing his claws into the blood Guardian's chest without mercy.

There was no help for Varros now; the fire and ice Guardians combined were just too much for him-especially in his already extremely weakened state from fighting the dark angel and drakkhon.

Even more proof came when Ash turned his pupiless auburn eyes on the man writhing on the ground and cast him a perfunctory glance.

The instant those eyes focused on him, Varros all but sobbed with pain as he felt the contracting poison and fire inside his wrecked body increase in potency and quicken its journey to his heart.

"This is so much more satisfying then just killing him quickly," Sehto commented cheerfully, a slight sneer pulling at his frosted lips.

His partner let out a vague breath of laughter, a barely there smile briefly creasing his pale, crimson-touched lips before they fell again into an unreadable line.

The wolf lashed a fierce jab at his 'opponent' 's chest and was pleased to hear him cry out again. Without waiting, he slashed his claws through the material of Varros' red shirt a second time, creating three unsightly gashes across his chest that started bleeding almost immediately.

Hopeless. That's what this is. Varros thought grimly as he lay there in mortal agony, screaming, and trying desperately to shut the pain out, but it came to no avail and this pain was absolutely unbearable; he just wanted it to stop.

As if reading his mind, Ash chose that moment to hiss in his head, *`Don't worry, Hawk, this will be all over soon. Very soon.'*

The fire Guardian focused his laser-like gaze on Sehto, who got the message instantly and shot out the blade from the toe of his boot.

"No vitals, remember, Howl," Ash told him out of the corner of his mouth, barely moving his lips.

Sehto nodded before twisting his leg around and bringing the blade into contact with Varros' right arm. The prone limb jerked up at the contact, almost nailing Sehto in the eye, but the ice Guardian managed to dodge it, grinning tauntingly the entire time.

Fire surrounded him threateningly and Varros fought to keep his eyes closed.

Red light exploded in front of the blood Guardian's enhanced vision and forced him to have to clap his gloved hands over his eyes to block it out.

White-hot pain licked at his insides, preventing him from remaining still, even being frozen in his current position.

"I think the end is near, Hawk, and you should be more than glad of that," Sehto said slyly, smirk evident in his cold tone.

Varros deigned not to respond, instead attempting to regain some semblance of dignity in this situation.

Needless to say, that attempt came to no avail.

"Stem your comments, Howl, and remember the plan," Ash intoned coolly, gaze dead focused on the battle happening before him; he had eyes for nothing else.

Sehto just scoffed at Ash's order, but obeyed nevertheless, lapsing into silence and giving the signal for the others in Xaliden's employ to retreat somewhere further away.

`You know what happens now, Howl,` Ash declared in Sehto's head and the corners of Sehto's mouth twitched. *`Absolutely,`* he replied, brushing a strand of cobalt hair off of his white forehead before looking down at Varros, still writhing violently on the ice, eyes closed and clothes heavily lined with ice.

It's almost time. Sehto thought, running his forefront incisor slowly over the bottom of his lip in anticipation.

Frost-laced air was freezing the flames around him in place and melding them together with his 'wings', creating a violet icicle mass that was doubled and jutting out of his back.

Ash came to stand beside him, twin feathered masses of crimson fire spreading behind him to a full span of over thirty feet and arcing so that they were aligned with Sehto's ice 'wings'.

The two men shared a quick glance for confirmation before clenching their fists at their sides and thinking exactly in unison, "*Omnis componentis.*"

Clashing red and blue glows burst out around them and both began to change and surround Ash's almost deadly still, tall form.

Like Sehto's 'wings', the glow around the fire Guardian became a flashing violet, jarring him into looking just that much more threatening.

Sehto drew out a slightly exaggerated breath as his diamond-pale eyelids fell shut and the majority of his powers combined with Ash's, increasing his strength practically a hundredfold.

This combining left only enough of Sehto's power to sustain his life.

"Fuck, that hurts," he muttered, grasping at his knees to try, and keep himself upright.

`*It won't last, Howl. You know that,*` his companion reassured him without emotion.

Sehto grimaced. `*Yeah, easy for you to say,*` he shot back.

Ash shook his head and curled his now virtually pulsing hands into fists. Raising both of them, he called out in a cold, clear voice, "The pits of Hell will take form right here and right now."

There was a violent rumble beneath the ground as the ice covering it began to crack to make way for acidic, livid auburn flames, mirroring the ones filling Ash's eye sockets.

The temperature dropped below zero and the indigo, lightless sky morphed into a bloody crimson; the air filled with the stench of seared flesh.

Despite the fiery inferno, the air was so far below freezing that it was hard to believe that this was Hell.

Flames flared out of every crack in the still-frozen ground, not melting the ice, but rather combining with it and making it stronger.

But, as Varros was consumed by the reconstruction of the pits of Tartarus, he stopped feeling his previous pain and instead, was filled with a cold emptiness.

Ash knew exactly what Varros was feeling and pushed harder at his powers, conjuring up more fire into his svelte hands, the flames the colour of Arctic pack ice.

Beside him, Sehto kept up a constant stream of power transference from him into Ash's system.

'*That's enough, Howl.*' Ash told him after a minute and Sehto let out a grateful breath, leaning heavily on the nearest tree in an effort to replenish himself.

Ash gave him a swift look-over and spoke.

"I think it's time I took over, Howl, so I can put the rest of our plan into action," he stated, his tone, or lack of one, clashing magnificently with the smouldering of his eyes.

Sehto was only too happy to incline his dual-toned head, and he took a deft step back, leaving the final two Guardians facing each other across the vast expanse of fire of ice.

All of a sudden, the bone protruding out of Varros' black wing retreated into its proper place and the skin over his various injuries re-knit itself until he was completely uninjured and wound-free. But even so, he stubbornly remained lying across the ice until Ash spoke again.

"Get up, Hawk," he commanded, voice completely void of emotion.

Varros finally re-opened his eyes and answered with obvious mistrust, "Why?"

"Because Lord Xaliden has ordered me to kill you in a fair fight; it's also why I healed you, and why I won't fight you while you're on the ground," Ash explained dully, "So get on your feet."

Outsmarted, Varros cautiously stood up for the instant onslaught of pain; but when it didn't come, he stood up straight, garnet eyes seeking out his opponent.

Ash's pale lips creased in a vaguely mocking smile as he surveyed the hawk critically. "Ever since I first found out about this Guardians prophecy, I've been waiting to see the strength of the other three and I must say, the dark angel and Howl are quite impressive," His mocking smile widened "The exception is you. You've disappointed me, Hawk."

"Well, sorry to disappoint you even more, but this speech of yours, moving as it is, is boring me, so if we're going to do this, let's do it before I fall asleep," Varros cut in monotonously, brazen even in the face of death.

Ash let out a singularly humorless laugh, eyes never leaving Varros' face, even for a second. "As you wish," he conceded with fake countenance, pretending to bow as he advanced in Varros' direction, deceptively relaxed.

That facade broke when Varros was within striking range and Ash threw a handful of blue fire directly at him.

It was blocked, however, by Varros' left hand, which he managed to raise at the last second.

Ash inclined his metallic-blue head mockingly. "I stand corrected. But that still doesn't mean you stand a chance against me," he drawled.

"We'll just see about that!" Varros all but snarled, extending his grey talons, and raking them at Ash's exposed throat; but Ash caught his wrist, twisting it around like a toy and throwing Varros away from him like a bag of trash.

"You're not trying," he chastised in mock reproof, clicking his tongue disapprovingly as Varros picked himself back up off the ground, "Why is that?"

"I don't know what you're talking about," the blood Guardian spat vehemently, cradling his wrist protectively close to his body.

Ash shook his head again, as if dealing with a slow child instead of a former legendary assassin. "Oh, I think you do," he contradicted Varros smoothly, eyes shooting sparks from their sockets, "But if you insist on playing stupid, then I guess I'll just have to force you to give me your best."

The phoenix wasted no time in carrying out his words and aiming his flaming foot at Varros' legs, kicking his feet out from under him and spinning a second kick at his opponent's head, snapping it sickeningly to the side.

His hands erupted with cobalt flames, illuminating Ash's ivory features and making him look positively inhuman.

He rammed his left hand into the hawk's sternum, causing him to scream out as the fire scorched his shirt and his skin.

In an effort to get Ash off of him, Varros snapped his leg up, sinking his foot into Ash's stomach and pushing him to the side.

Panting, Varros and Ash got back to their feet slowly, refusing to take their eyes off of one another as they did so.

"Good, now we're having a real fight," Ash commented seriously, eyes flashing, mirroring the auburn flames around him.

Varros didn't even bother responding before launching again, driving the heel of his palm into Ash's chest-but Ash didn't even flinch.

Instead, Varros had the breath compressed out of him as he was buffeted on all sides by white-hot flames.

"*Shiiiit,*" he groaned loudly, biting his lip to keep from screaming out.

That groan quickly turned into a yell as Ash let a tendril of fire entwine around his prostrate body and singe straight through everything to get to his skin.

When the fire released him, he gave himself no time to recover before he was at Ash's throat, completely forgetting about his powers and just lashing out with his fists.

Ash, however, somehow managed to block every single one of his attacks with such ease that it was as if he wasn't attacking at all.

When Varros was spent, all Ash did was push him back and he fell to his knees, breathing hard and clutching at his thighs.

"Despair is making you weak, Hawk," Ash said in a cool monotone, "I would have thought you would be feeling anger at me. After all, I did make you kill the only person left who cared about you in the most brutal, underhanded way possible-"

He didn't even get a chance to finish his sentence before Varros leapt up at him again, driving his head into Ash's middle.

They both drew parallel to the ground and Varros kicked out blindly, tears of anguish filling his eyes and blurring his vision.

Ash smirked as he dodged Varros' kick.

So, this was what utter misery looked like; it wasn't very fetching, he had to say.

Given that Varros wasn't thinking clearly, he was able to easily dodge every attempt at an attack Varros made.

"You...*complete*...asshole....Kiernan," Varros spat out venomously, voice literally shaking with suppressed emotion as he punctuated each word with an effortful punch.

Not a single hit made contact, however, and Ash was left completely unharmed.

With another blind kick, Varros reeled back, tears still streaming down his pallid, flushed face.

"Do you take pleasure seeing people in such pain, you sick freak?!"he demanded through clenched teeth, angrily wiping his eyes on the back of his bloodless hand.

Ash merely surveyed him emotionlessly, arms crossed over his chest and chin tilted slightly upwards, deigning not to answer.

Varros wasn't having any of it.

"Well, do you?!"he exploded furiously, balling his shaking hands so tightly into fists that the knuckles turned white.

"Hn," Ash breathed, eyes glinting behind his contrasting bangs.

The blood Guardian growled low in his throat, clearly livid at his opponent's answer, or rather, his lack thereof. "You two-faced son of a bitch, I ought to kill you with my bare hands right now," Varros snarled, getting more and more worked up the longer Ash simply stood there, not saying a word.

At Ash's side and steadily gaining his strength back, Sehto stepped forward, blue-tinged lips pulled back to reveal his canines/ "Just try it, Hawk."

"Do not interfere anymore, Howl," Ash cut in quietly, gaze still dead focused on Varros as he spoke, "This is my fight now; that was the plan, and I suggest you stick to it or suffer my...displeasure."

Sehto shot him a quick look before doing as he was told and backing off.

Ash let out a silent breath, snapping his fingers so that the flames in his hand returned to crimson. "Now how about we finish this, Hawk? I have a schedule to uphold," he said in a bored tone.

The hawk bared his teeth. "Gladly," he spit, launching himself at Ash before the fire Guardian had a chance to defend himself.

Varros' foot smashed into the side of Ash's flawless face, causing his head to snap to the side, sending droplets of blood spattering through the air.

Ash grabbed Varros' other foot, though, before *it* could make contact, dabbing delicately at his bleeding lip with a finger.

"I'm surprised, you actually managed to wound me," he said dully, tongue coming out to lick the last of the coppery substance from his mouth.

Varros angrily wrenched his foot out of Ash's grip and snarled, "There's even more where that came from, bastard!"

Ash launched his head backward as Varros' fist shot out toward his face; he caught the arm by the elbow as it passed over him, pulled it down and accompanied that by sinking his own flaming fist square into Varros' face in what could accurately be titled as "the punch heard all around the world".

A pained scream erupted from Varros' mouth when he heard the loud crunch that notified him that Ash had broken his nose yet again.

Pinching the broken appendage, he glared as Ash stepped away from him, releasing his arm as his ivory fingers began mimicking Sehto's earlier spinning of a scalpel blade with such accuracy that it was almost hypnotic.

But what was truly hypnotic was the fact that Ash's split lip had already completely healed without even leaving a scar.

Varros was staring; this guy was a total paradox to him. He was able to prevent himself from attaining scars and yet there was an entire compilation decorating not only his midriff, but his throat as well.

When he finally regained his composure, he decided to indulge in his sarcastic nature.

"What's the matter, Kiernan? Can't even take a single hit?" he taunted, still attempting to stem the blood flow emitting from his nose.

His response came in the form of a flat stare that betrayed nothing. No emotions, no pain- nothing.

In the background, the other "Apocalypse-bringers" watched this scene calmly, amusement dancing across the coffee-coloured features of the dark angel.

"Come on, *phoenix,* aren't you even man enough to answer me?" Varros called, lifting his fingers from his nose to check if the bleeding had stopped.

This time, the fire Guardian knew exactly what he was going to say to Varros' attempt at insulting him.

He turned away from Varros, shaking his head before heaving a theatrical sigh.

"You're pathetic, Hawk, resorting to crude remarks to try and get the better of me; you're almost not even worth killing," he stated quietly.

Before Varros could say anything, he'd whipped around, lightning fast, and added, "It's too bad for you I've already sworn to do so."

He kicked up off the ground, hurling himself straight toward Varros' unprepared form.

Time seemed to slow for the blood Guardian as Ash came flying towards him, flaming right hand outstretched.

In those smouldering auburn eyes, Varros saw his very life flash before him and he was so enthralled that he almost didn't notice when the fire hit his bared chest.

The impact knocked them both to the ground and agony instantly took hold of his body, forcing scream after scream out of his open mouth as it filled with blood from his still-bleeding nose.

As his back hit the ice and he continued to scream[gurgle] and began to choke on his own blood, images flashed through his head and he squeezed his eyes shut, but they kept coming.

Memories consumed his brain; faces, jumbled voices and sounds, colours, places, they were all blurring together before his crimson eyes-but soon, certain faces began to stand out;

Candor, the man he'd loved, first as his best friend, then as his lover;

Maiaa, his sweet foster mother who had raised him as her own, even though he had been created to be a monster;

Iove, the prophecy-keeper and his surrogate uncle, who he realized now had only been trying to protect him by keeping all of those secrets;

Niral, the vile snake who he had been stupid enough to trust for half his life;

The other three Guardians, the ones who had chosen to forego destiny and betray him so completely and ruthlessly;

And above all, the faces of every one of the victims of his assassinations, the ones whose lives he had ended, whose livelihood he had stolen and whose bodies he had broken.

These were the faces and the people who had defined him and the entirety of his sordid life.

He'd known he was never meant to be normal right from the day he had been conceived, but neither in his wildest dreams nor his worst nightmares had he ever imagined this: that he would end up being responsible for the complete and total annihilation of every race that existed on both Earth and Vanadis.

Failure had never been part of the agenda, but it was inescapable now.

He'd fucked up.

He'd fucked up big.

Because not only had he succeeded in destroying both worlds, but he had also managed to murder every person who he'd ever cared about.

Now there was nothing left for him to do, except die.

Let it end. He thought desperately as the pain in his chest increased steadily by the second. *I have nothing left to live for. The worlds are over.*

And those words were all too true.

The border was destroyed and the two worlds were now on a deadly collision course that spelled disaster for every race inhabiting them both.

He, Varros Hawk, had become the harbinger of annihilation.

And now he was going through the final stages of his own death.

On the ground, I lay

He could feel the ice underneath his back...

Motionless in pain

He could no longer move any of his limbs...

I can see my life flashing before my eyes

White light was blinding him...

Did I fall asleep? Is this all a dream?

"This was always your true destiny, Varros Hawk," Ash's smooth, lilting voice breathed in his ear as the pain built to a crescendo, forcing out a final agonized scream as the life went out of him and then...nothing.

Varros Hawk died.

CHAPTER 22 PART II

Hell

A single minute.

That was all it took for every race, save for Eidolons, on both worlds to be summarily eliminated–as Sehto had witnessed with his powers–without the ones doing the eliminating having to actually lift a single finger.

The army of Eidolons appeared at the former sight of the border dividing Earth and Vanadis to witness what was sure to be the most fateful event the worlds had ever seen; as soon as midnight struck, so did the Merging.

The ground shattered into pieces.

Ice broke beneath the army's feet, giving way to explosive flames that caught on anything and everything they could reach.

Fire and smoke consumed the already acrid air, filling everyone's nostrils and lungs instantly with the overwhelming scent of sulphur and burnt trees.

The melted ice turned into a relentless, flowing body of water, flooding everything on the ground while the flames went for everything above it, destroying it all, slowly and painfully.

Darkness overtook the crimson sky overhead, making the surrounding demolition look just that much more tragicomic under the lightless expanse of pitch black.

All the while, the aptly named Apocalypse-bringers just stood there, off to the side and looking completely unfazed by the utter destruction currently occurring right in front of them-and the worst was still yet to come, in the form of another ground-breaking explosion, this one actually causing the ground to break.

The previously frozen ground split in two, one side fire, the other ice-and, everywhere in between, nothing but water.

This truly was the Merging, brought on by the group of men and women who set no store whatsoever by any prophecies, true or not.

And it was the drakkhon lord that had started it all.

The sounds of water clashing with ice rang out through the night while fire roared out smoke in order to complete its quest of destruction.

Every element combined and destroyed everything in its path, leaving nothing intact but the ground.

There was a brief lull, during which silence reigned supreme and then....the final breakdown.

Fire.

Ice.

Water.

Darkness.

That was how the worlds ended.

And, when it had all cleared, only the ground remained solid enough to walk on.

Xaliden walked to the very centre of the carnage, dark lips curved in a satisfied smile.

His army, Therrian, Uronis, Sehto, Ash, and all the other Eidolons joined his side, the dark angel and his companion wearing twin triumphant expressions, the others merely remaining coolly expressionless.

The five men were looking out at the vast, decimated wasteland, divided in half as the only way of discerning one world from the other.

Both worlds, ripped asunder and the border utterly gone. Every race inhabiting both annihilated and currently burning in the fiery pits once known as the underworld(as far as they knew).

The drakkhon lord then spoke, voice echoing out in the deathly silence, "This is what we've waited for."

He stepped out of the virtually impenetrable darkness with Uronis and Therrian following after him before speaking again in that same quiet, yet carrying baritone, smooth as crushed velvet.

"The Guardians have failed and the border has been destroyed. And with the rest of the races annihilated, both worlds will fall once again under our control," he declared fiercely, his statement making Uronis crack a faint smile, "And the future now belongs to us,"

He turned then to the motionless dark angel, cocking his head to the side like a curious child, "Is this what you saw, then, dark angel? You predicted the Merging and you helped bring it about,"

Therrian's black-tinged lips twitched into a smirk. "I did predict the Merging, but the way it happened in my vision, all of the Guardians died and, as you can see, we were able to usher it in with only a single Guardian's death," he surmised matter-of-factly, leaning against the nearest tree, and folding his brown arms across his black-clad chest.

Now beside him, Ash and Sehto shared a knowing glance, twin pale faces unfathomable.

"So now we've settled our bargains with you," Sehto spoke up, facing Xaliden with a neutral expression, "We have no further allegiances to you and the next time we meet, it won't be as allies,"

He turned then to Ash, who had adopted a position identical to Therrian's, with his ivory eyelids shut over his auburn eyes.

"What about you, Kiernan?"

Ash offered no immediate response, merely lifting his eyelids and tilting his head slightly upward to show he was listening.

"HOWLtd is disbanded, which means your contract is terminated and you're no longer under obligation to me, so what are you going to do now?" Sehto elaborated, eyes of liquid ice surveying the phoenix piercingly.

Ash angled his upper body across the tree trunk as he appeared to consider the wolf's query, ivory features completely unreadable.

Finally, he spoke up, "You have an idea in mind,"

It wasn't a question, but Sehto nodded anyways, "We know each other's style and compliment each other's powers well. Provided you have no objections, we could be partners,"

"Do mercenaries have partners?" Ash quipped, arching a metallic-blue eyebrow smoothly. Sehto grinned, "There's no rule that says they can't. So, what do you say, *Ash*?"

He held out a hand to the fire Guardian.

Ash looked at the outstretched hand for several minutes, considering, before eventually clasping it with his own.

"Very well; partners it is, then," he accepted with an acquiescent nod, furling his crimson wings back into his trenchcoat at the same time.

Sehto copied him and his twin masses of ice retreated into his back.

The clashing red and blue of their eyes still remained the only source of light in the black terrain. They both looked at Therrian, who had been watching them the entire time.

The dark angel caught their gaze and looked at the ground, smirking slightly.

"I still have a commitment to Lord Xaliden, Howl," he stated quietly, "Plus, I don't think the whole mercenarial gig would work out for me; I do actually prefer being under someone's command, since left to my own devices, I get quite bored,"

"So, we'll be fighting you, too, then?" Sehto said with a vague smile building on his frosted lips.

Therrian's smirk widened, "Unfortunately. Don't you dare hold back the next time we meet,"

Sehto cast a quick glance at his companion before answering confidently, "You don't have to worry about that; Ash and I have no intention of ever holding back. Until next time, dark angel,"

Ash simply inclined his head before both he and the ice Guardian disappeared into the lightless night, leaving behind the peculiar mixed scent of water and smoke.

"Was that true?" Uronis' voice asked from behind him.

Therrian tilted his head back to face the drakkhon, "I'm not in the habit of lying about things like this, Uronis," Uronis chuckled quietly, "Smart choice, dark angel,"

It was Xaliden's turn to pose a question, "I think something's still left to do. Uronis, are *you* still committed to serving me?"

"I helped bring you back, Lord Xaliden, "Uronis supplied curtly, "Why do you suppose I would do that if I wasn't intending on remaining on as your servant?"

Xaliden and Therrian both smirked.

"I expected no less an answer from the new drakkhon lord," Xaliden commented with satisfaction, "I believe commendation is in order,"

The rest of the Eidolons, Ibis, Ayxh and Zadith near the front of the queue, joined him and all of them, including Xaliden, bowed their heads in respect.

Uronis smiled his first real smile and declared, "Rise, my army, because now we have taken back what is rightfully ours; the two worlds are one and this new world...belongs to us!"

An explosive cheer rose up around him as he raised his gloved fist in the air in triumph.

"Since Vanadis is no longer the worlds of assassins, we should re-name it to suit its new rule," Xaliden suggested with a slight gleam in his coal black eyes.

Uronis dropped his hand and pressed his dark lips together in a thin line, thinking the suggestion over critically. Finally, he nodded, "I think that's an excellent idea; and I also think I already have the perfect name in mind,"

"And that is?" Xaliden quipped, cocking a dark eyebrow curiously. The drakkhon grinned, "*Eidii,*"

Xaliden inclined his black head in agreement, "A fitting choice, *General,*"

Uronis smiled at the title and turned away so no one could see the amusement dancing in his eyes.

He felt a hand on his arm then and Therrian's voice spoke to him, "Looks like you got what you always wanted; the privilege to lead,"

"And you have the privilege to serve, dark angel," Uronis added without looking at him, "You don't have any commitment to me, but I would appreciate your services,"

Therrian retracted his hand and bowed his mane of steel-white spikes, "And you have them, General,"

"Thank you, Therrian," Uronis said sincerely with a small smile creasing his dark lips.

"No gratitude necessary," Therrian waved away his thanks dismissively, "After all, we enigmas have to stick together,"

"Heh, of course," Uronis chuckled lightly, returning to the forefront of his army.

"I personally think we shouldn't have let Howl and Kiernan go off alone; we could still use their powers," he commented to Xaliden, who came to stand beside him with a flick of his fingers.

"They can still be used," Xaliden offered, "for a price, though."

Uronis scoffed, "Price is no issue; if Howl wants power, he can have it with no complaints from me," "It wasn't power that won us this battle," Therrian declared matter-of-factly, ivory orbs daring anyone to contradict him.

"True," Xaliden concurred. "It was numbers and overall strength."

"Having all those different powers combined didn't hurt, though," Uronis mused thoughtfully.

Therrian shrugged, "If we need Howl and Kiernan again, I have the means to summon him, so there's no loss there,"

"So how does it feel to be a Guardian responsible for the destruction of the border, not its sealing?" the drakkhon asked smoothly.

Therrian hooked his thumbs in the silver chains hanging from his belt and answered in complete honesty, "It feels perfectly...satisfying; after all, I never did believe much in prophecies or destiny."

"It seems none of the Guardians did and chose to take their own path instead," Xaliden observed.

"Except for Hawk," Therrian interjected.

Xaliden nodded in agreement. "Yes, and notice how he's dead," he said pointedly, "And all of the others have become stronger than him,"

"By siding with you," the dark angel finished for him, crossing his arms over his black-clad chest in finality, closing the subject.

"So, what are your first orders, General?" Xaliden questioned with an indulgent smile pasted over his brownish, thin lips.

Uronis faced the army of Eidolons, all awaiting his orders. "Prepare yourselves," he declared in a clear, echoing voice, "Our dominance over the new world, *Eidii,* begins now!"

EPILOGUE

The Offer

When I'd first become immortal, I had, oddly enough, always found myself imagining what dying would be like. I didn't know why; maybe I had just liked thinking about the impossible. Or maybe I'd just liked being morbid.

Whatever the reason, I had always imagined it to be quick and painless. I thought that when I died, everything would be over. I thought that here would be nothing but silence and solitude.

I couldn't have been more wrong about that.

It certainly hadn't been painless and it definitely hadn't ended in silence. When I had died, all I could hear were the screams of all those I had failed to save ringing in my ears. I had felt as though every part of my body was on fire; I had been cold and hot all at the same time and what felt like shards of glass had been piercing every single inch of my skin.

A scream tore itself from the back of my throat; if this was a dream, I wanted to wake up right now-because this, this was agony.

This was my own personal Hell.

And when I opened my eyes, I found out just how true those words really were.

I woke up in a fiery red sea of burning, writhing corpses, all wailing at the top of their non-existent lungs in a macabre, sickeningly beautiful symphony. In opening them, I discovered that I had eyes and, though the pain had finally stopped, the screaming in my ears had not.

*Where am I?*I wondered. I was lying on a cold, hard surface and the air was permeated by the scent of burning flesh. I rose unsteadily to my feet and cast a slow, scrutinizing look around, but I could see nothing but a barren, flaming wasteland surrounding me on all sides.

With a sickening jolt, I suddenly realized where I must be: the remains of the underworld. Which meant I had been killed. And by another Guardian of the border, no less.

I clenched my jaw at the indignity of that recollection. I couldn't believe that, after everything, I had survived only to die at the hands of someone who was supposed to be my ally-and all so they could bring on the Merging and rule the new world born from the death of Earth and Vanadis.

Without conscious thought, I began to walk. I was somehow still wearing my cloak, but I didn't seem to be wearing anything underneath. Yet, I didn't feel cold or hot anymore-I felt nothing but my anger and indignation.

Had I really been such a terrible person that not even trying to save the two worlds from total annihilation had been enough to redeem me? Did I really deserve to burn here in this inferno forever?

Then a thought struck me. Or did I have a chance at repairing this?

I bit my bottom lip, lost in that feeble scrap of hope. I knew it was probably a long shot, but stranger things had happened than people coming back from the dead. And I was not any ordinary man, anyways; I was, or at least I had been, a Guardian of the border. It was my job to make this right.

Coincidentally, when I finally paid attention to what my body was doing and stopped, I found myself standing before a place I'd never thought I'd be seeking out intentionally: the headquarters of the dreaded underworld council. My hands curled into fists at the sight of the ominous building; my father was in there. I highly doubted that he would consent to helping me, but I wanted answers. So I had to try.

I steeled myself and walked inside.

The building looked woefully out of place in the emptiness of the land from outside, but inside, it looked perfectly in place. I crossed over the threshold and into the household of the living dead immortals.

I felt myself thinking that walking through the underworld had been bad enough when I was still technically alive; but walking through it now that I was dead was somehow even more unsettling-because now I had no way of leaving if I lost my nerve.

The familiar voices of despair were calling out to me again; I could hear them hissing in my ear and trickling into my brain, not giving me even a second's peace. I knew they didn't think I even deserved closure; they wanted to consume my soul and they wouldn't stop until they did so.

Clenching my teeth, I forced myself to keep going and followed the drab, stone transit whilst trying to shut them out to the council hall. Conveniently, all of the other council members were absent, save for the one I was actually looking for.

There, sitting in what I assumed was his allotted chair at the head of the cylindrical glass table, was the specter of my surrogate father.

Caius Halcott.

But his posture and expression were not at all the ones I'd expected him to have now that I'd finally died. His back was slouched over and sagging; his shoulders were hunched forward and his translucent grey face looked pallid and drawn. I could think of only one word with which to describe what his current mood appeared to be: disappointed.

My forehead wrinkled in a frown. That didn't make any sense, though. All Caius had ever desired was my death. Now it had finally happened and he was disappointed? I'd never been an expert on emotions, but even I knew that that was a little strange.

The decor matches his demeanour, I observed, a rueful smile curving the corners of my dry mouth as my eyes took in the expectedly monochromatic hall, absent of any form of colour or life.

I watched the dejected immortal for several more minutes before finally deciding to step forward into the light, and, when I could no longer bear just standing there, made myself known.

"Hello, father," I greeted the former human without emotion, schooling my features carefully into an expressionless mask.

Caius slowly turned his head to look at me, his face slackening. "So, you really are dead, Hawk," he declared lowly.

I was instantly taken aback by his uncharacteristically despondent tone, and my confusion severely deepened. I had a million questions running through my head at that particular moment, but only one made it out of my mouth. Well, two, technically.

"How come you aren't pleased? Wasn't this the very thing you professed to desire ever since I killed you and your wife?" I asked, doing my best to keep the sneer out of my voice.

I tensed when his granite eyes flashed almost dangerously-but he didn't make a move, except to shake his head.

"You owed me your death at my hands, Hawk, for being the one who killed me. For that, I deserved to kill you-not anyone else, no matter how fitting it may have been," he explained flatly.

I shook my own head; but in my mind, I sensed an opportunity to bring up the topic that I really wanted to discuss. Caius himself had probably thought of it already. I was just making the first play.

"So, what do you intend to do about it, then?" I challenged fiercely, daring him to give me the answer that I wanted.

Caius met my determined gaze head-on and he downright read my mind.

"I know you desired this death even less than I did," he stated in a matter-of-fact tone, "So I have an offer for you, and if you are wise, you will take it..."

Printed in the United States
By Bookmasters